Pauline Nostitz, Ferdinand von Hochstetter

Travels of Doctor and Madame Helfer

in Syria, Mesopotamia, Burmah and other lands - Vol. 1

Pauline Nostitz, Ferdinand von Hochstetter

Travels of Doctor and Madame Helfer
in Syria, Mesopotamia, Burmah and other lands - Vol. 1

ISBN/EAN: 9783337246655

Printed in Europe, USA, Canada, Australia, Japan

Cover: Foto ©Andreas Hilbeck / pixelio.de

More available books at **www.hansebooks.com**

DOCTOR AND MADAME HELFER'S TRAVELS

VOL. I.

TRAVELS

OF

DOCTOR AND MADAME HELFER

IN

SYRIA, MESOPOTAMIA, BURMAH

AND OTHER LANDS

NARRATED BY PAULINE, COUNTESS NOSTITZ (FORMERLY
MADAME HELFER), AND RENDERED INTO ENGLISH
BY MRS GEORGE STURGE

IN TWO VOLUMES

VOL. I.

LONDON

RICHARD BENTLEY & SON, NEW BURLINGTON STREET

Publishers in Ordinary to Her Majesty the Queen

1878

PREFACE.

THIS unpretending work is intended as a tribute of well-deserved affection.

Dr. HELFER was a young Austrian physician and naturalist, who, between the years 1830 and 1840, was impelled by an irresistible love of exploration and research to leave his country and travel in the East, until he met his death by the poisoned arrow of a savage off the Andaman Islands, in the Bay of Bengal. Dr. HELFER had furnished reports to the East India Company, which were written and printed in English, on his observations in India, particularly in the Tenasserim provinces, the Peninsula of Malacca, the Mergui Archipelago, and the Andaman Islands. They were afterwards translated into German by Count Marschall, in 1860, for the Imperial Geographical Society of Vienna. Most of his journals were unfortunately lost by shipwreck; only a small portion of them appears in these volumes.

Countess PAULINE NOSTITZ, however, is the spirited and adventurous lady, who, then the wife of Dr. HELFER, accompanied him in all his travels, and in these pages she now erects a monument over the grave of her first husband, the naturalist, who fell a victim to his ardent pursuit of knowledge.

This memoir and autobiography derives increased interest from the exciting narrative of the Euphrates Expedition, under the late General, then Colonel Chesney, in which HELFER and his wife took part, as well as from the graphic and lively descriptions of the life of Oriental women, into the mysteries of which a lady traveller could obtain glimpses denied to a man.

We are therefore grateful to the Countess for not having longer withheld the memoirs of a meritorious Austrian naturalist and traveller, with whose destiny, during a series of eventful years, her own was bound up, and we doubt not that the public will welcome a work which contains so much that is instructive and entertaining.

FERDINAND VON HOCHSTETTER.

VIENNA : *July 1872.*

PREFACE

BY

COUNTESS PAULINE NOSTITZ.

MANY were the exhortations that reached me, after my return from India, to publish my travels. Not only friends and acquaintances, but magnates in the scientific world, among whom were Alexander von Humboldt, and Karl Ritter, the latter publicly in his 'Geography,' have repeatedly urged me to give them to the world.

But for long years I could not bring my mind to arrange my notes. Profound sadness overcame me whenever I took the pages in hand which carried me back to the past. The melancholy end obscured the bright scenes with which these memories are interwoven, and, sad at heart, I laid them aside again.

There was, moreover, another reason for the delay. My husband promised Colonel Chesney, Commander of the Euphrates Expedition in 1835-6, not to publish any report of it until he had published his own. But our share in the Expedition formed far too essential a part of our adventures to be omitted from the story of them. It was not, therefore, until Chesney's 'Narrative of the Euphrates Expedition' appeared in 1868, that I felt released from that promise, and in a situation, by the publication of the following sketches of my beloved husband's life and travels, to raise a monument to him after his own heart, and at the same time to solace my-self by the fulfilment of a sacred duty.

The results of my husband's researches, which would have so greatly enriched science, are unfortunately lost. The greater part of his writings on Syria went down with the steamer *Tigris* in the Euphrates; a second portion disappeared on its way to Europe, whither it was to have been conveyed in safety. All that remains in his handwriting is a short extract from his diary, kept during the voyage down the Euphrates, three scientific reports on the Tenasserim provinces and Malacca, and a number of botanical and entomological notes, but in so concise and unconnected a form, that they could only have been deciphered by himself by the aid of his excellent memory. What I have myself stated in these pages on the various races of Syria, their manners and mode of life is mainly based on cursory observations in the apartments of the Oriental women, to which I had free access.

The chief interest of the narrative of the voyage to India, and our residence there and in British Burmah, lies not so much in the descriptions of those countries, as in our personal adventures.

Although my notes can scarcely form an essential contribution to geography or ethnology, I hope that this unpretending and faithful narrative of destinies and modes of life, not of every-day occurrence, may awaken sufficient interest in the travellers, even amongst those unknown to me, to ensure it an indulgent reception.

Countess Pauline Nostitz.

NOTE BY THE TRANSLATOR.

It may at first sight appear that the distance of time at which these travels were undertaken must detract from their interest; but it has also some advantages, as it renders them to some extent historical, and has prevented too much detail in the record of them. Travelling in some parts of the East was also of course far more adventurous, especially for a lady, forty years ago than it is now. The date, however, must be borne in mind by the reader; manners and customs have doubtless changed among the English in India, as elsewhere, and on some other subjects the state of things is very different from what it was then. More, for instance, is known of the Karens, and probably Christianity has spread to a wider extent among the Burmese than the authoress thought likely, although I believe missionaries have not found Burmah a very promising field.

The original work closed with Dr. Helfer's death, at the end of Chapter VII. of Vol. II. After the publication of it, the authoress was induced by the warm interest her narrative had excited in Germany, and the repeated solicitations of many friends, to publish, last year,

a small volume as a sequel, giving a sketch of her expe-
riences after her husband's death. This forms part of
the present translation, from Chapter VIII. of Vol. II. to
the end, as it was thought that those who had followed
the fortunes of the authoress thus far could not fail to
be interested in learning something of her subsequent
history.

CONTENTS

OF

THE FIRST VOLUME.

SYRIA AND BRITISH BURMAH.

CHAPTER I.

YOUTH AND STUDENT YEARS.

JOHANN WILHELM HELFER was born at Prague on the 5th of February 1810. He was gifted with an active mind and an extraordinary memory, and, even in childhood, showed a special taste for the study of nature. Instead of joining in the sports of his companions, the boy occupied himself, in the spacious grounds and gardens of his parents' house, with the observation of plants and animals. In watching the various characteristics of the latter he would amuse himself for hours together. The most minute beetles attracted his special attention—a taste which he preserved through life. From his ninth year he collected beetles and butterflies, and arranged them systematically.

In the diary which he even then kept with conscientious punctuality, those were red-letter days on which he had been successful in collecting. He invented methods of his own of collecting the smallest beetles, scarcely visible to the naked eye, from the shrubs and flowers, and of sifting and washing them from the decaying vegetation in the plantations. He was soon very expert at it, and surpassed his older companions.

As he belonged to a family in good circumstances, he was allowed to cultivate his taste for music and modern languages. Music was a pleasant companion to him through life, and his fine voice and melodious phantasies on the piano made him everywhere welcome; while his unusual talent for languages was afterwards of great service to him on his travels.

At sixteen, he began his studies at the University of Prague. He devoted himself to medicine, the auxiliary branches of which accorded with his tastes, though he had an aversion to the calling of a practising physician. Even in his studies he followed his own devices: it was impossible to him to attend the academic lectures regularly; monotony of every kind paralysed his mind and repressed his energy. For weeks together he sometimes neglected to attend the lectures, thereby incurring the severe censure of the professors; but he afterwards surprised them by passing a brilliant examination, having more than made up for what he had lost by diligent private study. The vacations were devoted to botanical and entomological excursions in Bohemia and the adjoining countries.

Notwithstanding his aversion to the practice of medicine, he resolved, after his academic studies were finished, to attend clinical lectures at the most celebrated hospitals; for which purpose in 1830 he went to Vienna. Before this, however, he attended a meeting of German naturalists at Hamburg. Still very young, and in no way entitled to enter the circle of *savans* as a Member of the Society, he succeeded, through friends, in making acquaintance with the most eminent men in his department—a piece of good fortune to which he often recurred with pleasure.

Many passages in his diary show that he was much occupied with the idea of travels in remote regions. But, singularly enough, forebodings of his fate are mingled with his projects. Thus on the 30th of January 1830, transplanted in imagination to Calcutta, and revelling in the idea of penetrating into the unexplored regions of India, he wrote in prophetic mood: 'But why draw aside the veil of futurity? What is for my good will be allotted to me. Who knows, when I yield to the delight of dreaming of travelling in India as a naturalist, whether I might not start back in alarm if the future were unveiled to me?'

His forebodings were only too surely fulfilled:—on that very day ten years, his love of research was the cause of his early and violent death.

The visit to Hamburg had a decisive influence on his after life in another respect. A curious combination of circumstances led to my first meeting with him. He who acknowledges a belief in a Hand that guides our destinies, will not fail to trace it in our involuntary meeting. Others may see only chance in it; however that may be, it gave an undeniable direction to our lives.

When Helfer, on his return from Hamburg to Prague, was about to enter the diligence at Berlin which went through Herzberg and Elsterwerda to

Dresden, he found all the seats occupied by the naturalists returning to Southern Germany. His holidays
were at an end, he could not wait a day, and therefore
resolved to take another diligence, which, in those days,
when there were no high roads in that region, took its
tedious way, twice a week, through the sands of Lusatia,
by way of Baruth and Luckau to Dresden. On that
day I was intending to go, by the same opportunity, to
visit a friend at Dresden. A letter from my friend,
postponing my visit, had been lost while we were on a
tour—the only one which we had missed. Thus, owing
to there being no room in the diligence at Berlin and
the lost letter, Helfer and I, whose different positions
and family circumstances would otherwise scarcely have
made an acquaintance possible, met on our journey.

I first saw Helfer's youthful and attractive form in
the passengers' room in the little town of Sonnenwald,
where I was waiting, with my escort, for the diligence
from Luckau. When we got in, he gave me the front
seat, which he had previously occupied, and took his
seat opposite to me.

The natural effect of a diligence dragging wearily
through the sand is either to send the passengers to
sleep or to make them beguile the time as best they
can. We chose the latter, and preferred to walk
rather than be jolted over the roots of trees through
an endless heath covered with firs; and thus, wading
in the sand and beneath the scanty shade of the stunted
trees, we began the journey of life together, which was
to end amidst the luxuriant verdure and under the
palms of the tropics.

Our conversation soon turned on Helfer's favourite schemes. Full of the impressions received at Hamburg, he spoke enthusiastically of projects of travel for the future, to which I listened with all the more attention, because from childhood I had always felt the greatest interest in foreign lands, and travels were my favourite reading. Youthful enthusiasm for his pursuits lent a peculiar charm to Helfer's almost girlish appearance. I was greatly interested in his conversation, so different from that of most young men of his age. I felt a sympathetic curiosity as to whether his schemes would ever be fulfilled. When I expressed this interest, flattered by the attention with which I had listened to him, he begged permission to inform me from time to time of what happened to him, which I readily granted.

Amidst this talk Dresden was reached, where we took a friendly leave, as Helfer immediately continued his journey to Prague. I little thought that this fleeting travelling acquaintance, to which I attached scarcely any importance, would have such lasting results, and was all the more agreeably surprised when, after some little time, I received Helfer's first letter. He told me that he was going to Vienna to continue his studies in practical medicine. But, accustomed to employ every leisure moment in entomological excursions, and not finding much booty in the neighbourhood of Vienna, he left it before long to finish his studies at Pavia. His talent for languages soon enabled him to graduate in Italian. In November 1832, the faculty there bestowed on him the degree of Doctor of Medicine and Surgery.

Like a bird escaped from a cage, he rejoiced to be released from scholastic fetters. He longed to go southwards, where he expected to reap a rich harvest for his studies and collections. The funds at his disposal did not allow of any extensive projects, but he would not at any price give up his newly-acquired liberty; he therefore declined an offer at Milan to accompany a wealthy English family as travelling physician, and set out alone. Passing through Genoa, Pisa, Florence, and Rome, in January 1833 he arrived at Naples.

After a short stay there he sailed for Palermo, where he was very kindly received by the Austrian Consul, and proceeded to Malta. Here he made acquaintance with John Morgan Leader, Esq., who took a great liking to him and invited him to join his travelling party, which consisted of artists and antiquarians. Helfer returned with them to Sicily. There the young men spent a highly enjoyable time together. Helfer also gave himself for a time to social pleasures, but never lost sight of the graver purposes of his life.

During this Italian journey a regular correspondence was kept up between us, which, as Helfer's diaries show, was not without a beneficial influence on him. His glowing descriptions of Southern Italy were received with the greatest interest by me, and my sympathy with his aims and projects acted as a spur to him to carry them out and as a preservative against the allurements by which he was surrounded.

His means did not allow of his remaining longer abroad, and as he did not choose to be dependent on

Mr. Leader, they parted as warm friends. He did not, however, refuse a challenge from him to accompany him the next year on a voyage to South America, for his doubts as to his vocation for the practice of medicine had increased.

After a short excursion to the island of Pantellaria and the north coast of Africa, Helfer left Palermo on the 31st of July 1833, laden with ample collections. He landed at Marseilles, and did not take the direct route home from Paris, but came to pay me a visit at Dieppe, where I was then staying. During the three years of our acquaintance we had kept up a constant correspondence, but had only once been permitted to meet for a fortnight. His life was in great danger on his way to Dieppe. The heavy French diligence, on which he had taken an outside seat, was overturned and Helfer was thrown on the paved road and received a severe wound in his forehead. He arrived at Dieppe with his head bound up, but so far recovered that nothing interfered with the pleasure of our meeting.

Unfortunately it only lasted for a few days. Helfer received letters from home recalling him immediately. Family circumstances had occurred, which required that he should be declared of age and assume the guardianship of his younger brothers and sisters. These events also made a sudden change in his prospects. His duties required that he should reside at Prague, and he saw that he must settle there and practise as a physician.

The greater his antipathy to this calling, the more urgently he felt the need of endearing his home by domestic happiness, and of finding in it a substitute for the wishes he had renounced. No one, in his opinion, could confer this happiness on him but myself, who had shown so much sympathy with his aspirations.

In the spring of 1834 he opened his heart to me by letter, and prayed me to be his companion for life. I was long in making up my mind, for I foresaw that sooner or later Helfer's love of travel would assert itself, and I did not wish in that case to be an obstacle. I therefore at first declined his suit, while I encouraged him not to lose sight of his special aims in life. But I must confess that this duty, as I thought it, required great self-command. I loved and esteemed the suitor, and to be united to him was my heart's desire.

But Helfer was not to be repulsed. Sure of my affection, he persuaded me that I was necessary to his happiness; so I consented, and our marriage was celebrated in June 1834, at Dresden.

After a considerable stay with my mother and brothers and sisters, whose affection Helfer quickly gained, he took me to his charming home. Its arrangements were just to my taste—elegant and comfortable, but not luxurious. I was as happy as I could be in this pleasant little home, and devoted myself to it heart and soul. I thought I had run into port for life.

Helfer's practice soon became considerable, and he had the pleasure of success in many a difficult case. But experience of it only increased his dislike to the medical profession. At the same time he began to feel that Prague, attached as he was to his native land, was not the soil in which his mental powers could thrive. There was a spirit of caste, which was an embargo on all free social intercourse. Even the scientific men had no acquaintance beyond their official intercourse.

Such a life was opposed to all Helfer's intellectual requirements. It was impossible for him to endure it long; but, tied by twofold duties, he tried to conceal his feelings. His secret discontent, however, did not escape the eyes of a loving wife : I observed that in unguarded moments a shade of melancholy beclouded his naturally cheerful countenance, and it caused me no little anxiety.

During the early days of marriage a wife is only too ready to imagine that every uneasiness in her husband concerns herself and is a symptom of waning affection. For a long time I sought in vain to discover the cause of his depression. He evaded my questions, and would not allow that he was concealing anything from me. But at last, seeing that I was hurt by his silence and that my cheerfulness was failing me, he gave vent to his feelings, and exclaimed, ‘I cannot endure the fatal constraint of the life here. I long to be out in the world and in the country.’

As Lot's wife, driven from her home by angels of wrath, was turned into a pillar of salt when she turned and beheld the destruction of all her soul had delighted in, so for a moment did I stand petrified and speechless when I saw the quiet, cosy, domestic life, which had become so endeared to me, in ruins. A future of endless wandering opened before my eyes. I was certain that only in this would Helfer find satisfaction ; and at the same moment I resolved that his longings should be gratified.   I would accompany him on his travels.

It was a happy thing for me that the elasticity with which nature had endowed me made the sudden revulsion more easy to me, and that the comforts of our pleasant home had not extinguished my own desire to see the world.   I was able to answer at once, with a smile, ' Well, then, let us travel.'

It was Helfer's turn to be astonished now.   ' What ! ' he exclaimed, ' would you really leave your native land and follow me on arduous journeys ? '   ' Why not ? ' I replied.   ' You know that I am as fond of travelling as you are.   I should like far better to see the world than to be buried here in the monotony of everyday life.' He still hesitated to accept the sacrifice, as he called it, and it was only when I playfully reminded him that our first acquaintance had been made on a journey, and assured him that an adventurous life was also to my taste, that with beaming looks he agreed to it.   We resolved to leave Prague, and travel together in distant lands.   When, and whither?   To America, Africa, or Asia ?   These were the next questions, considered as cheerfully as if we had been discussing a party of pleasure.

Helfer's preference for Asia, which had been so little explored, the land of his youthful dreams, carried the day.   A totally different direction having been laughingly given to our lives in the course of a few minutes, we now devoted our attention to the project, and the mode of carrying it out, with all the seriousness which it demanded.

His idea was to acquaint himself thoroughly with particular parts of the world and to turn them to account for his collections, which would require considerable sojourns in one place. Then he did not wish, if possible, to diminish his patrimony by so costly an undertaking as a journey in the East: he wished to acquire means for it by turning his medical knowledge to account. According to European notions, this was a singular idea, but a plan by no means impracticable in the East, where a hakim enjoys the greatest respect and is welcomed everywhere. The staff of Esculapius is a better weapon for the European traveller, a greater protection, and a more effectual aid in difficulties, than the best revolver or the most ample means.

Helfer thought Smyrna the most suitable place to gain a footing on the soil of Asia. He could acclimatise himself in this half European, half Asiatic city—transform himself into a semi-Asiatic,—and then, if fortune favoured, penetrate farther eastward.

No sooner was this plan settled, than we proceeded to carry it out.

The management of the family affairs, as well as of his own property, Helfer deputed to a legal friend ; and thus released from all ties of duty, he could devote all his energies to preparation for the journey.

I had the pain of parting from my beloved mother and brothers and sisters before me, and of course wished, before so long a separation, to see them again.

Although Helfer dreaded my mother's disapproval of our plans, he readily accompanied me to her estate of Zinnitz, in Lusatia. He was agreeably surprised to find that she not only did not oppose our project, but even encouraged us to carry it out.

My mother, no doubt, felt the parting painful, but she did not let us see it. Endowed with a strength of mind seldom given to our sex, and, with all her affection for her children, having always kept up a lively interest in passing events and the world at large, she forgot the temporary grief in her interest in Helfer's schemes. She followed us already in thought into unknown regions, and often became so deeply engrossed in it that the present was forgotten.

Helfer employed our stay at Zinnitz in carefully testing the successful homœopathic treatment of our medical man. Although he was, from his medical studies, an allopathist, he perceived the great advantage of homœopathy for countries where there are no druggists, or only bad ones, and where the most skilled allopathist is often powerless from want of the necessary medicaments. Having convinced himself of the efficacy of homœopathic treatment, he studied it thoroughly, provided himself with a complete stock of homœopathic medicines, and thus enabled himself to treat the sick without the druggist—an invaluable power in the East, to which we were afterwards much indebted.

Accompanied by my good mother's blessing, we went first to Berlin, whither I had been summoned by the Princess Marianne, Consort of Prince William, brother of Frederic William III., that I might introduce my husband to her. I had had the pleasure, as a young girl, of receiving great kindness from this lady, who was equally distinguished by goodness of heart and mental endowments. I had had the privilege of spending many morning hours with her alone in her boudoir, and owe much to her stimulating influence. She showed the greatest interest in our plans of travel. I had to engage to send her reports from time to time and especially to give her the results of my persona. observations on the condition of Christians in the East

I also took leave of another no less distinguished lady in Berlin—Madame Levy, who, I am proud to say, had been a motherly friend to me. Her intercourse with the distinguished men from far and near, who met at her house, had kept her mind bright up to a late age. In order to forward our project she gave us an introduction to her sister, the Baroness Eskeles, at Vienna, which, in many cases, was a real talisman to us.

This interest shown in our plans by estimable people could not fail to encourage us. We hastened back to Prague and made our preparations with great energy. As we intended to settle for a considerable time at Smyrna, we thought it desirable to take with us all portable articles for housekeeping.

In the arduous task of packing these I was assisted by my faithful Lotty—a servant such as I wish every household possessed, especially every newly-founded one. Brisk and active, she performed her duties amidst singing and laughter. She surprised me one morning with a chest packed in the night, as she said she could not bear to see me troubling myself with it.

One day I observed with astonishment that she was packing up her own things too. When asked about it, she declared modestly, but firmly, that she was going with us, whether we would or not. This *was* unexpected. How could I have imagined this devotion in the pretty, lively girl who had only lived with us ten months? I tried to dissuade her—represented to her the difficulties, the absence of pleasures of every kind, the impossibility of conversation even, amongst foreigners: it was all in vain; she persisted that she would not leave me, not even if she were a burden to me. That, however, she could not be, for she was not only an indefatigable servant, but had become a true friend. Touched by her affection, I embraced her, and told her that I gladly accepted her offer. Great was her delight; more diligently than ever, early and late, she pursued her labours.

I cannot refrain from giving a few particulars of so unusual a character—our most helpful, assiduous, and ever cheerful companion.

During the war which desolated Saxony in 1813, Charlotte lost her home and parents, and, with about three hundred other orphans, was committed to the care of strangers. She was taken by a country clergyman near Leipzig and brought up with his own children. She shared their lessons, and thus received an education far above that of a servant. When the needs of a growing family made the support of a stranger a burden to the pastor, she resolved to earn her own living, and, recommended by friends at Dresden, entered my service. As our only servant, she performed the numerous duties required in every household, however small. After spending the morning in washing, cooking, and cleaning, and the afternoon in needlework, she employed the evening in writing to her friends, or in her diary.

I should only be giving expression to my gratitude to Charlotte if I devoted more time to describing her; but the purpose of these pages does not permit it. I must, however, dispute the prevailing idea that education unfits people for domestic service. My experience has taught me the contrary. He who takes an interest in the education of his servants (by which, doubtless, the cultivation of the mind is to be understood) and really cares for their welfare, will train up useful and devoted attendants.

CHAPTER II.

FROM PRAGUE TO SMYRNA.

AFTER all possible care had been taken for those we loved and were leaving at home, and the needful arrangements had been made for a long absence, the day of our departure arrived—the 17th of April 1835,—an ominous Friday, which had been fixed on, I know not why, in spite of the remonstrances of our friends.

It is always affecting to tear oneself away from scenes amidst which a happy portion of life has been passed. It was doubly so in our case, for we were going to meet an untried future, and return was very doubtful. Though we had adopted our resolution with firmness and made our preparations with joyful anticipations, yet both failed us when the moment came for the last grasp of the hand, the last look ; when our eyes fell for the last time on the comfortable home, and with averted looks and downcast eyes we crossed the threshold, not knowing whether we should ever cross it again. Though Helfer had hastened the preparations as much as possible, he was deeply moved when the moment of parting came.

We started at four in the morning, just as dawn was breaking ; and Prague's ancient edifices looked even more imposing than in broad daylight. The carriage passed slowly through the Vienna gate. There we halted, and the last farewells were said to friends who had accompanied us thus far; and now the postillion struck up his morning hymn and we started at a quick pace for the unknown world.

Bohemia, mostly so beautiful, does not offer much that is interesting on the old Vienna road, and we sat engrossed in our own thoughts till we reached Znaim. The fair was being held there, and there was a great concourse of people. The booths stood so thick that the large post-carriage could hardly find room to pass. As the postillion was making his way close to the houses, and had to turn a sharp corner, the carriage was over-turned with a great crash. It was heavily laden, and some time elapsed before it could be got up again. What horror seized us, when it was discovered that a woman had been crushed beneath it, and now drew her last breath and expired! She was a fruit-seller, and had been sitting on the spot where the carriage was overturned. We were deeply moved by this painful occurrence, and the more so as she was the mother of four children.

No one, however free from belief in omens and pre-sentiments of evil, can fail to feel a shudder when so frightful an accident happens before his eyes at the outset of an adventurous enterprise.

Pale as death, my excitable Lotty exclaimed: 'O bad Friday! If only we had not set off on a Friday!' Our sympathy turned to the children so suddenly left motherless, the two eldest of whom came running to the spot. We put our hands into our travelling purse, and Lotty, with her usual practical sense, forgetting her fright and ill omens, put the money in her hat, and, taking the children by the hand, made so successful a collection among the crowd that a considerable sum was handed over to the magistrate. Somewhat relieved, we continued our journey towards Vienna.

After about thirty hours' travelling, we approached the old imperial city which I only knew by description.

My heart beat joyfully at the sight of the mighty Danube, with its well-wooded shores and the finely-formed hills. My eyes devoured the landscape as far as the narrow post-chaise windows permitted, until we reached the Rothe Thurm gate and drove in between the mean-looking shops. The imperial city no longer looked imperial. Its aspect is different now, thanks to advancing civilisation, and the æsthetic taste of the Viennese.

We stayed a few days to get introductions for Trieste and Smyrna. Madame Levy's letter procured us a most kind welcome in the house of her sister the Baroness Eskeles, which made our stay highly agreeable.

Well provided with introductions, we left Vienna and proceeded slowly on our way.

There was no railway then, by which you can hasten through the Mürzthal in a few hours: our journey with a *voiturier* took eight days. But then we saw all the beauties of the Steiermark at leisure. Helfer was rejoiced that they gave me so much delight; it convinced him that the journey would not be a sacrifice, but a pleasure to me, which was a great relief to his mind.

On the 5th of May we reached Trieste, and, like all travellers, ascended the heights of Optschina to enjoy the view of the city beneath, washed by the waves of the Adriatic.

I was charmed with the shores, with their villas and gardens, and still more so with the deep blue of the sea, so much finer than the greenish grey colour of the Baltic. My eye swept over the waves to the distant horizon, seeking the coast of Asia, on which I was soon to set foot.

We were so well provided with introductions that we were sure of a kind reception in the best houses at Trieste. But this did not detain us. Impatient to reach the goal of our journey, we hastened our departure, and, as the Austrian Lloyd's did not then exist, we had to embark in the Austrian brig *Elizabeth*—a very small and by no means inviting craft, but the only one just then in the harbour for Smyrna. The arrangements were so primitive that passengers had to take their own provisions. We laid in a stock for two weeks—the usual length of the passage between Trieste and Smyrna,—in which Lotty's help was most valuable. If I had had to do it alone, we should have been badly off. After having two large coops filled with poultry and considerable quantities of coffee, sugar, and rice put on board, we thought we were amply provided for; but 'man proposes and God disposes.'

On a splendid May morning we were accompanied to the vessel by friends we had made at Trieste. Herr

Napoli, an entomological friend of Helfer's, presented me with a glittering keen-edged dagger, with an ivory handle, in a green sheath. 'On a journey like yours,' he said, 'you may be threatened with great dangers: the dagger will protect you in case of extremity.' He then showed me how it was to be most safely handled and used. Amiable as he was, it made him appear to me almost in a dubious light. However, I accepted the gift with thanks, though not without a certain aversion; it was the first dagger I had ever had in my hand. I afterwards made better friends with it, and it gave me a feeling of security in many situations; but, thank God, I never had occasion to use it.

There is always a vast deal of bustle connected with the sailing of a ship. Even if the cargo and heavy goods are shipped beforehand, there is much that can only be done at the last moment. Every sailor, even of the lowest grade, has all sorts of little affairs of his own to look after before leaving port for a long absence; for each carries on a little business on his own account, and with all the more zest, because it is done behind the captain's back.

The narrow passage from the landing-place to the ship was crowded with people. Women, and even children, pushed in to bring their husbands, fathers, or brothers some profitable article of trade : fancy handkerchiefs, mirrors, red fezes, cut glass, or some private store of provisions, in addition to the ship's hard fare. Everything was quickly grasped, and still more quickly concealed, for the captain's eye was everywhere, and he sharply chid every interruption of regular work.

Our turn came at last. Our huge chests, containing materials for an establishment, were hoisted in, and jammed, as well as might be, into the small space for passengers' luggage. We had to provide for our own comforts in the little cabin, for everything was wanting. This we left to the indefatigable Lotty, and remained on deck.

When the bridge was withdrawn, the last link between us and home, in the widest sense of the word, was severed. We were leaving not only the land of our birth, but the quarter of the world, the language, manners, civilisation, and modes of life with which all our ideas were associated. Our feet no longer trod mother earth; we had confided ourselves to a frail craft on a treacherous element; unfathomable as the waters beneath us was the future.

The sails were spread, the anchor weighed; the vessel heaved and then cut rapidly through the waves; land gradually receded from view until but a few specks were visible to my tear-bedimmed eyes. 'Adieu, Europe!' said Helfer, and grasped my hand in deep emotion. 'You are giving up much for me, Pauline; henceforth we shall be all in all to each other—thrown upon ourselves entirely. But, do you know, it is just that which makes me so happy.'

How could the expression of this deep, this perfectly-satisfied affection, fail to compensate me for sacrifices which really were no sacrifices at all? how could I but be ready to go with him anywhere? A pressure of the hand assured him that, by his side, I also was perfectly content and happy.

It was the gods' decree that we should taste all the discomforts of a voyage on this first occasion, and that our courage should at once be put to the test.

Light breezes prevailed when we left Trieste, and the little craft made a few miles daily by dint of tacking, until a complete calm put an end to all motion except rocking up and down. Our Dalmatian captain, in true seaman's fashion, tried to whistle the winds into favour, at first in gentle tones, but they waxed louder and shriller until his ill-humour found vent in a storm of curses. It was fortunate for me that, being ignorant of the Dalmatian language, I heard nothing of this outburst but the sound.

Our stock of provisions was fast diminishing. Many of the fowls and ducks had died. The cook assured us that they died of sea-sickness; and there were no signs of violence. Very sea-sick myself, and, in this most distressing of all conditions, nearly bereft of my senses and believing that I was near death, I did not doubt that this had been their fate, and almost envied them the speedy termination of their sufferings. But Lotty, who was not so ill, and soon recovered her energies, shook her head incredulously about the sea-sick fowls. ' There must be some other explanation of it,' she said, ' and I'll soon find it out.'

The next morning she left her couch before daybreak and disappeared. Not long after I heard two contending voices: one of them was Lotty's, scolding some one violently in the purest Dresden dialect, who, not understanding this sweet tongue, was answering her in Dalmatian. They were vying with each other in their mutually unintelligible utterances, until the captain put an end to the strife, and it was explained that Lotty had seen a sailor take a live fowl out of the coop and crush its skull between his fingers. Just as he was putting it back into the coop, as if it had died of sea-sickness, she stepped out of her hiding-place, having caught the culprit in the act, who was now handed over to the enraged captain. Helfer had some difficulty in assuaging his wrath and in obtaining pardon for the thief; the captain could not understand that it was no satisfaction to me to see him severely punished.

This epidemic among our poultry was unfortunately discovered too late: only a few lean fowls were left, and there was no prospect of reaching land.

Trusting to our abundant supplies, we had invited a young *attaché* of the French Consulate at Syra, who did not relish the captain's dried fish, salt meat, and biscuit, to be our guest. We now had to have recourse to these delicacies ourselves, though they were most repulsive to me, owing to continued sea-sickness.

Helfer, on the contrary, proved from the first his adaptation for a voyage round the world: he had not a moment's illness, nor was the sailors' fare distasteful to him. With cheerful mien he stood on the prow, gazing towards the land of his future researches, or sat studying in the cabin. The fatigues of travel never robbed him of his cheerfulness, never affected his health; he seemed to be made of steel, invulnerable by any hardship. It was only in his intercourse with men that he was irritable and easily lost his equanimity.

Two weeks had passed amidst bad weather, calms,

and privations, and we were still far from land. One morning we were awakened out of the profound sleep into which one sinks on the open sea, by dreadful cries. We dressed and hastened on deck.

What a spectacle met our view! Three sailors and a little black boy were tied to the four guns we had on board, and their bare backs were being unmercifully lashed with strong cord. The captain was standing by and urging on the operator by crying out, 'More! Harder!'

For a few minutes we stood speechless with surprise and horror. At length I exclaimed: 'For God's sake, captain, what has happened? Do stop; you will whip them to death.' 'Not till the dogs have confessed,' he replied coldly and firmly. We saw that there was nothing to be done. Helfer, in fear for me, led me down into the cabin, where we stopped all openings as well as we could to keep out the sound; but we only succeeded in deadening it. At length the lashes ceased, and a whimpering sound was heard, still more heart-rending than the previous cries.

Helfer went on deck, and learnt that part of the cargo, which consisted of coffee, had been stolen. It was not the value of it which so enraged the captain, but the fear of losing credit in the mercantile world. The culprit had not taken whole bags, but some coffee out of every bag, hoping thereby to escape detection. As the captain had to deliver the coffee by weight, his honour would have been at stake if each bag contained less than the invoice stated. He would have been taken for dishonest himself, and would have lost the confidence of the owner of the vessel. The idea of this danger, which he had only escaped by the accidental discovery of the theft, highly incensed him; and, trembling with rage, he swore that every one of the crew should be punished till the culprits were discovered; and he kept his word.

My remonstrances and entreaties were all in vain. The next morning the flogging began again, and ended without any confession. A small bag of coffee had indeed been found in the berth of the little black boy; but it had plainly only been put there by the real culprit to divert suspicion from himself.

This obstinacy enraged the captain. When the scene was renewed on the third morning, I could bear it no longer: my whole nature revolted against being the witness of such cruelty; besides, I dreaded an outbreak between Helfer and the captain. Conscious of his authority as master of the vessel, he had answered all Helfer's remonstrances with defiance. I knew my husband too well not to fear that his self-control would give way, and I feared the consequences. We were not far from some of the scattered islands near the coast of Greece, destitute of inhabitants or vegetation, which rise abruptly out of the sea. While Helfer was deep in his books in the cabin I hastened to the captain. I did not fear him; for even the roughest man cannot divest himself of a certain deference to an educated woman. I said to him, in a resolute tone: 'I cannot compel you to desist from your ill-treatment, but neither can you compel me to witness it. I wish to have a boat to land us and our goods on that island.' He smiled at first, for he took my demand for an empty threat, and said : ' You can't go there ; you'll be starved.' But my resolution was taken, and I answered : ' I would rather bear any hardship than witness these scenes. Vessels are so often passing here, that I may hope soon to be taken up. You have no right to detain us in your vessel against our will ; and if you choose to do so, we shall not fail to inform against you at the proper place.'

The captain was alarmed, and no longer doubted that I was in earnest. He did not like the idea that his passengers should leave his ship and take refuge on a barren rock, to escape the sight of his cruelties. His heart had been untouched by the cries of his victims, but he trembled at the risk of having himself and his vessel brought into disrepute. It was interesting to observe his countenance, unused to dissembling, as he struggled between rage and reflection. At length the latter gained the day. He gave orders to release the men until he ran into the harbour of Syra, where he would have them up before the Austrian Consulate.

Who was happier than I ?—on my own account as well as on that of the poor men, many of whom were undoubtedly innocent. I was rewarded by a grateful look from every eye.

A favourable wind had arisen meanwhile which soon brought us in view of Syra, this city of the future, rising as it were out of the sea.

With eager eyes we looked towards the first Greek city, the first Greek soil we were to tread. Our expectations were not disappointed as we entered the harbour. To anyone coming from the centre of Germany, and who knows the East only from books and pictures, even Syra seems to have a non-European character. The island, hilly throughout, consisting of black rock and covered with sparse vegetation, somewhat resembles a hill of lava. Old Syra, about a mile from the shore, built on a rounded hill in the form of an amphitheatre, with its flat roofs, its churches and the convent on the summit, is highly picturesque. New Syra or Hermopolis, extending along the sea-shore, seems to rise immediately out of the waves; and its origin accords with this impression.

When the War of Independence had deprived many of the Greeks of their homes, some of them, particularly the inhabitants of Chios, who were driven from their island, found refuge at Syra. It was they chiefly who built Hermopolis; and in a short time, from the increase of its trade and population, which rose from 16,000 to 40,000, it became, next to Athens, the most important city of Greece.

We were delighted to leave the confined space and close air of our vessel. Helfer, full of hope, from the peculiar formation of the island, of finding new insects, landed as soon as possible, and he was not disappointed: the gleaming wet sands swarmed with the various insects that frequent such spots. The beautiful *Staphylinidæ*, with their bright-coloured wing-sheaths of greenish bronze and steel-blue edged with gold, hovered in countless multitudes over the sea in the sunshine, as if they enjoyed the play of colour produced by their reflection in the water. As we were not to stay long at Syra, the time had to be turned to the best account for collecting specimens. Helfer left it to me and Lotty to catch the *Staphylinidæ* in butterfly nets, while he sought out the almost invisible but interesting beetles in sand and moss. In spite of the glowing noonday sun we diligently pursued our fugitive prey, and did not observe at first that we were being attentively watched.

Among the many vessels lying near the shore was an English war-schooner, on the deck of which a telescope was directed to us. The unusual spectacle of ladies at midday on the beach, running and jumping in the pursuit of insects invisible from the vessel, had excited the captain's curiosity. We could not be natives, as a matter of course : no Greek lady would ever think of walking at this time of day, even if she ever wandered as far as the shore ; nor would she ever depart from her slow, shuffling gait, least of all to catch insects on the wing.

The young seaman, who took an interest in other things besides his profession (not often the case with Englishmen, who mostly pursue one thing only, and that thoroughly), soon discovered the motive of our singular movements, and was curious to get a nearer view of the ladies collecting insects in this temperature.

He landed and walked up and down, but at a respectful distance. What else could he do ? There was no one to introduce us ; and without this indispensable ceremony no Englishman can bring himself to begin an acquaintance. A Frenchman or a German would have soon found out the way—would have made himself agreeable and have offered his help, but would probably as soon have forgotten the objects of his curiosity, and have transferred his interest to something else. Not so our young Englishman. The greater the distance he had kept, so that we took but little notice of him, the greater and more lasting, as it afterwards appeared, had been his interest.

Heated and tired, we sought for a *locanda* where we might get rest and refreshment. The latter was but poor, for a *locanda* at Syra (at that time at any rate) did not offer much that was inviting; still it was a great boon to rest once more on *terra firma*, and I enjoyed the sweetest slumbers till towards evening.

Helfer, who required less time to refresh himself, had meanwhile gone into the town to deliver a letter of introduction to the American missionary, Mr. Robertson. He had been very kindly received, and brought an invitation to me to spend the evening. Nothing could be more agreeable than to spend a social evening after several weeks on board ship, and to make acquaintance with a, to me, new and interesting class of men, who, impelled by religious and humane enthusiasm, had left their homes to contribute their mite to the regeneration of the classic land of Greece. The American missionaries aimed not so much at converting as at instructing, and had established schools for boys and girls in which they were taught their own language and the elements of knowledge on the Lancasterian system. Our short stay, and my ignorance of Greek, prevented my testing the efficiency of this instruction; but I was told that the abilities of the young Greeks and their desire to learn kept pace with each other, and that their progress was surprising.

The schools were not then interfered with by the Greek clergy, as Mr. Robertson was wise enough to keep aloof from dogmatic controversies. Unfortunately, conversation with Mrs. Robertson was difficult, as she spoke as little French as I did English ; and it was only by the aid of a third person that we could understand each other. More guests soon arrived, and among them two English naval officers, one of whom we at once recognised as the stroller on the sands in the morning. He immediately availed himself of the opportunity of being introduced in due form, and naïvely said that he had observed us through the telescope, and the wish to make a nearer acquaintance had brought him here, where he was sure we should be found.

Captain Owen Stanley was commissioned to make charts in Greek waters. This arduous task, in which the best charts of those seas originated, had long detained him in the Grecian Archipelago, so that he was quite at home there. The acquaintance of this young man, as highly educated as he was amiable, was a great advantage to us, for he obligingly offered to be our guide next day through the island.

Early in the morning, Stanley and the second lieutenant, Helfer and I, started on our expedition. The island is of a most desolate character. It consists of black rock, destitute of vegetation, and has so little fertile soil that it cannot even provide the inhabitants with fruit and vegetables, which are brought from the adjacent fruitful island of Tino.

The way for a long time was difficult, over hard, black, sharp stones, painful to the feet, and scarcely any path was traceable. But we beguiled the way all the more with conversation, in which our young guide distinguished himself by his playful humour, and we learnt that he was the son of a man of high mental culture, afterwards Bishop of Norwich. He had left us in doubt as to our destination. I had begun to fear that the whole way would be equally difficult and uninteresting, when, on rounding a projecting rock, we stood at the entrance of a valley, narrow indeed, but thickly planted with orange and fig trees, pomegranates and cypresses, winding like a stripe of verdure among the black rocks. The citron trees were in full bloom, and at the same time laden with golden fruit; their glittering leaves formed a strong contrast to the dark foliage of the cypresses, which looked solemnly down on the youthful bloom and fragrance beneath them. The heights were covered with cactus in blossom, and their brilliant hues amidst the foliage formed a splendid sight.

We were in the Vale of Coimo. It appears to have been formed by the hill having been rent asunder; and, secluded from the rest of the world, it is a little paradise in itself. What a resting-place for a weary pilgrim, after the turmoil of life, or how well adapted for the contemplative life of a philosopher! But no such dwellers did we find there: only a common-place Greek peasant, who was astonished at my delight; he could not imagine what there was to admire so much. But so it ever is: man is only charmed with what he does not possess; what he has without trouble, loses its attraction for him.

The good man, flattered by my admiration, took us to the terrace of his house, whence we had a view over

the greater part of the valley.   He brought me plums,
fully ripe even at that season, large edible citrons,
which were new to me, and cucumbers, which in the
East are often eaten undressed like other fruit, and
are very cooling.

In spite of all these glories, there was no accommodation for strangers—no benches and tables for serving
Sunday visitors with coffee, beer, etc., such as every
pleasant spot in the neighbourhood of a German town
can show in only too great profusion.   Wert thou in
my country, happy valley, pleasure-seekers of all ranks
would flock to thee; thy rocks would echo the grandest
concerts (for two groschen), and thy idyllic vale would
be the promenade of pleasure-loving beauties!   There
is nothing of all this here: it is seldom that the foot-
step of a solitary traveller breaks the stillness, which is
not even enlivened by the singing of birds.   The male
population of Syra is too much engrossed in business, or
its political and national regeneration, to find time for
pleasure, and the women, with their full figures, their
slippers, and shuffling gait, have most likely never
wandered so far.

The Greek women differ very little from the Turkish.
Though the yoke of the Turk is thrown off, it has
weighed too long and heavily upon Greece—has pene-
trated too deeply into family life—for the effects of it to
be easily effaced.   The Turkish element is much more
obvious among the women than the men.   Like the
Turks, they are almost entirely confined to the interior
of their houses; like them, they spend most of their
time sitting idly on their divans, smoking the *nargileh.*

Their only care is the rearing of children: the men even manage the kitchen department; for they go to market, and there is mostly a man cook : there are very few female servants, and they are of little use. Even the appearance of the Greek women reminded me more of the Turks than of the models of a Phidias. Though the form of the face is regular, and the straight line of forehead and nose recalls the antique, the features are too strong, the expression too masculine, and the short, somewhat corpulent figure too graceless, to remind one of the descendants of the Helens and Aspasias.

The men, on the contrary, though mostly short, are well formed. The antique form of the foot is remarkable, even among the common people : the instep is so arched that the hollow is perhaps an inch from the ground. They are not a little vain of this beauty, and a Greek dandy takes pains to enhance it by wearing European boots; but by artificial exaggeration it sometimes reminds you of the arch of a bridge. Their vivacity, the quick pace at which they walk, their loud and rapid mode of speaking,—make them very unlike the dignified, taciturn Turks, and reminded me rather of the French, with whom they seem to have much in common, and they are fond of taking them as models.

If, after the lapse of so long a time, during which the Greeks, with their excellent abilities, have made rapid progress, and great changes in manners may have taken place, this slight sketch should not be correct, the errors will be deemed pardonable.

Having rested and refreshed ourselves, we proceeded on our way. Stanley mentioned the southern shore as the object of our walk, and led us straight across the island.

We soon had to leave the shady valley and to take the narrow path on the inhospitable black rock. We were getting very tired, and the, to us, unwonted Grecian sun began to be more and more intolerable. But before long the refreshing sound of the sea met our ears : only a few steps farther and its blue waters came in sight and surrounded us with their cooling atmosphere, while the soft moist sand was pleasant to our burning feet. 'Here,' thought I, 'we might rest, if there is any shade;' and just at that moment our amiable guide turned round a projecting rock, and our astonished eyes beheld a blue and white striped tent. Soft benches invited to repose, and a well-spread table, such as can only be provided from the stores of an English ship, with fresh fish and southern fruits, looked most inviting. Stanley had had this comfortable resting-place arranged by his sailors in the early morning, and was delighted at the success of his surprise.

Some hours passed quickly away over the refreshing repast and amidst pleasant chat. For the first time I encamped in a tent, entertained by English hospitality, and for the first time tasted English ale and sherry. I little thought that this playful impromptu would soon be my daily mode of life.

Towards evening we returned by a shorter, but still more difficult, way to the town, Helfer well laden with insects, in the search for which we had helped him. For him a day was not a successful one if he had not added to his collections : this day was doubly fortunate through the friendship which had arisen between him and Stanley, which afterwards afforded us many a pleasant hour. In token of our gratitude we allowed the merry *Staphylinidæ*, which had been the origin of our acquaintance, to sport undisturbed on the shore.

I was pretty well tired, and spent the next day in my room, preparing for continuing our voyage, pinning out the insects, and pressing and packing the plants. Helfer, who never left a neighbourhood without ascending to the highest point, made an excursion to the summit of the mountains. Here follows his own description of it:

'To-day I made an excursion to the highest point of the island which had attracted my attention. The path, at first leading over loose stones, was soon lost altogether. I climbed over rocks and crept through clefts, and feared it was too late to reach the top by daylight; but I climbed on and on, until at last, to my delight, I stood on a little pyramid of stone which marks the height of 3,400 feet. Before me, far off in the sea, lay the island of Tiros, the verdure of which, in contrast to the black masses of rock beneath me, looked very inviting; in the dim distance Delos was lost in the crimson hues of the setting sun. But it was only for a short time that I feasted my eyes on the distant views: they were soon directed to earth again in search of the minutest insects and plants.'

The next day we embarked on board our brig again, better provided than before. When we parted from our amiable host of the Vale of Coimo, he promised before long to follow us to Smyrna, whither the survey

for charts would take him. We were happy to find
our captain in the best of humours. He had discovered
who had stolen the coffee, and thus his own honour was
safe from suspicion.   A favourable wind arose and bore
us swiftly onwards.

CHAPTER III.

RESIDENCE AT SMYRNA.

ON a fine morning in June, under a bright blue sky, we steered round Cape Kara into the Gulf of Smyrna, the beauty of which is justly praised and compared to that of the Bay of Naples. The bay was spread out before us, surrounded by gently-rising hills, clothed alternately with tall cypresses, olive trees, and cornfields of varied hues of green. Illumined by the rising sun, Smyrna itself was seen at the farthest end of the bay, with its flat roofs, gaily-painted houses, and slender minarets in picturesque confusion. Higher up were the white tombstones of the Mussulman cemetery, overshadowed by dark cypresses. Beyond this again, is the old Roman aqueduct, whose threefold arches, bidding defiance to eternity, extend majestically over the Turkish city, to which, with its gaily-painted and carved houses it produces the strongest contrast. But we were not long to enjoy the fine prospect and to yield ourselves to the reflections called forth by the contrast between the past and present. As we neared the harbour we observed the yellow flag on the masts of all the vessels —the signal of the plague !

The ships lay motionless. No sound of oars, no

eries of chaffering trades-people : the harbour was still as death, though it was full of shipping. All our crew exclaimed : 'The plague!'—a fearful word, which calls up all the horrors of the desolating malady, and perhaps makes it sound doubly terrible to those who know it only by description, like every danger which one has not courageously looked in the face. A general tumult ensued on board. All rushed on deck to see the fatal signal for themselves, and, having seen it, each one cast down his eyes as if annihilated, and fell into deep dejection.

All the hopes of the crew of being released from hard work, privations, rough usage—the ship's slavery, in short,—if but for a few days, and of enjoying a short respite on green mother earth were at once at an end.

The captain rushed about with the vehemence of passionate natures, ready to explode like a rocket. The whole crew were assembled, and we too were summoned, to hear the strict regulations to be enforced : No one was to leave the ship to return to it again ; all intercourse with land or with other vessels was strictly forbidden, and if anyone secretly disobeyed he would be liable to the penalties of the ship's discipline ; no trading, no taking in of provisions—in short, no intercourse whatever was to be allowed with the Smyrniotes. The danger of infection rendered such entire isolation necessary, and we could say nothing against it.

Our situation was far from enviable. Entirely ignorant of the precautions to be observed, and laden with household goods, which we could not possibly take on shore with us at once, we knew not what to do.

No help was to be looked for from the captain. He was beside himself, and stormed about in doubt whether to cast anchor or at once to turn his vessel round. But at length the disadvantages to himself of the latter course decided him to remain.

In our helplessness we resolved to have recourse to our letters of introduction; and from amongst a large number selected that to the Baron Van Lenep, the Dutch Consul, whose hospitality had been specially lauded. In a letter sent with it, Helfer described our dilemma, and begged for his protection and advice. One of the police boats was called, which at such times keep watch over the maintenance of the sanitary regulations, and are the medium of the necessary communication between the vessels and the shore. The captain, who handed the letter to the police officer at the end of a long staff, congratulated us on having so powerful a friend, who would not fail to take us under his protection. The consideration in which the European Consuls are held in Smyrna is, in fact, very great. Their advice and co-operation in all the affairs of the pashalic is highly valued; their consular policy and the precision and promptitude of their mode of conducting business, form a striking contrast to the easy-going fashion in which Mussulmans manage their affairs.

All orders for the Consuls are executed without delay, even by the Turks; and scarcely an hour had passed before a consular boat, with the Dutch flag, approached, and was saluted by our captain with great respect.

Baron Van Lenep was so obliging as to send his chief secretary, M. de Trauliette, to us. But even he was not permitted to come on board, but handed up his chief's letter from the boat, which was seized by our captain with tongs and steeped in vinegar till it was almost illegible. The baron offered his services in the kindest manner. But precisely what we wanted we hardly knew ourselves. 'Release from shipboard,' sighed I; 'And some place of safety,' added Helfer.

'Put yourselves under my protection,' said our friendly envoy. 'I know what you want; only trust to me.' 'With pleasure,' we replied. In some situations it is the greatest boon to be delivered from deciding for oneself, and to follow the guidance of another.

We were at once let down into the boat, in which, however, the otherwise very polite young man offered me no assistance, but kept at a distance in the middle of the boat while we took the stern.

Lotty sent an anxious glance up to the vessel which contained all our property, hitherto carefully watched by her. M. de Trauliette answered her looks with the comforting words: 'The luggage will be well taken care of.' At a signal from him the oars were dipped, and the boat was dexterously steered between the numerous craft. Everyone hastened, however, to make way for the consular flag.

We soon reached the shore and set foot upon the soil of Asia. How I had looked forward to this moment! How reverently I had meant to greet the classic ground where Homer had composed his immortal poems! But now a dirty rabble surrounds the traveller, falls upon him, shouting and scuffling, and takes possession of him and his effects. Mountains of goods of all sorts and sizes, just unloaded or to be loaded, were lying about; porters were bending under their heavy burdens; camels, lean and weary, having come long distances, had laid down to rest ; others were being laden ; asses, bearing their daily lot, sadly drooped their heads ; baskets of fruit or fish sent forth good or evil odours according to their contents. Turbaned merchants stalked solemnly about in the midst of this confusion, testing wares with critical eye. Everyone was armed with a stick, and took good care to avoid contact with every person or thing, and roughly kept off with the stick those who came too near. Amongst it all the police stormed about, exercising their office by cracking their whips right and left, not caring whether they hit the innocent or the guilty.

I stood bewildered by this strange confusion, and hesitated to proceed. 'Do not fear,' said M. de Trauliette encouragingly ; 'you are under my protection.' Two of the consular police went first with their signal, and two behind. The crowd respectfully made way ; for the commonest Turk knows the dignity of a Consul, and the most fanatical Mussulman in Smyrna would not think of refusing the respect due to him. Thus we arrived unmolested at the Locanda de Nave, on the shore.

If an Italian tavern is repulsive to us Germans, from its want of cleanliness and comfort, how much more so an *albergo* in Turkey !

We were conducted up a dark, dirty staircase to a large room on the first floor. The walls, which were of wood, and the floor were coloured dark brown ; a

table of the same and a few chairs completed the furniture.   Two small closets opening out of it contained
bare bedsteads.

'Here,' said M. de Trauliette, 'you are in safety.
This is a clean house' ('clean,' in this sense, means
that the house is in quarantine, and protected from
infection); 'but you must not touch anything that is
handed to you, except wood' (wood is not considered
a medium of infection); 'not a handkerchief, nor a
towel, nor a bed : all these things are especially
dangerous.   You must also keep aloof from the servants of the house : that class of persons is not to be
trusted.   Food will be placed on the table close to the
door, from which the empty vessels will be removed,
so that the waiter will not have to enter the room.   It
will also be best not to allow your servant to leave the
room : you cannot tell whether proper precautions
will be observed.'   With these words he closed several
side doors, handed me the key, and added, 'When
you go out, fasten the main door, so that your servant
may not be tempted by curiosity.'   Therewith he gave
a significant look at Lotty, who stood looking on with
an air of astonishment.

We had listened to all this with open mouths and
bewildered looks.   The scene was tragic enough, and
yet I could not forbear from ironically exclaiming : 'So
this is what you call a clean house and being in a place
of safety !'

'Certainly,' M. de Trauliette replied, shrugging his
shoulders.   'It is the best house that we have, for it
was placed in quarantine at the first outbreak of the

plague ; but you can never rely upon servants. However, you cannot stay here long. I will at once look out for a more suitable private dwelling.' He then handed to me and Helfer two long, stout sticks, giving us to understand that we must not go into the streets without them, and must ruthlessly keep everyone off from us, taking special care that our clothes did not come in contact with anyone. ' It would be better, however, not to go out at all. Strangers are generally too scrupulous in the use of the stick, and are likely to get into danger.' With this he took his leave.

My Lotty had already begun to busy herself with the luggage, which had meanwhile arrived, and had prepared a bed for me as well as she could. Tired to death I lay down, and did not awake till late next morning from a profound and peaceful sleep. One sleeps a great deal on board ship, but the slumbers of a sea-sick person are not refreshing, and the awaking is most uncomfortable. The only remedy is to make a resolute effort, to hasten out of the close cabin on deck, to inhale the fresh sea breeze at dawn, and, deep in contemplation and adoration inspired by the splendour of the rising sun, to forget one's pain and misery.

After we had partaken of our modest breakfast, with all precautions, and were discussing how we could best arrange our life under these uncomfortable circumstances, the door opened, and a pleasant-looking little gentleman entered, followed by the house servant, who most respectfully announced him as ' M. Van Lenep, Consul of His Majesty the King of Holland.' Surprised by this polite attention, we advanced to meet

him and to express our thanks,—which I was about to
emphasise by a shake of the hand, but was alarmed to
observe that the kindly expression of his face suddenly
changed, and, retreating a few steps, he put his hands
behind him.　We looked at each other in silence for a
moment, when he said, ' Pardon me, but during times
like the present all contact is dangerous and must be
avoided.'

' What do you mean ? ' I said.　' Would a shake of
the hand be dangerous to you or to me ? '

' To both,' he replied.　' You cannot know whether
I may not be already infected, and you, although you
have but just landed from a clean ship, may have come
into dangerous contact with your first step on shore.
I am come to assure myself of your health with my
own eyes, and to help to provide you with another
dwelling.　I regret that the epidemic does not permit
me to offer my own house, but it is in strict quarantine,
and needful caution forbids us to open it to anyone.'

He even declined the proffered seat, and, obviously
uneasy at being in a place not wholly free from suspicion, to which he had only been brought by the tra-
ditional politeness to strangers with an introduction, he
took leave, with a renewed request that we would stay
indoors until we should hear from him in the course of
the day.

The precautions against infection during the prevalence of the plague are very comprehensive, and
strictly observed among the European population.
The abodes of the wealthier families, generally shut
off from the street by a high wall, the gate in which

forms the only means of ingress to the often spacious interior, are kept strictly closed : all intercourse with the towns-people is forbidden. The gate is opened to no one, and the master himself takes charge of the key. Provisions are brought by special dealers, who go through the streets with them in the morning and knock at the gate, when a sliding shutter is opened, and, for greater security, the goods are received by the master himself. They are thrown through the opening into a vessel of water inside before they are touched by the receiver. Loaves, eggs, vegetables, even live fowls, are thrown in. Everything must pass through the purifying element before it can be touched and cooked.

But in spite of this isolation the pestilence does sometimes find its way into the best families, causing unspeakable distress. The dread of infection is so great that it destroys the feelings of humanity and rends the closest ties. Everyone flies from a person seized by it ; the infected house is deserted ; husbands and wives, brothers and sisters, are separated ; the mother even leaves her sick child to the care of Greek nurses.

In the afternoon M. de Trauliette appeared, commissioned by his chief to conduct us to a really clean, and, what was more, a German house. The migration was at once effected, and before long we were in the pleasant and very neat house of a clockmaker from Nuremberg.

How attractive the white bed hangings, the clean floors, the carefully dusted furniture, looked to us !

The large cabinet was filled with cut glass and many-coloured bowls. There were even some Easter eggs. I took it all in at a glance ; and how it reminded me of home! I had not imagined that so short a separation from my beloved country could make a German middle-class house look like an Eldorado. It is thus that we learn abroad to appreciate the advantages of home.

The good people—a busy little old man, and his wife, as broad as she was long,—gave us a most kindly welcome. Her beaming face was encircled by a plaited white cap, and with her white apron she was the very picture of a cleanly housewife. Herr Hoffner had been settled many years in Smyrna. He took care that the Turks did not get quite behind the age in their reckoning of time, and his wife took in travellers, who, like ourselves, desired cleanliness and security. Both carried on a thriving trade.

The very next day Helfer began his entomological excursions in the neighbourhood. He also sought opportunity to see patients suffering from the plague and to try remedies. For this purpose he obtained access to a Greek convent in which a plague hospital was established. He was readily taken round by monks who had recovered from it, and so were not liable to infection. But when he announced his intention of administering remedies and making observations, he was gravely told that it was not permitted : fate must not be interfered with. No appeal to reason no argument, availed against these truly fatalistic principles. He tried to give remedies secretly to some of the sick, hoping that if timely taken they might shorten the course of the disease—that is, hasten the breaking out of the carbuncles, and thus save the patient. He told me that in one case he had succeeded ; but further observations were prevented, as his visits to the hospital were forbidden.

Smyrna has three entirely distinct populations : the Turks, the Greeks, and the Franks. With the Turks, who are by far the most numerous, I made no acquaintance, as it is considered so dangerous to enter the narrow, dirty lanes of their quarter, that anyone seen in them is shut out from other intercourse. The Greeks inhabit a quarter of the city to themselves, and their houses, built of wood and framework, gaily painted and adorned with carvings, have a pleasing appearance, but look as if the first breeze would blow them away ; though, from the yielding nature of the wood, they really stand the often-recurring earthquakes better than the massive stone buildings, which are rifted and split, and fall completely into ruins.

The Greeks are the vital element in the civic organism. The retail trade is almost exclusively in their hands. I could not, however, make much acquaintance with them either, owing to the restrictions on intercourse. But I was struck with their appearance. Clad in the white fustanella with its many folds, their richly-embroidered vests, long white shirt sleeves, the broad girdle holding a pair of pistols, the red fez with its blue tassel,—they looked more fit for the stage than for making bargains. But this is their favourite occupation, and they are said to display all the cunning of their classic ancestors.

The Franks are mostly descendants of Italian or French families who have settled here, and have partly intermarried with the Greeks and partly kept their descent pure. They prefer to be called Europeans, even though they only know Europe from the traditions of their forefathers. They are proud to wear the dress coat of the West as a sign of their origin; nowhere is so much importance attached to this article of dress as in Smyrna. It is the key to good society, to the houses of the Consuls. To have access to them is not to be despised, for the Consuls are a power which, under some circumstances, can measure its strength with that of a European great power. The Pasha would not think of taking any measure of importance without consulting his good friends the consuls. He rules ostensibly, with their quiet co-operation. So it was at all events at that time.

It soon became known that a German physician had arrived. Sufferers who had long tried in vain all the means which the Smyrniote disciples of Esculapius could offer them, hoped for aid from a doctor who had really studied and taken a degree. A few cures, effected without any great medical skill, increased the favourable opinion of Helfer, and fame soon pronounced him a miraculous doctor. Not only the higher and more wealthy classes sought his aid, but the lower grades of the people, even Turks, who usually commend body as well as soul to Allah, flocked to him, though with more faith in the wonder-worker than the physician.

The little room in which he had to see patients was

soon too small, and the crowding in the limited air space became intolerable. When the time allotted for the audiences was long past, and fresh patients were still arriving, he often escaped by the back door.

As medical practice was only a secondary object with him, he did not wish to be too much tied by it, and to be hindered from botanical and entomological excursions. But while we lived in the town these were out of the question, and we therefore resolved to leave it. We found accommodation in the house of a missionary of the English Church (though he was a native of Würtemburg) at Budja, the summer residence of most of the English families, between two and three miles[1] from Smyrna. We retained our rooms in the good clockmaker's house, as a place of call, and Helfer saw patients there three times a week.

Budja is a charming spot. The pretty country houses are scattered in picturesque confusion amidst the shade of olive trees and cypresses interspersed with oleanders and myrtles. Winding foot-paths led from one to another, for there were no carriage-roads. Mrs. Verry, wife of the English Consul, had had a road made from Smyrna to her country house at Budja, but it was so rough that the drive in her carriage (the only one in Smyrna) was not very enviable, though so unique a possession made her very distinguished. All the social intercourse at Smyrna is carried on by means of

---

[1] English miles. Distances are given in English miles throughout the translation with as much accuracy as I can command, reckoning the German mile at 4½ English, and the rather indefinite 'stunde' at 2¼. Dr. Helfer generally uses the English mile.—Tr.

that most patient and unjustly despised animal, the ass.
What would Smyrna be without its asses? They not
only convey all the necessaries of life to the inhabitants,
they are the only mode of conveyance : they carry the
men to business, the ladies to pay visits. One sees the
pretty Smyrniotes, in their finest clothes, riding on
donkeys to a ball. On the occasion of such festivities,
they may be seen riding through the streets of Smyrna,
the back of the head covered with the becoming red fez
with dark blue tassel, beneath which flow thick braids of
blonde or chestnut hair, their fair brows adorned with
fresh flowers, and the wavy ball dress covered with a
mantle. And how gently and carefully the well-trained
animal bears the belle ! how much room his back affords
for her ample robes ! Not crushed and crumpled in a
carriage, as with us, does she alight from her palfrey :
casting off the mantle, fresh as a rose she steps into the
well-lighted rooms. It is quite worth while to attend
an assembly of young Smyrniotes decked out for a ball:
a prettier sight can hardly be imagined. The admix-
ture of various European types which is unmistakably
evident, gives to the Asiatic, regular, but somewhat
rigid features of the Greek women a peculiar charm and
loveliness, which is wanting in the straight lines of the
pure classic style. Then there is the joyousness of
these fearless and innocent children. I never saw such
unrestrained laughter and merriment combined with so
much natural grace.

Our stay at Budja, in the house of Mr. Jetter the missionary, was as pleasant as it was interesting. For the
first time I made acquaintance with English family life;

for, although modified by foreign ways and usages, it still retained its English character in its agreeable aspects. Only I could not acquire a taste for the strict observance of Sunday. I could not understand why the whole day should be spent in religious observances. At first I was disposed to regard the absence of every cheerful sound, of all secular music, the abstinence from any but religious reading, as evidences of an exalted state of mind, and to admire it; but when I became better acquainted with this family, and found them *ennuyées*, or napping over a religious book during my afternoon calls, and knew how they longed for the cool evening and the walk then permitted, I thought our German Sunday, with its morning service and cheerful recreation in the afternoon, was more in keeping with the right proportion between things divine and man's nature, and that it gave to each its due. Afterwards, when in England, I found the key to English Sabbath-keeping in the religious sentiments of the people, which cannot fail to inspire respect. The solemn observance of the whole day is not a doctrine imposed upon the people by those above them, but a religious necessity deeply rooted in their hearts, which the upper classes respect and to which they conform. I have myself laid aside my needlework when the servant came into the room, in order not to wound her Sunday feelings.[1]

---

[1] It will be a novel idea to most English people that our strict observance of Sunday is a concession to the feelings of the working classes, and may be taken as an instance of the difficulty of understanding foreign customs. As will be seen in the sequel, Mme. Helfer, when in England, was a guest in the house of the Prussian Ambassador, where it is possible that she may have observed something of the conformity she speaks of.—Tr.

Much of this will be changed by time, which changes all things,—whether improved, remains to be seen.

An incident with Lotty nearly put an unpleasant end to our stay at Mr. Jetter's at Budja. I had strictly enjoined upon her to conform to the customs of the house and to abstain from all secular employment on Sunday. She generally sat, poor thing, sadly weary, under the shade of the plane trees outside the door, with a devotional book by her side, but she was not given to read long together. One Sunday she was joined by the Greek servant of the house, on whom solemnity was also enjoined. They sympathised with each other as well as they could by means of words and gestures, about the melancholy Sundays; each told the other how different it was at home, and Lotty, overcome with the memories of many a country dance, and wishing to show her fellow-sufferer the delights of a jig, sprang from her seat, struck up a Vienna country dance tune and whirled and swung herself in time to it, making quite a clatter on the smooth pavement. Suddenly a stentorian voice called 'Stop!' to her, in which, though hidden from view, she recognised that of the strict master of the house. His face flushed with anger, he overwhelmed her with reproaches about immorality, Sabbath-breaking, and similar expressions, which sent the poor thing in tears to me. I had great difficulty in appeasing the reverend gentleman; he would not listen to my assurances that she meant no harm, he considered it an insult to his pious household and his spiritual calling. Finally, his wife and Helfer came to the rescue, and by our united efforts peace was restored. But I never saw my Lotty merry in that house again.

We were invited by Count Hoschpie, a nephew of M. Van Lenep, to his romantically situated summer residence, Sedi Koui, four or five miles from Budja, called the Dutch Village, and, in company with several young ladies, friends of the family, we made an excursion thither, of course mounted on well-trained and gaily-caparisoned donkeys.

The path led through a fruitful plain surrounded by picturesque hills, clothed with myrtles, oleanders, arbutus, gum trees, and ilex. The foliage and blossoms, and the rich cornfields were a wonderful sight, and presented a blending of colours such as can only be produced in the temperate Ionian climate, without extremes of heat or cold.

The count received us alone, and was anxious to make up for the absence of the lady of the house by his own amiability. He seemed to enjoy showing his art treasures as well as his knowledge of them. Besides a whole genealogical tree of family portraits, he had a considerable number of fine paintings of the Dutch school.

After we had feasted on these treasures, food for the body was not forgotten: sherbet, delicious fruits, pastry, and the never-failing *glico*[1] were offered us. But we were soon disturbed by the sound of horses' hoofs and the clang of arms outside, and by the entry of Turkish police soldiers. With the pomposity peculiar to them,

---

[1] A jelly made of various fruits, offered, with a glass of water, to every visitor at any time of day.—Tr.

but with ill-concealed awe at seeing M. Van Lenep, they respectfully asked permission, with folded arms and many prostrations, to search the house and grounds. No Turkish official can enter a Consul's house without his leave, not even to take a notorious criminal into custody.

A Jew had recently been assassinated in the neighbourhood, which had been for some time insecure, and the assassin was said to have taken refuge here. Permission having been given, and the good Mussulmans having quaffed goblets of fiery wine with much satisfaction, they proceeded to search for the murderers, but with so much noise, and care not to incur danger themselves, that I was reminded of hare-shooting at home, and the care taken to keep out of the line of shots. Of course no brigands were taken; they had had plenty of time to make off.

Nothing daunted by this incident, we set off on our return in the highest spirits. Mlle. d'Yong, daughter of the Danish Consul, a very pretty and lively girl and a bold rider, took it into her head to boast of the qualities of her donkey. This gave rise to a little contest, as no lady liked to have her ass undervalued. I was amused and reminded of the wagers at our races at home, and half in jest proposed that the animals should decide for themselves, by running a race. The proposal took, and, as we were in the open plain, it was carried out at once. But however well trained, it is not easy to bring a cavalcade of asses into a line. I, who did not join the race, gave the signal for the start—one, two, three,—and away sped the animals and their riders. If no sparks were struck, ribbons, hats, flowing locks, and dresses flew about, presenting a sight as comical as it was pretty. The greatest difficulty was, however, at the end of the course. When a donkey is once roused out of his lethargy, and is in full trot, it is impossible to keep him in a particular course or to stop him at a certain point, and all missed the mark. Thus the comparative merits of the asses, like many other problems, remained an open question.

As the plague brought from Constantinople is not so virulent, and does not last so long, as that from Egypt, after a time it ceased to disturb men's minds at Smyrna. There was less restriction on intercourse, and our friend of Syra, Captain Owen Stanley, could venture to run his schooner into the harbour of Smyrna, and to continue his surveys. His arrival was a great pleasure to us and of great importance to me, for to his instructions in sketching I owe a collection of sketches, very imperfect, but still interesting. Helfer found in him a willing companion for ascending the Tartali, the highest of the chain of mountains encircling Smyrna. We were also joined by several gentlemen, who had often projected the ascent, but, with their accustomed love of ease, had never performed it. We chose a bright moonlight night, to escape the heat of the day and that we might see the sunrise from the top.

Mounted on horses, asses, or mules, we set ourselves in array, and rode through an extensive plain, the careful cultivation of which surprised us.

Pomegranates, orange and fig-trees alternated with various crops of grain, until we reached the village of

Burnar Bashi, whose pretty dwellings lay peacefully amidst the dark groups of trees in the moonlight. Thence we began the ascent and were soon in the deep shade of thick woods on the slope of the mountain, which rises abruptly from the plain.

The path, if path it can be called, winding between lofty walls of rock and along steep precipices, became more and more difficult and unsafe, from rolling stones ; it was fortunate for those inclined to be giddy that the darkness concealed the deep gorges, the edges of which the beasts obstinately chose to take. Unmoved by their riders' fears, they will obey no admonitions either gentle or severe. It is best to leave them to themselves, as they rarely make a false step. Towards midnight we reached the summit. We felt the great change of temperature very keenly, in spite of cloaks and a quickly-kindled fire. The height measured by Helfer by a barometer was 5,180 feet.

Wearied with the exertion, we took a short rest, from which we were awakened about four by the first light of dawn, and eagerly watched for the crimson hues of the rising sun. Words fail to describe the beauty of the scene from this point.

The ball of fire lighted up the wooded hills and vales extending far to the eastward, chasing the deep shadows in which they had been veiled. Now here, now there, a mountain peak appeared in the rosy light. The mists dispersed, and, assuming wondrous forms, sought refuge in the deep, narrow valleys. Towards the west extended the Gulf of Smyrna, set in its lovely shores, and almost closed in by wooded islands ; beyond these the eye roamed over the boundless sea.

Smyrna, lying apparently at our feet, with its slender minarets, its bright-coloured houses, its harbour full of ships with their pennons streaming in the breeze, lent life to the scene, and brought back the mind, lost in the contemplation of nature, to prosaic realities. Unfortunately we could not long yield ourselves to this, for we had to take advantage of the cool of the morning for our descent.

The concourse at Helfer's medical audiences increased from day to day; but so also did the envy and wounded pride of the native doctors—mostly Greeks. In spite of their ignorance, they had hitherto maintained their professional dignity; but they now saw their interests threatened by a young stranger, who neither sought practice nor intercourse with them. No wonder that they bore him a grudge and considered how to get rid of their obnoxious rival.

A report was gradually spread that Helfer's life was in danger; but the author of it could not be discovered. Before long he received threatening letters, warning him not to continue his practice. He, however, disregarded them, as well as the remonstrances of our anxious friends, and continued to see patients on the appointed days. His carelessness lulled my fears, until one day he showed me a sheet of paper which he had found on one of his walks, fixed to an arbutus, on which were the words: ' Take care! Not long wilt thou go to heal the sick by this road; thy hours are numbered!' The paper might have been just affixed; the foe was probably lurking near, to see whether it fell into the right hands, and what effect it produced.

This incident roused us out of our security, and the more so as we were told of many instances of the revengeful malice of the Greeks. It often slumbers for a long period, but at last takes unerring aim at its victim, even after the lapse of years.

Helfer no longer went out unarmed, and was always accompanied by an armed servant in his walks to the town. But these precautions would probably not have protected him; for who can always be prepared for a foe in ambush? Just then, however, a providential circumstance, or at any rate an unexpected event, occurred, which put a sudden termination to our stay in lovely Budja, and had an important influence on our after lives.

During one of our visits to the city, our loquacious host told us with beaming face, that during the last few days he had lodged two very distinguished guests, who, if we would permit, would dine with us. We had no objection, but paid little heed to this pompous announcement, as we knew that our Nuremberger's love of truth had not been improved by residence in the East. We were therefore the more surprised when the door opened and two young men entered, both very handsome, and in rich Turkish costume. With the fine features and contemplative look of the dark eyes, shaded by long lashes, peculiar to the Asiatic, the fine curly beard, the swelling lips and beautiful teeth, was combined that expression of mental activity, indicative of European culture, which is usually wanting in the Asiatic. Thus their appearance combined the advantages of East and West. We were still more surprised by the dignified ease with which they addressed us and carried on an interesting conversation in French and English. It was something quite extraordinary. We were curious to learn what country could have produced these marvels, and where they had been brought up. In answer to our inquiries they told us that they were nephews of the celebrated Dost Mahomet Khan, Ruler of Cabul. They related to us their history circumstantially. Their mother, a princess distinguished by her mental powers, had been brought up at Ispahan, and had been intimate with the ladies of the English Embassy, from whom she had imbibed from childhood a taste for the English language and European culture. They spoke with great affection of an elder sister, who had been carefully educated by their mother, and whose instructive conversation attracted them to the apartments of the harem even after the age at which, according to usual Oriental customs, they would have been excluded from them. They had a great desire to see Europe, the land of intelligence and of the arts. After the death of their father, they took advantage of their independence to gratify it, and in order to see and observe unmolested, they had gone first to England and then to France, incognito, as British subjects, under the names of Hunter and Brown. They were now on their way back, enthusiastically intent on introducing European culture and manners into their own country.

Their remarks and criticisms on our social institutions were most striking and piquant. They had not been dazzled by the advantages of Europe, but had preserved an open eye for the absurdities of our social

life and fashion. If James Morier had met with them,
we should perhaps have had more volumes of his celebrated book, ' Hajji Baba in England.'

A few days later we again met our new acquaintances at a *fête* in the ' Great Paradise,'—a pleasure
resort of the Smyrniotes. They had been invited by
the English Consul, and were treated by him and the
élite of the company with great consideration. If we
had had any doubts about their identity they would
have been dispelled by this, as the English Consul was
in possession of their papers. However, we did not
need any confirmation of our own impressions.

The lovely young lady world hovered like gay
butterflies round these two *raræ aves.* Song and dance
and lively chat were intermingled without constraint.

Uhli Khan, the elder of the two Affghans, behaved
with the gravity and dignity of a true Asiatic prince:
he scarcely deigned to glance at the ladies, and only
seemed to take pleasure in conversing with men, and
in the music. Selim Khan, the younger, was evidently
torn by conflicting feelings : he beat time involuntarily
to the music, and his eye roamed with pleasure among
the circle of ladies who roguishly invited him to dance.
But his Mussulman ideas of manly dignity would not
permit it ; for, according to these, dancing is only for
slaves and women.

We learnt to appreciate our interesting friends more
and more. The books they had with them showed
their culture, and good taste in literature. English
classics, Addison, Johnson, and Steele were their
favourite reading ; their conversation consisted mostly

of descriptions of their country, their hopes and projects for its improvement. Their narrations had a great charm for Helfer, and he expressed a playful wish some day to travel in those regions. But the seriousness that lurked beneath the jesting tone did not escape me, nor how much the pressing invitations of both the Affghans to accompany them increased his desire to go. They took a great fancy to Helfer, and greatly regretted that they must soon part, and that they could not have the aid of his acquirements for their projects. They described their uncle, Dost Mahomet, as a man who highly valued Europeans, and granted them perfect security. They also told him that the journey, under their influential protection, would be quite devoid of danger. They intended to take the caravan road through Baghdad to Basrah, to take ship for the Indus, and to go up by the river to Cabul. They said that their influence was great on the lower Indus, as their uncle was in alliance with the Ameers. To defray the expenses of the journey, they carried, after Oriental fashion, precious stones and pearls.

I observed that Helfer sought to conceal his desire to accompany the princes from me, and I became convinced that the stay at Smyrna, pleasant and promising as it had hitherto been, would have no further charms for him. Still he did not express any wish to travel farther with them, and we certainly should not have done so if an accidental circumstance, so to speak, had not again ordered it otherwise.

On account of the heat, I rarely accompanied Helfer on his daily rides to the town, and consequently had

not observed the deep impression which constant intercourse with the Affghans had made upon him. But
one morning, as he was bidding me adieu, our hostess
came and pressingly invited me to accompany her to a
Greek *fête* in the town. I was not at all inclined to go,
made various excuses, and finally urged that my donkey
was lame ; but the kind lady had forestalled this objection, and had had her own best donkey saddled for
me. So I could do no otherwise than go.

This ride was a turning-point in our lives : had it
not been for it we should probably never have reached
India ; perhaps should have been living in Smyrna to
this day.

In the city we met the Affghans, whom Helfer had
not seen for several days. They told us that they had
found a vessel for Beyrout, which was to sail next
morning, and that they were now preparing for their
departure. Had it not been for this accidental meeting,
we should never have seen them again, as time would
not have allowed them to come out to Budja to take
leave of us. My eye rested on Helfer as he heard the
words ' take leave,' and the effect they produced on him
did not escape me. He turned pale, and, making a
pretext of business, hastily left us. I had seen enough
to know what it cost him to give up the journey to the
interior of Asia, and, as it had always been our ulti-
mate intention to go there, it seemed to me unwise to
miss so favourable an opportunity. I therefore at once
made up my mind that we would go, and proceeded
to lay my plans accordingly. I begged our friends, if
possible, to postpone their departure for a few days ;

and, as they were delighted at my decision, they were very ready to do so. Selim Khan hastened to the captain of the vessel to induce him to wait, in which he found no difficulty. Helfer soon returned, and had apparently regained his composure. But never shall I forget the expression of his countenance when I met him with a smile and said, ' What do you think? We are going with them.' He looked almost hurt that I should jest on a subject which so deeply agitated him. But when I explained to him that I was in earnest, that an arrangement had already been made with the captain, and that it now depended solely on himself, he could not conceal his delight, and agreed without delay.

So our lot was decided once more, and we were to sacrifice our peaceful abode at Smyrna to Helfer's love of exploration, and to go forth to meet an uncertain future.

He who once gives himself up to an idea is unconsciously and impetuously carried away by it ; on and on it leads him, and his dazzled eyes cannot see whether it is towards attainable ends or delusive phantoms. It was an idea that had torn us from a peaceful home and beloved friends, and an idea that induced us for the second time to leave a life of social pleasures and devoid of care in a splendid climate. People often ascribe the events of their lives to destiny : I should rather ascribe them to devotion to a ruling idea. If it had not been for this, how different might have been our life at home, our stay at Smyrna !

Only two days were allowed us for preparations,

and it was well; for I could not part without sorrow from the many friends I had made. They at first eagerly tried to dissuade us from our project, but, finding that we were immovable, they did all they could to help us. Herr Dutil, the Austrian Consul, allowed the sale of our goods by auction to take place in his courtyard. It was a half-comic, half-tragic spectacle to see the things I had become attached to passing into other hands. The ladies did not scruple to buy even caps, bonnets, dresses, and ribbons that had been worn, if they thought them modern and becoming. The whole lot was soon bought up, and, to our surprise, sold for more than they cost.

Another no less tragi-comic scene waited me— assuming the dress of a Turk. Safety and propriety enjoined the laying aside a woman's dress. In the East, women can only travel in closed litters, or, if on horseback, completely veiled; and they are of course shut out from seeing anything and from all intercourse. But I did not wish to go through the beautiful world awaiting me, either packed up like a bale of goods, or swathed like a mummy: I wanted to see, hear, and learn, and this was only possible in the garb of a man.

My female friends assisted in transforming me into a mamaluke. Each one helped to array me in some article of the unwonted attire. When the turn of the fez and turban came, my thick hair could not possibly be thrust into it (besides, under the heavy Persian shawl material, the heat would have been intolerable); but not one of them could bring her mind to use the scissors, not even the spirited Marie Perdey, of half Greek, half

English extraction; and when at length I seized the scissors myself and with a resolute hand severed the switch of long hair from my head, there was a sound of sobbing and lamentation as if they had been bewailing the dead. It was a ludicrous scene, but perhaps, under other circumstances, I might have cried too.

When at length my toilet was completed, by placing a dagger and two pistols in my broad girdle, and I looked not unlike a young Turk, I was introduced to the circle of acquaintances assembled, among whom I found Helfer, also in the costume of a mamaluke.

We both looked so different that we scarcely recognised each other, and might therefore hope that strangers would not find me out, but that we might be taken for brothers.

CHAPTER IV.

THROUGH BEYROUT TO LATAKIEH.

THE vessel in which we had taken our passage was an Arabian one. He who has seen an Arab vessel knows what that means; and no description will enable one who has not to form a conception of it: the dirt and discomfort are indescribable. I was therefore not a little astonished on the morning of our embarkation to find a clean deck and a well ventilated, clean, and nicely arranged cabin. For this most agreeable surprise we were indebted to our dear friend Captain Owen Stanley, who, with his sailors, had introduced perfect English order on board our Arab coaster. The captain had looked on with absolute indifference, only exclaiming, ' Inch Allah ! '

The sails were spread, the wind was fair, the anchor weighed. But now a painful parting awaited me— from my devoted Lotty. Not long before she had engaged herself to a respectable German master saddler settled at Smyrna ; they were to be married in a few days. Having followed me on board she could not tear herself away : she embraced me in tears, and, falling at my feet, entreated me not to leave her behind ; she would rather forsake her betrothed and give up a home than part from me. It was with the greatest difficulty that I persuaded her to join her betrothed, who was looking sadly on from the shore ; and I am glad that I did so. She is happily married. Enabled with the household things I left her to keep a really clean home for strangers, she is well off, and has had her sons brought up to be clever tradesmen, who have visited the Exhibitions in London and Paris. I still receive letters from her, bearing witness to her affection.

After a stay of nearly three months, we left Smyrna, where much hospitality had been shown us, on the 29th of August. We were again the victims of the treacherous winds and waves, for the very next day after passing the island of Vurla, contrary winds set in and we were soon becalmed.

The voyage was a tedious and unfavourable one. Although the vessel was a coaster, we saw nothing of the coast except the tops of the mountains of Anatolia. But the time passed pleasantly away in the study of the Persian language, in which the Affghans instructed us, as a knowledge of it was indispensable in their country. Besides, their conversation was most interesting ; there was no topic on which they could not express an opinion with sound sense and judgment, and their remarks were often witty and striking.

We were not permitted to land at Rhodes. The European consuls had, on their own authority, placed it in quarantine for mutual protection. After a seven days' voyage we reached Cyprus and cast anchor, a mile or so from land, in the harbour of Lanarka, which is only a roadstead and affords no shelter. We were disappointed in not seeing the luxurious vineyards which yield the fine Cyprus wine : at all events there were no vineyards in the part of the island we saw ; nothing but a saline and sandy soil, destitute of vegetation.

Two things only interested us as precursors of the southern zone. A few date palms, which, stunted as they were, deluded us into the idea that we had entered the paradise of a perpetually mild climate, should never more suffer from cold, nor see the earth covered with its winter winding sheet. Vain dreams! Before long we suffered more from cold than we had ever done in our Northern climes.

The other object of interest was a bright red scorpion, which made such rapid movements over the hot sandy roads that I sprang out of its way in alarm. I regarded it as a specimen of the poisonous reptiles which excite our childish imaginations in books of travel. But in this also I was mistaken, for in later wanderings in the thickets of tropical forests, I do not remember to have seen such a venomous reptile.

It had been our intention to leave the vessel, which was bound for Beyrout, here, to proceed by boat along the coast to Latakieh, and to go thence to Aleppo, the rendezvous of the caravans we were to join.

The strictly enforced quarantine regulations, however, under which the whole coast had been placed by Ibrahim Pacha—according to which no vessel not coming direct from Europe was permitted to land anywhere but at Beyrout—made this plan impracticable. So we had to submit to the inevitable, and go on to Beyrout.

Early in the morning of the 12th of September we

came in sight of it and saw the Phœnician coast in the early dawn. I quote the excellent description by Carl Ritter in his 'Geography,' which cannot be improved upon :

' A uniform range of dark blue hills rises above the water, while the purple clouds of sunrise light up the sea with fiery hues. If you approach it at sunset, however, the snowy peaks of Lebanon are visible, illumined with rosy light, and in losing sight of them the sailor takes leave of Syria.

' On a nearer approach, the features of the hills become more distinct : valleys and ravines are seen clothed with oak, fir, and cedar. Villages appear as specks of light on the declivities among the vineyards and olive gardens.

' During light winds, shoals of medusas are seen near the coast, and flying fish hover over the water to escape from their enemies the sharks.

' Above the city rise terraces clothed with the most luxuriant productions, from the palms in the warm plains near the coast to the regions of perpetual snow. Next to the palms come citrons, oranges, pistachios, walnut trees, olive woods, and mulberry plantations. On the borders of the plain there are fields of grain, rice, and cotton ; these are encircled by vine-clad hills, and the majestic pines mark the boundary of the cultivated land, which is enlivened by the songs of blackbirds, thrushes, and nightingales, and the loud cries of the bee-eater with its brilliant plumage.

' On the highest point of the mountains, with their prosperous communities and numerous flocks and herds, the order of pines attains, on the borders of the rich Alpine pastures of Lebanon, its noblest form in the famous cedar forest of Jebel Makmel.'

The institution of quarantine, hitherto unknown in Mussulman countries, contrary to their religion, and consequently under the supervision of the foreign consuls, was very strictly observed. It has four times protected Syria from the plague.

We had scarcely cast anchor when an officer of public safety came on board and gave us our choice, whether we would perform quarantine on board ship, in which case guards would be placed over us, or in the lazaretto.

Heartily tired of our voyage, we chose the latter, and were at once conducted thither by the guard, without going near the town, which was almost concealed by foliage.

The quarantine buildings were on a pretty high rocky promontory, against which the dark blue sea broke in waves of foam. Fresh sea breezes, intermingled with those coming from the heights of Lebanon, encircled the place: there could scarcely be a more healthy or pleasanter spot for a lazaretto. But the building was in a most unfinished state: 350 Egyptian soldiers were at work on it and the grounds.

Through the influence of the French Consul, to whom Helfer had sent his letter of introduction, two rooms were allotted to us which were intended for the ladies of the seraglio of Soliman Pacha, the famous general of Mehmed Ali, a native of France.

We pleased ourselves with the idea of the far-famed luxury of a seraglio, but were greatly disappointed : we found nothing but bare walls and clean floors—a great privilege, however, in Syria.

We made ourselves as comfortable as we could ; we put bricks together for the support of a table, and placed a door on them for the top. Window frames served for seats, and, with our ship mattresses upon them, for beds also. Dinner was to be served upon a straw mat, if any dinner was to be had ; about this, however, our guard did not trouble himself in the least.

Fortunately we were allowed to wander about freely in the whole quarantine space, and, from the defective fences, had free access to a large vineyard adjoining. The grapes were most inviting, and hunger overcame all scruples about tasting them. They were so delicious and satisfying, that we felt ourselves already in the promised land which was so near.

At length we found the owner, to whom we confessed our theft and offered remuneration, at which he was much surprised. He not only entirely declined it, but helped us to procure more substantial food from the city during our quarantine.

Our hospitable neighbour was a Druze, and through him we made acquaintance with the character of this people under its best aspect. He possessed lands and numerous flocks among the mountains, and only came down at the time of the vintage, for the liberty-loving Druzes are not fond of leaving the hill country. Through frequent intercourse with the city and connection with its trade, he could speak the Turkish language fluently, which was a means of communication between him and Helfer.

The Druzes are a fine race, full of energy, dowered with good mental powers, brave, honourable, and hospitable. The traveller or fugitive who seeks refuge with them is sure of a safe asylum.

As owners of their mountain lands, they consider themselves as independent lords of the soil, and cultivate it diligently; whereas the inhabitants of the plains are only tenants under Government.

Although outwardly they profess Islamism, they hold doctrines of their own, which they keep a profound secret. They receive with interest the teaching of Christian missionaries, and have even established schools in connection with the American mission among the mountains. The missionaries would be able to labour much more effectually among them if it were not for the jealousy of the Christian Maronites. The Maronites, although no national or external differences exist between them and the rest of the inhabitants of the mountains, are distinguished by their religious fanaticism; they are under the bigoted rule of their priests, who cover their beautiful country with convents; and to them they offer the best fruits of their industry.

To our regret we were prevented from making any excursions in the neighbourhood or from visiting the city, which, from its historical interest, we should have liked to see; but it is little in accord with the charming environs, and the style of its buildings is like that of most of the cities of the Levant. The streets are dark and crooked, the houses mean and rough ; one would never suppose that some of them are inhabited by millionaires.

The great mosque, built by the Christians, formerly the church of St. John, which served the Crusaders for their church festivals, towers above the houses and the thick foliage. It brings before the mind's eye the past history of this once important city and its varied destinies. Founded in very early times, it was enlarged by Roman emperors ; and, selected by Herod Agrippa as the seat of his voluptuous court, Beyrout became the scene of bloody festivals, in one of which 700 criminals slaughtered each other for the amusement of the spectators, and even Titus celebrated his father's birthday here by the execution of some thousands of rebel Jews.

It is curious that it was upon this blood-stained soil that Roman learning established its seat. Up to the sixth century the most renowned legal school of the empire, known for its moral strictness and discipline, flourished at Beyrout ; it reared the first jurists and statesmen, and was called a Mother of Wisdom. But this prosperity was not to last. What was not destroyed by the hand of man was ravaged by the fearful earthquake of 529, which desolated nearly the whole of Syria, and in which the greater part of the inhabitants and students of Beyrout lost their lives.

The city has never flourished since that time. It fell in turn under the dominion of the Arabs, Crusaders, Turks, and Druzes, and was alternately rebuilt and destroyed.

This went on until, in 1840, the English fleet expelled Mehmed Ali's troops.   In spite of all these disasters, however, Beyrout entertains hopes that, if a regeneration of the East should take place, it would again be one of the most important points of these classic shores.   Its favourable situation in the centre of the Phœnician coast, its natural beauties, the fertility of the soil, as well as the industry and capabilities of the inhabitants, justify these hopes.

Perhaps the time may not be far distant when these gifted but fanatical people, misguided by Islamism and bigoted monasticism, will again attain prosperity and true civilisation.   But then they must not be objects of petty jealousies among European powers, and Christian missionaries must aim less at making proselytes than at educating men.

We were disturbed in our peaceful asylum and diligent study of Persian and Hindoostanee by a rumour that a regiment of Egyptian soldiers was coming to perform quarantine there.   The report was confirmed on enquiry of the French Consul, who told us, with many assurances of sympathy, that we could not keep the rooms any longer, for they would certainly be required by the officers   It was impossible to permit us to enter the town before the expiration of our term of quarantine, but, as a longer stay at the lazaretto was impossible, he would, if we would venture on secret flight, keep a vessel bound for Latakieh in the harbour ready for us.   We were referred to a fisherman, who would conduct us by a private smugglers' path to the shore and take us on board in his fishing boat.

Dangerous as secret flight from quarantine always is, it was doubly so under the ruthless rule of Ibrahim Pacha in Syria : a human life was nothing to him ; it was only the ambition to make a name for himself and to invest himself with a nimbus of European civilisation that induced him to imitate European institutions.

But no choice was left us. To stay was impossible; the flight must be risked. We reckoned chiefly on the laxity of our guards and their love of gold. Our neighbour, the owner of the vineyard, was won over to our project, from hatred of the stern ruler who monopolised every branch of industry and sorely oppressed the people, not by the proffered sum of money: this he entirely declined for himself, but did not refuse a backsheesh for his servant, who was to carry our luggage.

On the 19th of September we prepared for flight. It was very difficult to persuade the Affghans to it : in true Eastern fashion they preferred to submit passively to any inconvenience rather than courageously to escape from it. But on our representing to them that they must remain behind alone, and that coming from Smyrna they would probably be taken for Turkish spies, they consented.

The guards nearest to us were won. Our scanty possessions were concealed among the vine-trellises in the garden, and we ostensibly retired early to rest, closed the doors and shutters, put out the lights, and sat in profound stillness. Nothing is more calculated to damp the spirits and fill the mind with anxious forebodings than to have to sit idly in the dark while

awaiting the hour for a hazardous enterprise The
minutes seemed like hours; our hearts beat audibly; we
listened anxiously for every sound. Helfer must have
struck his repeater a hundred times before it indicated
the appointed hour of twelve. He led the way, keeping close to the wall, I followed, then Selim Khan, and
last his brother. The brightness of the night, which,
even when there is no moon, had so delighted me before,
was now alarming—we could recognise each other at
fifty or sixty paces off; but we reached the vineyards,
which concealed us from prying eyes, without waking
the guards, and there we found our guide, whom we
quickly followed by the appointed path to the edge of
the promontory. Here the fisherman, who had fastened
his boat below, was waiting for us with another active
man ; and this was necessary enough, for if we had
hitherto had only to exercise passive courage, we had
now to put it in action.

From a rocky cliff, sixty feet high, rising perpendicularly out of the sea, against which the waves beat
with a loud roar, a kind of stairway led down in a
slanting direction. The steps, worn and slippery and
several feet high, looked impracticable. 'Must we
climb down here? Impossible ! It is madness !' we
exclaimed. And yet it had to be done. Return was
out of the question : our guides would not have consented to it for their own sakes. Happily there was no
time to think about it. The fisherman seized me in his
nervous arms, and, as if I had been a feather, went
down the perilous path, up which, perhaps, he had often
carried heavier burdens of smuggled goods ; Helfer

followed, trusting to his own agility, and the Affghans closed the procession, submissively following their leaders. Not a word was uttered; each one knew that a single false step must be death. At length we reached a platform, where there was firm footing, and took breath for a few moments. We then went on more quickly, until we were in a little cave in which the boat was concealed. Who can describe our feelings when we looked up the giddy height and could justly estimate the perils we had escaped!

Having expressed our gratitude to the vine-grower by a pressure of the hand—for he still declined remuneration,—we got into the boat; and vigorous strokes of the oar soon conveyed us to the ship. But before we reached it, the sound of guns from the lazaretto gave notice that our escape had been discovered and that we were being pursued. Whether it was in earnest, or whether the guards were anxious to prove their watchfulness by giving alarm after the fact, we did not know; we, however, were safe on board the coaster.

The captain received us with all the respect due to the recommendation of a consul at Beyrout. He was a stout, prosperous looking Turk, attired in an orange-coloured silk caftan with green stripes, ample trousers. with a variegated pattern on them, and yellow slippers. His head-dress was a red fez with a huge green turban, the sign of a pilgrimage to Mecca. His thick curly beard reached to his breast. He had prepared his only cabin for our reception; but, alas, it had not been cleaned and put in order by English sailors! On descending the first steps leading down to it I staggered back, stupified by the combination of smells, which might have been accumulating for years. They arose from garlic, salt fish, tar, and oil, mingled with the scent of lemons, spices, rose leaves, and bunches of dried lavender. Beside all this, there was a crowd of human beings, mostly Jews and Egyptian soldiers.

Although our cabin was divided off from the rest of the space, the atmosphere was the same, and it was impossible to stay there a minute. Happily in the East there is never any lack of coverlets, rugs, and cushions, and with the aid of these we made ourselves comfortable on a part of the poop which was considerably raised above the fore-deck. We were separated by curtains from the rest of the passengers : only the captain took his place at the wheel near us, the two Affghans, and a smartly dressed Frenchman, who politely introduced himself as the head cook of His Highness Ibrahim Pacha, whom he was about to follow to Aleppo.

We could not lay in provisions when in quarantine, and had nothing to look forward to but the ship's fare— hard biscuit, dried dates, fresh olives, and old goat's-milk cheese,—of which I could not bring myself to partake till driven by hunger. Our Parisian cook, on the contrary, had with him a large store of provisions wherewith to prepare dainties for his master's table, and, having a capacious chafing dish, could, under any circumstances, prepare an inviting repast. The interest which I evinced in his skill seemed to flatter him not a little, for when the meal was ready he gave us a pressing invitation to partake of it. We felt no scruple about being entertained on the pacha's provisions behind his back, and helped ourselves freely to the delicate viands. This unexpected piece of good fortune, like so many others which had befallen us, raised our drooping spirits and revived our hopes. Man often thinks and feels very differently before and after a meal.

The captain turned the wheel mechanically backwards and forwards, without being able to see the prow of the vessel. The rusty compass did not move; which, however, he did not regard, for, when Helfer called his attention to it, he only nodded and slowly stroked his leg under the knee with the back of his hand—an inimitable pantomime, peculiar to the Turks, expressive of various things for which other nations employ many words; most frequently, however, it denotes contempt for what they hear, especially from the lips of a giaour.

Helfer remarked again that a ship could not be guided without a compass, when he coolly replied that the Great Bear was a surer compass to him, adding, with a mysterious smile, that he did not require any guide. I thought he meant that, being near land, he could see the right course; but he was trusting to other, invisible, aid.

After sunset—during which he reverently performed his devotions, kneeling on a fine carpet spread before him,—he took out of his doublet a painted tablet with characters upon it, and hung it round his neck. He then turned the vessel seawards, made the helm fast, and lay down to sleep as peacefully as a child.

Helfer could not refrain from asking what he was thinking of. 'Of going to sleep,' he answered, with perfect coolness. 'But who is to guide the vessel during the night?' 'The wind,' was the reply, as he turned on the other side. 'But if the wind should change, what then?' To this he vouchsafed no answer, but pointed to his tablet and fell asleep.

This time his amulet made good its claims: a fair wind took us during the afternoon of the following day into the harbour of Latakieh. How easily and quickly the voyage may now be made round this interesting coast by the comfortable steamers which provide regular communication in these waters!

There was an unusual stir in the harbour of Latakieh: hordes of Egyptian soldiers were being disembarked, lately enlisted, or rather taken prisoners, in their native land to fight for Mehmed Ali in Syria.

There were Nubians, with their flat, sphinx-like faces and narrow eyes, their coarse black hair, greased with mutton fat and wound round a kind of wick, hanging down to their shoulders on either side of their flat cheek bones, like a wig of spiral curls. Then came Abyssinians, tall and slender, with regular Caucasian features, but their skin of an ash-grey colour, their long dark eyelashes giving them an expression of profound melancholy. They were all in rags which barely covered them. They were driven, fastened two and two, along the distance from the harbour to the town. The road, planted with olive trees, and abutting on extensive gardens, forms a beautiful walk. The houses are almost hidden in foliage; only the mosques and a few date palms rear their heads above it.

But there was no time to linger over these novel

sights : we had to hasten to seek shelter, for the captain had told us on sailing that there was just then no room for strangers at Latakieh, all the khans, and even the private houses, in which we might have found accommodation before, being laid under requisition by the new ruler. Helfer remembered that the convents in Syria were renowned for their hospitable reception of travellers, and resolved, as an orthodox Catholic Christian, to seek shelter in a Franciscan convent not far off, to introduce me as his brother, and to beg quarters also for our Mussulman companions, who, of course, had first to consent not to mention the Prophet during their stay in the convent.

By the aid of a few piastres we found a guide, who conducted us to the large but desolate looking building. It was shut off from the street by a long, high wall, with no opening but one inconspicuous door. On this door hung a hammer, with which Helfer struck three hearty blows on the metal plate beneath, making the knocks resound far within.

We had not long to wait before a sliding shutter in the upper part of the door was opened, and an old monk cautiously stretched out his round face and bare head, which, however, he hastily withdrew on seeing four Mussulmans. He was about to close the shutter, when the Christian salutation, 'Laudatur Jesus Christus,' met his ear, and the expression of his face changed, as if by magic, from fear to surprise. He stared at us, uncertain whether to trust this greeting from a turbaned head, until Helfer explained in Italian that we were not enemies, but Frank travellers, who had only adopted the Turkish dress for safety, and begged for shelter because the city was full of Egyptian soldiers. The monk now opened the door and bade us welcome; but told us, with a shrug of the shoulders, that a roof and a hard couch were all he had to offer us, for he only lived on charitable gifts from Christian families in the town. 'Whether this,' he added, with a significant glance at me, 'will suit the young gentleman there, I do not know.' The old man showed much acuteness by the rapidity with which he had seen through my disguise; up to this time I believed that I had always been taken for a young Turk. But seeing my alarm lest he should refuse to receive me into the convent. he said to me, 'Come in; I will make it as comfortable for you as I can.' And he kept his word.

For fifteen years he had lived alone in the convent; for fifteen years no fire had been lighted in the great empty kitchen, the refectory had not been aired, the cells and corridors had not been cleaned: birds and spiders had undisturbed possession of them, and the windows were scarcely transparent. We passed through a long passage, the floor of which echoed our footsteps and broke the grave-like silence for the first time for many a day.

At the end of the passage, he led us into two adjoining cells, in no better condition than the rest; but when he opened the windows there was a splendid view over fruit gardens to the open sea.

The good old man was gratified with our admiration; he was proud that even his convent should have something beautiful to show.

He now hastened into the town, to some of the faithful of his little flock, to procure provisions for us, and soon came back laden with good bread, wine, and delicious fruits, followed by a servant, who brought soft cushions from the neighbouring house of a Christian merchant and prepared couches for us.

The next day Father Antonio, at our request, found us a travelling servant amongst his community. Pietro Giacomo, a native of Malta, was a shrewd and well-trained fellow. He was to be our guide to Aleppo, but first, convent cook, and he addressed himself to his task with great alacrity. The materials were soon collected for an ample dinner, a bright fire was kindled on the long desolate hearth, the refectory was swept and aired, the table laid, and at twelve o'clock dinner was served. I shall never forget the beaming face of the good padre as he took his seat as our guest at his own table, and seldom have I fulfilled the duties of hostess with more real satisfaction, or taken more pleasure in the enjoyment of my guests, than when I figured as housewife in the convent.

The old man's heart was opened, his eyes sparkled, and he was quite eloquent; he even became more sociable with the Affghans, of whom he had been rather shy, as he evidently regarded them as real Mussulmans.

Destined from childhood for the Church, he was brought up in the Seminary at Rome, then became a pupil in the mission school, and, in obedience to the superior, entered this convent as the youngest brother. It was at that time occupied by numerous ecclesiastics, and had an extensive sphere of labour. By degrees this diminished : the number of monks and their influence declined ; many were removed to other places, until at length Antonio closed the eyes of his last companion. For fifteen years since then he had lived alone within these gloomy walls, and had to be porter and sacristan and to wait upon himself at the mass. And yet how contented he seemed, and with what humility he submitted to his fate! 'It cannot be helped,' he said ; and therewith every earthly desire seemed to be stilled.

I cannot describe the deep impression the cheerful resignation of this monk made upon me, and with what humiliation I compared it with my own restless heart.

In spite of his isolation he was by no means apathetic : he listened with great interest to Helfer's narrations, and when cities and countries were mentioned he fetched an old book. 'Now,' he said, 'tell me all about them, and I shall follow you everywhere.' It was an old well-worn 'Gazetteer,' in Italian—the only book in the house except the Breviary and Missals. He studied it at his leisure, and thus lived in the world he had never seen.

The next morning he accompanied us as guide into the town, which contained many ancient ruins. Specially remarkable are the numerous catacombs, dating from the most remote times, on the north and west sides of the town ; they are excavated in the rocks, and are so extensive that there would be room for a whole generation in them. The number and careful construction of these catacombs afford evidence of the former large population and wealth of Latakieh. Bones are no longer found in them. One of the largest is called Mur Tekleh, after Saint Thecla, a martyr, who is said to have taken refuge in it. Saint Thecla's day is still kept by the Christians.

These catacombs served the early Christians, during the persecutions, as asylums and dwelling-places : they are very much concealed, are dry and roomy, and some even have wells in them.

The population of Latakieh is said to be from six to seven thousand, of whom about one thousand are Christians, one thousand Maronites and Armenians, and the rest Mussulmans. In addition to their ten mosques, the latter had lately built a splendid new one on the hill on which the citadel stands, in honour of their sainted Sheikh Mugreby, who is said to have made a pilgrimage to Mecca every week. It is approached by an imposing flight of steps, adorned with painted windows and a pulpit with fine marble steps. The chief mollah has to deliver here as orthodox a Mussulman sermon as possible every Thursday, and to stir up the people against unbelievers.

The town contains some well-built houses ; the consulates, bearing the flags of England, France, Italy, and other European powers, are specially handsome. The Christians regard them with great satisfaction, as, to the annoyance of the Turks, they find them a protection against insults from them.

Our host told us much of the fanaticism of the Mussulmans here, and described them as the most intolerant in Syria. 'They have several times plundered our convent,' he said : ' what they could not make use of and drag away they destroyed; but now that there is nothing left but the bare walls they leave us alone. They also persecuted the rest of the Christians, who were often obliged to fly and take refuge in the neighbouring island of Ruad.

The island of Ruad, the Aroa of the ancients, is a remarkable spot—a little rocky island rising abruptly out of the waves. It is the same as Arvad, mentioned by Ezekiel as allied to the Phœnicians.[1] Amidst all the political changes of the neighbouring continent its brave, liberty loving inhabitants have maintained their independence, which has enabled them to afford a secure asylum to many political refugees. The island is destitute of vegetation; it contains a mass of houses several storeys high, surrounded by a colossal wall built of huge blocks of stone, and it possesses a harbour which, from its natural situation and fortifications, bids defiance to the approach of a foe.

This hardy race of seamen became rich and powerful by means of extensive commerce. Formerly under kings of their own, and afterwards under presidents elected by themselves, the inhabitants maintained themselves as an independent little State, until, in the last war, it sided with the Turks against Ibrahim Pacha, who, as master of the coast, gave the word of command for sacking the island, and it was only saved by the English fleet. The inhabitants are renowned as swimmers and divers: it is to them we owe much of our finest sponge, which they detach from rocks at the bottom of the sea at a great depth. They cannot, however, remain so long

---

[1] Ezekiel xxvii. 8–11.

under water as the pearl divers of Ceylon. It is so exhausting that few even of these muscular men can stand it for more than a year.

We paid a visit to the Christian merchant whose cushions had furnished us with soft couches. He had evidently been apprised of our intention, for he had left the dark little office in which he spent the day engrossed in business, and had joined his family in the inner court, paved with marble, under the shade of chestnuts and cypresses. There were pomegranates and roses in bloom, and in the centre the waters of a clear fountain fell into an artistic marble basin.

These courts with their grateful coolness and shade are a great comfort—the only one, indeed, of which the dwellings of the most wealthy families can boast ; for inside the houses there is nothing but bare white-washed walls and divans of straw or reeds covered with cushions. The rooms are mostly dark and close, for they are seldom aired.

Three youthful forms and an older lady were sitting near the fountain, two of them occupied in winding silk ; the other, evidently the youngest, was weaving pomegranate blossoms into her sister's dark hair. She was a lovely creature, slender and graceful as a Hebe, her face of the finest oval, her complexion transparent and tinted with peach colour, her gazelle eyes shaded by long dark lashes, her brow by fair hair hanging in wavy locks, to the ends of which were fastened gold coins, producing a faint jingle with every movement. Although prepared for our visit, they were evidently surprised by our entrance : the ladies were embarrassed to find themselves in the presence of four Turks, and the lovely Hebe hid her face behind her mother, only raising her head from curiosity now and then to have a peep at us. The salutations with the master were ceremonious and reserved. Perhaps he did not feel secure, owing to former experience, from Turkish arbitrariness and greed, and Helfer's short communication as to the objects of our journey did not suffice to inspire him with confidence. At all events, he eyed us sharply and exchanged many suspicious glances with Padre Antonio.

With his hands crossed over his breast and the customary prostrations, Helfer introduced me to the ladies as his wife. For a little while they eyed me with scrutinising incredulity ; and only when he assured them that I had undertaken the journey of my own free will and from affection for him, and had from necessity adopted male costume, did they become more sociable ; but still they shook their heads. The notion of a woman travelling through the world in man's attire was too remote from all their ideas.

I saw that the little one had some scheme in her head, for she several times whispered some words of Arabic into her father's ear, looking archly at me. She might have spoken aloud, for we did not understand a word of Arabic. On Helfer's asking what she wished, the master said, turning to me : ' The silly girl wants to see you in a woman's dress, and would like to dress you herself ; you must pardon her childishness.' ' I will let her dress me with pleasure,' I answered. These words put some life into the group. The girls sprang from their seats and hastened into the inner apartments. They wore, buckled on to their feet, a kind of stilt-like stool with four thin legs about a span high, on which they balanced themselves with extraordinary ease and grace, like tendrils in the wind. The reason of this probably is that the marble floors are watered several times a day and are often quite wet. But I do not know whether they are in general use; I only saw them in this house.

The girls took me into their sleeping apartment, which, instead of beds, only contained benches covered with cushions. The eldest, who was about my size, fetched her smartest dress, while the two younger ones busied themselves in taking off the mamaluke garb so distasteful to them. After this had been done, a chemise, made of a kind of *crêpe de Chine*, with very long, wide sleeves, was put on; then pantaloons of pink satin, a tunic of thick flowered silk interwoven with gold threads, and over this a short sky blue silk jacket embroidered with gold. A costly Persian shawl, folded crossways, was tied round my hips, instead of thrown over the shoulders in European fashion, and fastened in a knot in front, so that the ends hung down long, while the two broad corners reached to my knees, looking not unlike a miner's leathern apron. Finally, I had to put on a number of heavy gold chains, richly adorned with gold coins, which reached to the waist. Now all was complete but the head-dress. My busy lady's maids sadly missed my long hair; and when I explained to them by signs why I had myself cut it off, they looked at me with amazement—almost aversion,—and tried to hide the defect by a little red fez and a bright blue gauze shawl, embroidered with gold stars, put on turban fashion. Thus decked out they were delighted with me; they admired and caressed me, danced with joy, and played no end of childish freaks. At last I was to be exhibited to my husband, that he might see how much more beautiful I was in this attire. They had even buckled on the stilts over my yellow morocco shoes; and as I could not walk in them without help, they took me under the arms and led me out in triumph to Helfer, who, of course, did not fail highly to admire my toilet. We were now quite sociable—I was treated like an old friend; coffee and chibouks, whose aromatic vapours were inhaled by the lady of the house, increased the general satisfaction, and it was late before we separated, after I had taken off my fine clothes. The girls looked sadly on, and, on taking leave, they could not bring themselves to embrace me, lavish as they had been of their caresses before.

How lovely these girls were, and how charming their unaffected childishness seemed, compared with the airs of the belles of European *salons*! But what was the fate that awaited them? They were all three betrothed, though scarcely grown up, to men whom they had never seen, perhaps more likely to inspire aversion than affection, and who, at all events, would be more bent on success in their commercial undertakings than on making their young wives happy. And this is still the lot of Christian women in the East.

We were warned on all hands to be on our guard, on the way to Aleppo, in passing through the territory of the Nazarenes. Although Ibrahim Pacha's iron fist ruled this race and punished every misdeed with ruthless severity, still their country was dangerous, and, but a short time before, no traveller alone would have ventured to go from Latakieh to Jebili, though the one place is in sight from the other. The Nazarenes and Ishmaelites, descendants of ancient native tribes, have the worst reputation as brigands. Is is said of them that they would not hesitate to rob their brothers or mother. Strongly built, and inured to every hardship and privation, always persecuted and oppressed by the rulers of Syria, they have yet enjoyed a kind of consideration, mingled with dread, among their mountain fastnesses.

The Ishmaelites, distinguished by their relentless pursuit of their enemies, were called assassins by the Crusaders, since many Christian princes and generals had perished by their daggers.

The Nazarenes have a considerable territory between the Orontes as far as the sea and Latakieh, with many almost inaccessible mountain strongholds, among which towers Massejed, the seat of their chief.

Both sects are opponents of Mahomet and worshippers of Ali, but they hate each other with a deadly hatred, and are always ready to betray each other to their common foe. Both keep their dogmas strictly secret, and cannot be induced to disclose their religious mysteries even by violence and torture.

The spiritual chief of the Nazarenes is considered to be infallible, and held in the greatest veneration. He who is elected to this dignity is instructed as a boy in reading and writing, and is taught to look upon martyrdom for his faith as the highest merit. No suffering will extort the sacred mystery from him. Amidst the cruellest tortures he will only reply: 'Try! cut my heart out of my body, and see if you find anything there!'

The characteristics I have given of these wild mountain tribes must be ascribed to the absence of all moral and religious training. Persecuted and despised, they are subject to the yoke of the fanatical followers of Mahomet, and live amidst ceaseless feuds among themselves. But, nevertheless, they exhibit many noble qualities and show great aptitude for culture. They are hospitable and polite to strangers who approach them with confidence, and who do not excite their rapacity by the sight of valuables. Their sheikhs, who exercise hospitality in the name of the tribe, they revere as saints, and erect numerous monuments over their graves.

The English Consul, Mr. Barker, who, after a residence of many years in Syria was intimately acquainted with the people, asserted that he had found Nazarene servants as faithful and honest as Christians and Moslems. They were brave, trustworthy, and industrious, even open and communicative; it was only on religious subjects that they were reserved, and could on no account be induced to make any disclosures.

Mr. Barker gave practical proof of his opinion of their aptitude for culture. After fifty years of active business life he retired into the plain of Suweidieh, which extends along the coast of Syria from the mouth of the Orontes, and eastward from Seleucia, for ten

English miles inland, inhabited by a mixed population, mostly Greeks and Armenians. By untiring efforts he turned it into a garden of Eden, whose rich natural products were increased by cultivation.

The huts of the inhabitants lie scattered on the shores of the Orontes, amidst plantations of oranges, lemons, and mulberry trees. They are a vigorous race, and the women handsome; they show more politeness and goodwill to strangers than to their Arabic speaking countrymen.

Barker introduced a system of high cultivation; the finest fruits of the earth flourished in his domains. Products of China, the Indian Archipelago, etc., throve here as in their native climes, and flowers of every zone adorned the grounds, from the plains to the summer country seats on Jebel Musa and Akra. He introduced the cultivation of the mulberry, Italian cocoons, and a better method of manipulating the silk—the production of which had greatly increased, and had become a source of prosperity to the people, who needed no longer to live from plunder, but could hospitably entertain strangers, like their master.

The Nazarenes were also ready to receive instruction from the English missionaries, so long as they sought only to teach, not to convert them. They had been disposed to establish schools, but had taken care that the boys should not be led to adopt another religion, by the instructions conveyed, before they could judge for themselves.

They always replied to the missionary, Mr. Thomson, to whom they were much indebted for their education, in conversation on their religion : ' We love Christ and Moses : your religion is the same as ours.' But no sooner had they attained their object—some remedy for their sick, perhaps,—than they mounted their horses and rode back to their mountains. The better educated among them, however, saw the advantages of more cultivation and the favour which they would thereby gain with the European consuls, and were said to be disposed to promote the establishment of a mission school near Latakieh. Let us hope that this has been accomplished, and that a blessing has rested upon it from above.

We had great difficulty in getting animals for ourselves and our baggage, as every riding horse or beast of burden was in requisition—by fair means or foul—by the myrmidons of Ibrahim Pacha, for the transport of his soldiers. Our Giacomo, however, well acquainted with all the mule drivers and their tricks, contrived to help us out, and succeeded in secreting five riding horses and a pack horse out of the way of the troops; but, in order not to run the risk of being robbed of them in the streets, we had to steal out of the city on foot.

CHAPTER V.

JOURNEY TO ALEPPO AND BIREJIK.

WE left Latakieh at daybreak on the 25th of September. Our good Padre Antonio had become attached to us, and our table had suited him so well that he was sorry to part with us; but, finding that his efforts to detain us were vain, he accompanied us to the convent gate. The vast building, with its inner and outer courts, lay still in deep shadow; perfect stillness reigned, broken only by the echo of our footsteps. He turned the rusty key and opened the creaking door, but before we passed through it, he placed his hands on our heads and, with agitated voice, gave us his benediction; he even extended it to our Mussulman friends. Then, turning hastily away, he closed the door, and therewith ended one section of our journey. We had found here a safe asylum and even kindness; it renewed our trust, and we went on in good heart, until, not far from the town, we found our beasts concealed in the thickets and mounted without delay in order to escape as soon as possible from the range of the soldiery.

We soon began to ascend the heights of the Nazarene hills by bad roads bordered with brushwood, mostly box and myrtle. Fine hills and luxuriant plains adorned with laurels, arbutus, plane, and cherry trees, opened to view. A few huts, built of mud or sun-dried tiles, were picturesquely concealed among them. But their inhabitants, although accustomed to ever new and increasing oppression, had deserted them, in order to escape by flight the hardest fate of all—being pressed into Ibrahim Pacha's army. All the men capable of bearing arms had fled to the mountains, where his myrmidons could not so easily follow them.

As far as the first station, Ghafâr Awenâd, the river of Latakieh, Nahr el Kebir (the powerful; so called from the rushing mass of water it often contains), had made way for itself through a rocky defile, through which our road lay ; but, being autumn, we saw only the dry pebbly bed.

After a ride of five hours we came to Baluligeh, or Bahlulie, where, on account of the healthy climate and fine scenery, the wealthy families of Latakieh have their country houses ; but they were now all closed and deserted. We found, however, grapes, cucumbers, and goats' milk, which, with the provisions we brought with us, furnished us with a refreshing meal.

Tiring as the ride had been up the steep ascent on our over-worked horses, we could not rest long: we had to hasten to reach a caravan before darkness set in, with the leaders of which we had agreed to make the journey together for safety, and it was still some hours in advance. It was late in the evening when we came up with it, and found our first night quarters, after a ride of about twenty-two miles, in Ghafâr Awenâd. Here we found Egyptian soldiers as outposts, but nothing but the bare walls of the large khan, which, however, may perhaps have offered more accommodation to travellers in former times.

We had scarcely performed a fourth part of the distance (about ninety-three miles) between Latakieh and Aleppo. Three days of hard travelling were before us, during which we should have to exchange the fresh air and verdure of the coast for a desolate waste. We therefore started very early next morning, and, after a pleasant ride of thirteen miles in the cool of the morning, we arrived at Jisi esch Sogher on the Orontes. Here the steep and lofty mountain chain closes in the valley of the Orontes so completely that it is filled by the bed of the river. It is spanned by a fine bridge of thirteen arches, which is crossed by all caravans between Latakieh and Aleppo. The Traun, between Gmunden and the waterfall, afterwards reminded me of the Orontes.

Near the bridge is a handsome khan, built at the expense of the Nazarene family Kaproli, and kept up for the gratuitous reception of poor and sick travellers. This generous hospitality, strangely in contrast with the manners of a robber race like the Nazarenes, is nevertheless one of their characteristics, and is shared by many uncivilised nations. They plunder whenever they can, and yet value hospitality so highly that they erect monuments to those who are distinguished for it.

In Niebuhr's time Shogher belonged to a powerful Nazarene chief, M'Kaddem of Baluligeh, who was then lord of the pass.

From Shogher, steep mountain paths lead to the

highest pass of the chain, from which you can see a great extent of the valley of the Orontes, and Shogher appears to lie almost perpendicularly beneath you. Towards the south the eye ranges over the fertile vale as far as Apamea, and beyond to the less lofty mountains of Jobr.   On this pass vegetation changes, the varied foliage and verdure cease, and you come to a desolate region of limestone hills with a rocky surface and scanty sheep pasture, very similar to the Karst of Trieste.   In some of the valleys and basin-like hollows you find fertile soil.   In such spots human beings have settled, sunk wells, and drag out a miserable existence. This treeless waste, with its rocky chasms, is a melancholy spectacle ; nevertheless the landscape is dotted with the ruins of churches, castles, and settlements of considerable size and solid construction—signs of a once numerous population which must have succumbed to some fearful fate.

The heat became almost intolerable, and instead of a refreshing breeze we had a hot, dry wind which cracked our lips and cheeks until they bled. To protect yourself against it, you must wrap yourself up as much as possible in thick clothing, not dress lightly as we do in Europe in warm weather. This is the reason of the native costume—the heavy mantle, the thick turban, and the double shawl of camel's hair which the Bedouin draws over his head down to his eyebrows, while he crosses the two ends over his face, so that only his dark flashing eyes are visible.

During the great heat, besides my cloth mamaluke dress and a cloak of the same, I put over my head a wadded silk cloak, which I had kept of my lady's wardrobe, and sat on my horse wrapped up like a mummy.

Wearily our poor horses dragged on. At every green spot I hoped for the longed-for rest; but the leaders of the caravan, caring less for themselves than for the beasts, pushed on to the resting-place for the night. It was nothing but a large meadow where there was pasture and water for them, but nothing at all for us.

Without our Giacomo we should have fared badly; but he exhibited brilliant talents as courier. In a short time he collected together from the camel drivers so many coverlets and cushions—whether borrowed or stolen I never knew—that he was able to prepare a comfortable couch for Helfer and me, divided by curtains from the rest of the company, while, with the provisions he had with him, he prepared a substantial meal.

For the first time I lay down to sleep in the free air of heaven; but although tired to death, the novelty of the scene kept me long awake. The eye ranged over the boundless distance, the deep blue arch of heaven, the countless stars. Around us flickered the fires, near which the guards comfortably smoked their pipes, wrapped in their black and white striped mantles, their faces glowing with the ruddy flames. The merchants were lying about in various groups, and their servants kept a sharp eye on their carefully packed goods. Among them lay the camels, freed from their burdens, their long necks stretched out even in sleep, their bells making a monotonous tinkling with every movement.

With their wise looks and soft eyes they gazed around, as if resigned to their fate of being patient burden-bearers for man over the burning sands of the desert, and willing, when he is ready to perish, to furnish him with the reviving draught by their death.

All the vast changes, amidst which for ages one nation has succeeded another, each in its turn to perish, having fulfilled its mission,—the great tragedies of which this country must have been the theatre, the indelible traces of which I had just witnessed,—crowded into my mind. Never had I felt so far from home, so entirely transported into another world, as at this moment. The past and future seemed to pass before my mind's eye, until at last fatigue gained the victory over phantasy, and I fell asleep amidst a jumble of Arabian fairy tales and German realities.

Our slumbers, however, were not of long duration. The first streak of dawn restored life to the sleeping group and aroused us also; and it was well, for when we tried to rise we felt quite lamed, and our clothes were wet through, so heavy is the dew and so great the decrease of temperature by night. We with diffi-culty regained the use of our limbs, and feared the worst for our health; but some hot coffee, the rising sun, and a morning ride of several miles, set us to rights.

That day's ride led us through a similar monotonous waste, sprinkled with numberless ruins. We ascended several times to small plateaux, rising terrace-like one above another, the desolation being only now and then broken by a wretched village or a few scanty cornfields.

Although in many parts the ground would repay cultivation, it remains untilled, owing to the poverty of the
inhabitants. The fellahs can only carry on farming
with the help of the wealthy Aleppines, who furnish
them with capital for implements and seed, and receive
part of the produce in return. Besides this, the poor
peasants have to pay high taxes from their produce to
the pacha. It is easy to see, therefore, why, under
circumstances so unfavourable, they cultivate as little
as possible of their land.

The Affghans, although accustomed to tropical heat,
did not bear the hardships of the march and the changes
of temperature so well as we did. Selim Khan became
so exhausted as to alarm us. He had only as yet been
acquainted with Asiatic luxury. We were therefore
rejoiced, on the morning of the fourth day, to see from
the plateau, although at a great distance, the minaret
of the ancient citadel of Aleppo. But we had first to
descend the plateaux, leading down to the desolate
plain of Aleppo, which extends northwards to the foot
of the mountains of Aintab, southwards to the heights
of Jebel el Has, and eastward to the Euphrates, about
thirty-three miles from Aleppo. The way was full of
natural hollows, deepened into holes by the hoofs of
the caravan beasts. Desolate as the aspect of this
region is in autumn, it is enlivened in spring with the
bright hues of a southern flora, when the bulbous
plants, deeply hidden amongst·the rocks, shoot up their
vigorous tufts.

About a mile before reaching the city we came to
a large cistern of excellent water. These wells, which

often have temple-like structures built over them, in such spots are the greatest boon to the weary traveller, not only for the sake of a refreshing draught, but from the shade afforded by the roof.

From this spot the whole of the arid plain, in the midst of which Aleppo is situated, can be seen. The city looked well, extending on the left bank of the Koik, or river of Aleppo, like a lake of stone, out of which the slender minarets rose, like nymphs from a bath, and broke the uniformity. From this point we could admire the beauty of the city without seeing the desolation within.

We approached the gates at sunset, and painfully felt the want of letters of introduction. Our isolation in quarantine in Beyrout and hasty flight had prevented us from obtaining any there for the consuls at Aleppo, especially the English Consul, who enjoys the highest consideration. It is most painful to be without them, as there are neither inns nor *restaurateurs*, in our sense of these terms : native travellers go to their country-men, foreigners to their consuls, and the lower classes either encamp in the streets or with the muleteers in the caravanserais. Besides, just now the latter offered no accommodation, as they were overflowing with Ibrahim Pacha's troops, which were preparing for a raid against the refractory Kurds and Turcomans.

We were in the greatest embarrassment when our mule driver asked where he should take us to. Helfer's proposal to ask the English Consul's hospitality without introduction, appeared to me, considering the strict formalities of the English, to be doubtful policy.

Perhaps by unceremonious intrusion we might forfeit his goodwill for the future. I therefore proposed that we should go on, and ask the first European looking man we saw for advice and temporary accommodation. I still had home-ish notions.

So we resolutely proceeded to seek shelter and supper somewhere or other. A twelve hours' march and a fast day were powerful incentives. We were fortunate enough before long to perceive not far off a dress coat with long tails, the wearer of which was gravely stalking along. At this moment it appeared to me like a signal of victory, though I am in general no admirer of this most unbecoming article of dress.

Helfer hastened at once to our European country-man and told him our situation and our wishes. He listened with distant curiosity, stepped into a house, promising assistance, closed the door and did not reappear. After waiting a few minutes Helfer returned, like one who comes back to his thirsty brothers after a fruitless search for water in the desert. People are curious, even in Aleppo, and our rather strange appear-ance had attracted a small crowd, who looked on from a little distance; but no one said a word. The tongue of the Oriental is not set so lightly as that of the Western nations. He thinks twice before he speaks, and meditates or dreams ten times more than he talks.

At length we learnt, by dint of repeated question-ing, that all foreigners must go to the English Consul— to the great lord. We had scarcely made up our minds to follow this advice when a peremptory 'halt' was called, and custom-house officers, whom Ibrahim Pacha's civilisation had conferred on Aleppo, laid hands on our baggage. All remonstrance, and assurances that it contained nothing but clothes were vain: to the custom house it must go, and our Giacomo, for safety, with it. The crowd of spectators had meanwhile increased, and a second dress coat was visible. Undaunted by the former futile attempt, Helfer addressed the wearer with a request that he would direct us to some shelter. This time he found commiseration for our dilemma. The gentleman commissioned one of the men standing about to guide us. For the promise of a few piastres he consented, and he led us through a labyrinth of streets which the growing darkness concealed from view.

As our guide only understood Arabic, we were cut off from all enquiry as to how and whither. After long windings in and out, we stopped before a great door, which was opened to his knock. He said a few words in Arabic to a little man who came forward, took his piastres and disappeared, whereupon the door closed behind us.

We found ourselves within a spacious court surrounded by a wall and other buildings. The chief edifice was lofty, though only of one storey, and had a large window in the middle extending nearly to the height of the house itself; the entrance was covered by a canopy, ornamented with gilt carving; the floor was a mosaic of costly marbles. A glistening stream rose high into the air from a basin of the same material, and played over vases of flowers; close by were two lofty cypresses, which served as roosting-places for a flock of gyrating doves, and roses and jasmines filled the cool evening air with fragrance.

We felt ourselves transported, as if by magic, from the desert into a fairy palace of delights and Oriental luxury. We simultaneously uttered exclamations of delight, and congratulated each other on reaching so promising an abode.

Our eyes now fell upon the man who had opened the door. He was a thin little gentleman, with red slippers on his bare feet, a long dark blue kaftan, an immense black turban, and a Jesuitical countenance. He introduced himself to us as an Armenian doctor of great repute, and as a still greater linguist: he was constructing a dictionary in no less than five languages, and he began to go with great deliberation into the details of his work. We listened for some time, not venturing to interrupt the flow of his language, for the wounded pride of a learned man is hard to heal. But seeing no preparations for supper, politeness finally gave way to hunger, and we both informed him that we were in great need of a substantial meal. If any one blame us for this, I wish him a twelve hours' ride for four days together over hard rock glowing with heat, and scanty fare. Our desire obviously embarrassed the old man: he smiled, turned this way and that, and after making various excuses, said that it was too late to make purchases; the provisions in the house were limited; a little rice and a few eggs were all he had to offer. Our sanguine expectations were sadly damped; but the words eggs and rice fell pleasantly on our ears, and, asking for nothing more, we only exhorted him to be quick, for we needed rest as much as food. Fatigue and hunger strove for mastery.

Our host disappeared, his slippers clattering all over the house. A corpulent old lady assisted him: she was not the lady of the house, she whispered mysteriously; *she* was young and beautiful, but never seen by strange men.

It was hours before the longed-for rice made its appearance. I could no longer sit up, my eyes closed with weariness; still the tyrant hunger asserted itself and would not be appeased. At length the master laid the table himself, and, in spite of our remonstrances, prepared to wait upon us. We replied to his invitation to take our seats with a 'Thank God!' Broken plates, rusty knives and forks, ragged table linen, in short, the whole equipment of the table in this fine house had caused our illusions to vanish. There must surely be some enchantment here, I thought. But we were too much taken up with the rice, which tasted delicious, to think much of anything else.

The meal ended, we exclaimed, ' To bed! to bed!' ' Adesso, signore,' was his reply; ' adesso vado a preparare il letto.' Fear of waiting for hours again made me follow him. He hastened panting through the rooms; they were all empty, but bore unmistakable evidence of former luxury. With some trouble he collected cushions enough to make tolerable couches. I had begun to feel rather awe-stricken in this great desolate house, whose owner seemed to me like a magician under the spell of some superior power; but fatigue soon overcame all alarms and caused me to fall

into a profound, refreshing sleep, not disturbed even by
dreams of enchanted castles or spell-bound princesses,
until at length the bright noonday sun awakened me,
and Helfer was at my side encouraging me to rise.
The hope of a cup of fragrant coffee made me hasten.
We were soon assembled for breakfast in the cool court
near the splashing fountain and the cypresses. Among
the shrubs was a host of chirping, twittering inhabitants,
with brilliant plumage, quite indifferent to our presence.
Greenfinches, bullfinches, red-throats, and other birds
unknown to me, fluttered round our heads and hopped
about on the marble floor as if they alone were entitled
to breakfast there; while pigeons, fowls, ducks, and other
poultry strutted about, now and then coming to look at
us, as if to ask if we were not going to give them their
accustomed meal. But we, poor creatures, were still
fasting ourselves.

About one o'clock the old woman appeared with
our breakfast—a small can, containing as much as a
good German bowl,—and told us that we must await
the arrival of our servant for dinner.

Giacomo's appearance with the luggage put an end
to our difficulties. He soon made purchases and
prepared a savoury meal, which we took under the
cypresses, and afterwards yielded ourselves to a sweet
siesta.

We had as yet had no means of solving the enigma
of the house and its inmates : our host went out early
in the morning, and the old duenna answered all our
enquiries with a silent shake of the head. Giacomo had
been too much taken up with cares for the outward
man to take much interest in our curiosity.

We were still sitting under the cypresses, deep in attempts to solve the problem ; each thought he had found the solution, but each was mistaken. The door opened, and a lady entered the court, who, after she had thrown aside the thick veil in which she was enveloped, displayed the dress of the Frank ladies of the better class : a dark silk skirt, open at both sides, bright-coloured silk pantaloons, and a little jacket richly embroidered with gold. Her dark hair hung down her back in numerous tails adorned with gold coins ; she wore a close-fitting cap ornamented with a kind of silver filagree work, and over this a blue silk handkerchief with gold stripes. The arched nose and eyebrows and long, dark, narrow eyes clearly belonged to the Armenian type.

Shuffling with her yellow slippers, she slowly approached us, and making a respectful obeisance, said at length, in Frankish Italian : 'I am Madame Salina, and wish to know whether you have seen my husband.' We looked in amazement at her and at each other : who was Madame Salina? and who was her husband? She rightly interpreted our looks, for, taking the seat offered her, she began, without further ceremony, and with the greatest ease : 'My husband is one of the first physicians here in Aleppo. A week ago he was called to see a wealthy merchant who was taken very ill on the way from Latakieh, and I have heard nothing of him since. I fear he has fallen into the hands of the barbarians who infest these parts and lay hands on whatever they can. I have learnt from Mr. Dimitri, my neighbour, that you are come from Latakieh, and you must have seen my husband on the way.'

This mode of obtaining news of distant friends—
which we Westerns, who jostle each other on the rail-
ways, scarce deigning a look at anyone, should, to use
a mild expression, consider rather ' green '—is in these
countries quite a matter of course, for travellers seldom
meet without asking ' whence ' and ' whither.'

We expressed our sincere regret that we could not
give her any news, as our caravan had avoided the
khans on the usual route, because they were full of
soldiers, and had taken a less frequented road.

Madame Salina, by her natural unassuming manner,
had made a very favourable impression on us, and she
was quite ready to solve the enigma of our abode. We
told her what had happened on our arrival, and of our
curious reception. She was evidently amused, and said,
with a roguish laugh : ' My neighbour has been playing
off his little game again and giving himself out for a
learned man, which he is very fond of doing. He is
only a barber, whom the English Consul has put in to
take care of his house during his long absence at his
fine seat on the coast.'

So this was the prosaic solution of the mystery!
And, in spite of ourselves, we were at the English
Consulate after all, although just now it was deserted
by its occupants.

It was now Madame Salina's turn to ask questions ;
and we at once, as concisely as possible, gave an account
of ourselves. She listened in silence, inhaling in long
puffs the aromatic vapours of the *nargileh* which had
meanwhile been handed to her. What we told her of
home seemed to make no impression on her, it was too

remote from the circle of her ideas. But as we approached Aleppo she became animated; and when we recounted the adventure with the coat she broke out in exclamations of disgust at such a breach of hospitality—a virtue held so sacred here. She asked for a more particular description of the delinquent, a mischievous smile spread over her face, and a low 'si conosce' escaped her lips.

To make amends, she asked us to dine at her table, which we declined, as Giacomo was able to provide very well for us. But the invitation to spend the evening with some friends and relations was very welcome, and at the appointed time we repaired to her house, which was not far off. We found a circle of ladies sitting cross-legged on the divans along the wall and smoking the indispensable *nargileh*. Their dress consisted of the Aleppo costume already described. Their necks were encircled by a large number of gold chains, which hung low down over the muslin handkerchiefs concealing the bosom. Their arms, so far as they were not covered by the muslin sleeves which appeared from under the jacket, were covered with gold bracelets. The turban-like head-dress was adorned with bunches of cord ending in tassels of real pearls. It was a very fine sight for a spectator initiated into the mysteries of the Levantine lady's toilet.

As we entered, each rose deliberately, one after the other, and, with her hand on her breast, made her salaam and then deliberately resumed her seat and her pipe.

Our unquestionably strange appearance did not

appear to excite any interest in them : they sat like wax figures, their eyelids half closed, and their countenances devoid of all expression.

I should have begun to feel ill at ease among all this still life, had not Madame Salina, with an alacrity which was all the more striking in contrast, taken Helfer and me by the hand and conducted us to another part of the spacious room. A roguish look beamed in her face as she approached a group of gentlemen and said, in a loud tone of voice : 'Come here, Mr. Franz, here are some countrymen of yours!' Dress coat number one, a fair young Bohemian, stood before us, blushing all over and unable to bring out a word in his dire confusion.

'Is that the way you receive strangers in your country?' she said to him, with assumed displeasure ; 'it is not our way. You were near bringing our hospitality into evil repute.' Herr Franz now stammered out a few words, excusing himself, from ignorance of the circumstances and fear of getting his partner into trouble, as he had taken us for agents of the pacha. But we cut his bad Frankish phrases short with a hearty welcome in German, and expressed our pleasure in having found a countryman in any way. Hardly had the words been uttered when a genial welcome met our ears on two sides, and four hands were extended for a German shake. Herr Pocher, from Leipa in Bohemia, who had long been settled in Aleppo as owner of a large glass warehouse, and Herr Klinger, also a Bohemian, music director in Ibrahim Pacha's service, introduced themselves to us.

Then followed enquiries about our beloved country, which both had left years before, and even Herr Franz, Herr Pocher's partner, became loquacious. But whenever four Bohemians meet, talk soon resolves itself into music, and so it was here. Instruments were quickly fetched, and several quartettes were given, with Herr Klinger as conductor, which Helfer followed by airs from operas as yet unknown here. Our improvised concert lasted till late at night.

I carefully watched the countenances of the ladies, to see whether the German music produced any impression on them. But not a trace of emotion was to be seen. There they sat, totally indifferent to it, exchanging a few insignificant words with each other, sipping the thick coffee out of little cups, and taking the indispensable *glico*. Their ears, dulled from childhood by the Turkish tom-tom, had no power to convey harmonious sounds to the mind. We, however, left this unexpected German musical entertainment in the highest good humour.

Early next morning Madame Salina came to take me a walk in the city, of which, owing to the darkness in the evening, I had not yet seen anything.

This once flourishing commercial city, the centre of intercourse between the East and the West, where the precious products of the tropics were exchanged for those of western industry, where vast treasures were stored, and reals not counted, but measured, the rendezvous of all the caravans of pilgrims,— this city, as it existed in my imagination from descriptions I had read, full of palatial commercial houses splendid mosques, and lofty minarets, with clean, well-paved streets—met my eyes with a scene of fearful desolation.

The earthquake of 1822 had ruined two-thirds of the city; it had not, however, as in the case of fire, reduced it to ashes, leaving not a vestige of its former glory, but large portions of handsome edifices were left standing amidst the ruins, making the surrounding destruction all the more conspicuous. Here was half of a fine building left standing, its interior, bearing witness to the luxury of its former inhabitants, laid open to view. There was half the cupola of a splendid mosque cut in two as if with a sword, its dome of azure adorned with stars of gold. The crumbling mud walls of miserable huts lay among massive constructions more or less ruined, whose granite blocks should have bid defiance to eternity, and by whose walls race after race, nation after nation had passed. The old and the new, the great and the small, palace and hut were jumbled together : all differences between the habitations of men were effaced. But man ever erects anew the barriers between the ruling and the serving class.

So the Aleppines, in spite of this fearful destruction, which, though not often to this extent, had frequently recurred, had taken heart again, and had begun to restore their homes. New huts and new palaces had already arisen among the ruins, and many modern improvements had been tastefully added to the old Saracenic style. The interminable bazaars were filled with wares as before. Indian shawls, silk stuffs embroidered with gold and silver, Persian carpets, Indian spices, European cotton and other manufactures, precious stones, pearls, Bohemian glass, cloth, and furs— all were to be found well classified here, and a stream of bargaining customers was for ever passing to and fro.

At first I was alarmed at the number of dogs, who, quite independent of masters, had quartered themselves under the booths of the bazaars, and apparently divided them into districts, for the observance of which they seem to have police regulations of their own. Woe to the four-footed offender who passes his boundaries! He is sure to be torn in pieces by the rightful owner. But they are harmless to human beings if they leave them alone; for although the dog, in the eyes of the Mussulman, is an unclean and contemptible animal, whose name he uses as the greatest insult, he never ill-treats him nor kills his young ones : this accounts for the large number of dogs in the East.

My companion did not at all approve of my costume; she would have liked to see me in one like her own, and in true woman fashion tried to excite my vanity by praising the pretty flowered materials, the head-dresses finely worked in silver, so becoming in her eyes. But finding that she could not persuade me to adopt a feminine dress again, she said that I must, at least to please her, buy a new mamaluke suit, one of the handsome sort made in Aleppo, of red cloth with gold embroidery. She had, however, the mortification of seeing me choose a modest green embroidered in black silk. She thought my taste incorrigibly bad.

I was afterwards her guide up to the castle hill,

which, like most of the Aleppines, she had never mounted, as the ascent is fatiguing and an order from the governor is required. This citadel, like many others in Syria, in the midst of the city, is a partly natural, partly artificial hill of from 150 to 200 feet high; the outside is entirely covered with masonry and surrounded by a fosse 60 feet wide and three-quarters of a mile in extent.

The citadel of Aleppo was very strong at the time of the Crusades; according to a Kufic inscription, however, it appears to date from the sixth century of the Hegira. The main entrance was under a strong arch, with three thick iron doors, which are said to have led, ages ago, to the inexhaustible treasures of Aleppo. The earthquake had made fearful ravages here, the greater part of the building was in ruins, the portions still habitable were imperfectly restored for barracks.

In the midst of these ruins was a watch tower, 60 feet high, and near it a draw well 288 feet deep; both, singularly enough, had been untouched by the earthquake. The well still supplies its cold crystal water.

From the tower we had a magnificent view of the neighbouring desert and its distant boundaries. Towards the south and east the eye ranged as far as the Euphrates; towards the west, to the mountains of Beilan; in the north, the majestic Taurus with their snow-clad peaks were visible. At our feet lay the city, the terraces on the roofs of the new houses adorned with flowers beneficently concealing the ruins; among them wound the river Koik, amidst blooming gardens and dusky olive plantations, from which pretty pleasure resorts peeped forth.

This splendid prospect was not without its effect on Madame Salina ; her prattle ceased as, for the first time, she gazed in wonder beyond the boundaries of Aleppo. Whether she was overcome by a sense of the greatness and beauty of the world I could not make out, she had no words for such novel sensations, and was not quite herself again till we entered the commandant's house to pay a visit to his wife. We had scarcely crossed the threshold when we heard a loud scream, and encountered two female figures hiding their faces in their hands. My mamaluke costume had frightened them ; they thought themselves exposed to the gaze of a strange man, but after Madame Salina had explained, they were pacified. They were mother and daughter—Nubian beauties of rather dark hue, with large black eyes, eyelids and eyebrows artistically encircled with black, their lips blue, and the nails of hands and feet dyed red. At first I disliked these painted faces, but when you are used to them, the bright colours seem to harmonise with the dark complexion ; it certainly would not become a northern blonde belle.

Here, also, the walls of the rooms were bare and thinly whitewashed, the women untidily and insufficiently dressed, but gold coins were suspended from their heads. Little distinguished as they looked, they spoke in a lofty tone. When Madame Salina expressed surprise at finding only one wife, she answered : 'I do not allow a second.' 'You do not allow it ? Your

religion and your laws permit it to the husband.'
'But I do not; I am a Nubian princess, and only
married my husband on condition that I should be
the only wife; if he took another, I should accuse
him before the pacha and return to my family.'

Whether her exceptional claims were well founded
I do not know; she looked resolute enough to assert
them.

After so much had been explained to her as she
could understand of our coming and going, and why I
wore a man's dress, we took our leave with polite
salaams and hand crossings.

Madame Salina had no children, of which she
often complained with tears, for it is only as mothers
that wives in the East feel their dignity and happiness.
This led to her not leading a very domestic life, and
she was often at the house of her elder sister, the
wife of our countryman Pocher, who was blest with
children. Here I had an opportunity of observing
the invincible indolence of eastern women. I used to
find Madame Pocher, although she had four children,
as well as her childless sister, sitting the whole day
cross-legged on the divan smoking the nargileh. Herr
Pocher made the purchases for the kitchen, which was
managed by a slave, who did just as he pleased in that
department as well as in the rest of the house. Even
Madame Pocher's own toilet, smart as it appeared to
view, was very much neglected. On going to rest, the
women only take off the outer silk garment and gold
embroidered jacket, and keep on their trousers and
other articles of dress. The thick roll of hair is only

combed out and fresh plaited once a week, and at other times merely smoothed with pomade. If only the coins suspended from it glitter and jingle, that is enough.

Under these circumstances the frequent use of the bath is very desirable. But I found the arrangements for it in the highest degree repulsive. The women regard the bath-room, filled with hot steam, as a place of entertainment, in which they walk about quite undressed, sit and chat, take sweetmeats and sherbet, and free from all restraint, they show great want of refinement. Induced to visit it by Madame Salina, and my own desire for a refreshing bath, I was so disgusted by the sight that met me on the threshold that I at once turned away and have never again entered a Turkish bath. I can, therefore, divulge nothing of the arts and mysteries practised there which are so highly extolled.

I mention as a fact told me by Herr Pocher, that in his business transactions he only made written contracts, as is customary with us, with Christian merchants, but never with the Turks, whose word was a better security than the most binding contract. What an admission from the lips of a Christian merchant!

The European community gave a ceremonious ball in honour of the new ruler of Syria. The order and security which Ibrahim Pacha had introduced, the severity with which he had punished rapine and theft and driven the Bedouin hordes back into the wilderness, had awakened great hopes of better times. The merchants could transport their goods in safety, and expected

to see trade restored to its former prosperity. New life
was stirring everywhere, although the unsparing con-
scription for military service had induced several
hundred young men to escape it by flight.

We received an invitation, and eagerly availed ourselves of the opportunity of attending a ball at Aleppo,
and of seeing the dreaded conqueror.

The festive hall, although spacious and brilliantly
lighted, did not come up to our expectations. Instead
of the smooth parquet floor of a European ball room,
there were carpets, of rare beauty certainly, but so soft
as to make it impossible for the feet to glide swiftly over
them. This, however, was no obstacle to the fair
Aleppine dancers; even for dancing they retained their
yellow slippers and their slow shuffling gait; they
did not array themselves in light ball dresses, but
rather overloaded their usual attire with additional
finery. Herr Klinger's baton directed a *Française*, and
the ladies shuffled solemnly up and down, backwards
and forwards, over the carpets, paying no heed to the
time of the music. Some young gentlemen of the French
consulate tried to introduce life and movement into the
dancing, but they had their *pirouettes* and *entrechats* to
themselves, and the close files of lady dancers shyly
made their way among their ranks.

After each *Française* there was a pause, during
which preserved fruits and sherbet were handed round.

His Serene Highness sat on a raised seat. He was
somewhat corpulent with strongly marked features and
a grey beard, and he wore the scarlet fez. The scene
seemed to amuse him; then his eye fell on Helfer and

me, as we stood a little apart from the rest. He was surprised to see Europeans in the mamaluke dress, the costume of his guard, and asked where we came from ; on being informed he expressed a wish to see us nearer. Of course they hastened to introduce us. 'Inch Allah!' he exclaimed, 'the lady is courageous! How do you like it here?' he asked through his interpreter, as he would not speak Turkish himself. 'Very much,' I answered. But when Helfer, in the course of conversation, asked if he would not like to see Europe, he knitted his brows and answered sternly, 'I am good enough for my country as I am.' Perhaps he thought that the question meant that there were some things he might learn in Europe.

I asked permission to pay a visit to the ladies of his harem. 'What do you want with the women?' he said. 'You had better see my soldiers; to-morrow is parade.' And I did see this parade, which exhibited the greatest possible variety of physiognomies and costumes ; but the troops had been well drilled by the French officers. Still more admirable, however, was the achievement of our countryman, Klinger, who, in a short time, had trained an excellent band composed of negro boys and young Abyssinians, and that day, in honour of us, nothing but German marches were played. While we were listening to these home-like sounds, his Serene Highness dashed up to us and asked complaisantly: 'Well, how do you like it?' but was off again immediately.

At the ball I had sat by a young lady, the regular beauty of whose profile had attracted my notice. How

lovely her front face must be, I thought, and longed
that she would turn her head. From the passivity of
Oriental women, I might have waited a long time, so I
attracted her attention by heaving a deep sigh. Good
heavens! what a sight. If I had just feigned a sigh,
an involuntary exclamation of horror escaped me now.
In her other cheek there was a deep hollow, and from
a spot in the middle deep seams diverged contracting
the whole side up to the eye, the lid of which was
pulled down, showing the red inside. Was it possible
that so much beauty and ugliness could exist divided
only by the line of the finely-arched nose! It was the
effect of the *bouton d'Aleppe*, a kind of carbuncle,
which, in Aleppo, and particularly in Diabekr, attacks
young women and girls on one side of the face, completely eating it away.

The cause of this disease is not known; in Aleppo
it is attributed to drinking the water of the Koik,
in Diabekr to dirt, and the sharp contrast between
summer and winter temperature. However accounted
for, the sight was not merely hideous, but alarming, as
foreigners, although less frequently, also contract this
disease.

We were greatly interested in making the acquaintance of several English officers attached to the oft-
discussed Euphrates Expedition. They had just returned
from a perilous mission to Orfah and Harran. Attacked
on the way by the Subha and Aniza Arabs, their
leader, Lieutenant Lynch, had by his presence of mind
contrived to turn their enemies into friends. They also
took up their quarters beneath Démitri's hospitable

roof, and we met first at breakfast. The little troop consisted of Lieutenant Lynch, the second in command of the Expedition, a clever diplomatist and expert in Oriental languages; his brother, a captain in the Indian army, Dr. Staunton, and Mr. Elliot. The latter was a Eurasian, the son of an English gentleman and a native Mohammedan woman, not of legitimate birth, which in England is of more consequence than elsewhere. He had, however, received a careful education in England. He was afterwards taken prisoner on board a Greek vessel by the Russians, and transported to Siberia. He made his escape, however, and reached Constantinople, where he exchanged the religion of his father for that of his mother, and became a dervish—a useful exchange for one who wishes to travel safely and comfortably through Asia. In every village, when one of these Mussulman saints arrives and blows his horn, the whole population assembles; even the secluded women come out to serve him and learn from him, for from his lips drop the sayings from the Koran. This pseudo-dervish wore a coarse grey robe, a broad girdle round the waist with a pair of pistols in it, a shawl of camel's hair round his head, and red leather boots, the sign of a polished saint, for a true dervish treads the glowing earth barefoot. A gazelle skin, thrown over his shoulders, served him as a mantle and a couch. Refined features and a bright dark eye gave evidence of higher culture than you would have expected from his garb. His adventures, which he soon related to us, excited our interest. He was one of those people who, richly endowed by nature but outcasts from society, live in perpetual conflict with it, and either conquer or perish.

These gentlemen also showed a lively interest in us after we had told them our plans and adventures, particularly Lieutenant Lynch. He had travelled much in Asia, and with a good English education he combined a taste for Asiatic hospitality and Oriental luxury, which, however, it is necessary to indulge in there to a certain extent for the sake of keeping up your dignity. Perfectly acquainted with the character, subterfuges, and intrigues of Turkish officials, he was quite a match for them, and was therefore often employed in negotiations with them. Like ourselves he had adopted the mamaluke dress, only his was richly embroidered. He was struck with our Affghan companions, and at first regarded them with suspicion. To my satisfaction, however, when I questioned him as to the grounds of it, he replied, ' The appearance of these men, with my knowledge of Asiatics, at first very much surprised me, and I was in fact disposed to regard them as impostors, who are to be found here as well as in Europe; but I am now convinced that they belong to the class of honourable Asiatics, who keep their word and conscientiously follow the rules of the Koran ; you may safely travel with them.'

Although we thoroughly trusted them before, this verdict from so experienced a connoisseur was very satisfactory, and removed the least shade of suspicion.

We had hoped to find Aleppo the chief rendezvous of the caravans, which either take pilgrims to the grave of the Prophet through Baghdad and Basrah, or merchandise into the interior of Asia, and to find an opportunity of making the somewhat dangerous journey in safety. But weeks passed without the least prospect of this ; the warlike state of things had kept everything at a standstill. An invitation from Lieutenant Lynch to beguile the time by an excursion to Port William, whither he was about to return, was therefore all the more welcome. We accepted it with the greatest pleasure ; we were as curious to see the mighty river which runs through Syria from north to south as to witness the opening of steam navigation upon its waters.

This bold and magnificent enterprise, which was carried out with iron perseverance, arrested at that time the attention of the world, and it could not fail to excite the greatest sympathy in Aleppo, which had só large an interest in it. Politicians and merchants beheld the dawn of a new era in the regular navigation of the Euphrates. The results, however, expected from the undertaking as a civilising agent, the blessings it was to confer on great and gifted nations groaning under a cruel yoke and sunk in fanaticism, its special purpose to restore the advantages of cultivation to those countries now lying waste, which once enjoyed paradisiacal abundance—these beneficent ideas which doubtless animated the heart and soul of the originator, were not, and have not to this day, been realised.

On a bright October day we left Aleppo. Every one had wrapped himself as well as he could in cloth clothing, and wound a shawl over the tarbush as a protection against the midday heat and the cold at night. We formed a considerable troop, calculated to inspire respect. We were preceded by two Turkish kawasses in rich costume, well armed with guns and pistols, and provided with the silver staff, the ensign of their dignity. Lieutenant Lynch followed at some little distance, giving me the place of honour on his left hand, then the rest of the gentlemen. I much enjoyed the ride with this stately convoy, so different from our previous mode of travelling, and the more so as the neighbourhood of Aleppo on the north is richly cultivated. Villages lie along the banks of the Koik amidst luxuriant gardens; the country was even adorned by an avenue of stately trees which would have done credit to European taste.

At seven we reached the village of a tribe of Kurds, to whom our arrival had been announced by our outrunner Mahomet, and he had secured night quarters for us. I was much interested in making acquaintance with this race, hitherto unknown to me. Unfortunately the darkness prevented me from distinguishing anything but a mass of habitations half below and half above the ground, the roofs of which were formed by black tents. We were received by the sheikh with great ceremony, with many salaams and much hand crossing, as signs of respect for the great lords, and he conducted us to the abode for strangers. Every village must keep one such for the reception of travellers who are under the protection of Government; if it has none, the sheikh must give up his own. It consisted of a square hollow sunk a few feet in the ground with a black tent stretched over it; two little openings represented the windows, but the door, always open, gave light. The floor was of hard trodden earth. It was prepared for our reception with rush mats spread along the bare walls, covered with soft cushions of silk and flowered cotton, red being the prevailing colour.

Our English companions, more accustomed to the usages of the country, took off their large red boots, put on yellow slippers, and took their seats crosslegged, which we with our less practised limbs did not succeed in doing. For supper, a carpet of varied hues was spread upon the ground, and on this were served pilaw (stewed meat with rice, the usual dish, and very good it is), sour milk (leben), apricot marmalade with fresh butter, which I found an excellent mixture, and splendid grapes. There was also flat plate-like bread, which, from the scarcity of fuel, is generally baked on a hard-dried cake of cow-dung well mixed with straw. The dough, shaped like this cake, is placed upon it, and the cake is immediately set fire to ; as soon as it is burnt away the bread is ready ; it is of a greyish colour and rather tough, and serves for plate, knife and fork ; you break a piece off the edge, take it between the three fingers of the right hand, dip it into the dish, and eat it with what you dip out. Some rusty old knives and forks, which had not been cleaned for a long time, were brought out in honour of us, and to show their advanced civilisation, but they seemed to me much less inviting than the hands carefully washed before every meal, and with which they are so dexterous in dipping up the food with the bits of bread, that no one touches another's place. Our host, invited by Lieutenant Lynch, took his place opposite to us, with some of the most distinguished of the tribe, and thus we sat in the Kurdish tent, taking the common meal with our fingers out of the dish, and very good we found it.

These customs may seem very uninviting to Europeans, but they are not really so. The Asiatics maintain so much dignity in all their actions and mode of handling things, that nothing seems rough or vulgar. These Kurds also showed their good breeding by not betraying the least aversion to partake of a meal with a woman, although they never do so with their own women. They go freely about unveiled, as is universal among the country folk, for they do most of the rough work, and there is not the strict separation of the sexes which is kept up in the towns, but they are not permitted to eat with the men, and have to wait on them.

The tent afforded space enough for part to be divided off by a curtain for Helfer and me. As usual, after a long ride, we were refreshed by sound sleep, and continued our march next morning. The sheikh himself accompanied us to the next village, where we were regaled with milk and fresh water, and took another guide.

Although there is no danger in this country of losing your way in forests, it is scarcely less difficult not to miss the right path, or rather to find a path at all, for not a trace of one is to be seen on the rocky ground, not a tree nor a plant grows in the arid soil, no mountain nor rising ground breaks the horizon; you do not see the villages until you are close to them, and perceive the black doorways in the burnt clay houses; the cloudless blue sky seems to rest on the greyish brown earth. I found this to be the case in autumn in the greater part of Syria. Others, who have traversed the country in spring, speak of the carpet of flowers, the abundance of purple and yellow crocuses and other bulbous plants, whose roots are buried deep in the rocky earth, secure from frost and heat, and when nature awakes, put forth numberless blossoms, without leaves, and change the country into a flower garden. It is always a mistake to try to describe foreign countries after only a rapid journey through them.

Towards evening we reached a tribe of Turcomans, who do not live in mud houses, but mostly in black and white striped tents. Apprised of our approach, they had erected a large tent for our reception. These tents, supported by six or eight poles, and often very spacious, are divided by a curtain separating the space for the women. The multitude of silk cushions and costly carpets, as well as the rich attire and dignity of the sheikh, bore witness to his wealth. We were received with still more ceremonious politeness than on the previous evening, and at supper had preserved fruits and sweet pastry, which could not have been home-made, but indicated intercourse with the town.

Lieutenant Lynch played the part of chief of our party with great dignity. He solemnly took the seat of honour. The attention he paid to me by handing me the first cup of coffee, attracted the notice of the numerous men present, whose curiosity had before been excited by my appearance. Observing this, he introduced me as his younger brother, thereby preventing any inconvenient inquiries. After supper we were surprised by the singing of two men, accompanied by a guitar. This ended, a girl of twelve years old entered the circle and executed a dance. With incredible agility and frightful distortions of the limbs and features she tried to express, now joy, now sorrow, to the great admiration of the native spectators, who followed her movements with breathless attention and involuntarily imitated them. I was told that the meaning of the song and dance was life and death.

It was interesting to notice the deep impression produced by this mimic acting, primitive as it was, among those present. When it was over, the Turcoman Terpsichore demanded a gift from each, and to the amusement of all, she urgently begged for one from our dervish Elliot, who refused to give, pleading poverty; he was only relieved from her importunity by our chief, who doubled his own gift.

I should have liked to pay a visit to the women's apartments, and to see life behind the scenes, but was precluded from it by my masculine garb and the part I had to play. But I saw enough of the unveiled fair ones, who, as curious as myself, often peeped between the folds of the curtains, and during the preparation of supper went about outside the tent, to obtain no very exalted idea of their charms. Stately, powerful, and dignified as the men are, the women are unattractive. They do all the rough and menial work. The expression of their faces, in spite of their piercing black eyes, is heavy, showing no activity of mind, and they are not so well nor so neatly dressed as the men. The ornaments they prize the most are earrings, and a very large ring, set with beads, in the right nostril. Gold coins are suspended from their caps, which are high, and broad at the top. Their faces are uncovered, except that they wear a broad bandage over the mouth.

We started early next morning. Our intention of visiting the ruins of the ancient Hierapolis involved a long march through the desert. The sheikh himself and a number of eminent men of the tribe accompanied us. They appeared to wish to inspire the Franks with a good opinion. Armed with long guns, pistols in their belts, and spears in their hands, with large bright coloured tassels on the top, which fluttered gaily in the morning breeze, mounted on swift steeds of noble pedigree, their black and white striped mantles hanging in ample folds over their shoulders, they looked like a troop of knights of bygone days. Some of them bore falcons on their wrists, their wise-looking eyes hooded for the chase. Who would not have felt as if transported into the middle ages?

After a march of several hours the cultivated land came to an end, and we entered on the desert, which had plainly only become a desert for want of tillage; industry could now, as in former times, reap rich harvests from it.

In the distance we saw herds of antelopes feeding, who fled as on the wings of the wind at our approach. These defenceless creatures, with their beautiful heads and soft beseeching eyes, find safety only in speed. Large flocks of birds of various kinds were flying southwards; noisily as they announce their arrival in spring, they leave their breeding haunts in autumn in perfect silence. No sound broke the stillness but the horses' hoofs on the rock. In order to display the dexterity of the riders and the fleetness of their steeds, the sheikh gave orders to his people to chase the flying game. The word was scarcely spoken when ten riders sped away, gradually separating, then forming a semi-circle till they vanished from view. After about half-an-hour, during which we had kept to a walking pace, some of the hunters came back in a measured gallop. Across the crupper of one of the horses lay an antelope, dead, but not wounded; it had not been killed by any weapon, but ridden to death. We were soon to get a nearer view of this method of killing game. From hither and thither the rest of the hunters now drew near. They appeared to be seeking something. All at once, not far off from us, we saw two young wild boars; the hunters sprang after them, drove them before them, and ran them down before our eyes, so that they were killed by the horses' hoofs. I should not have thought a horse could be trained to tread a living creature to death, but these horses seemed to be accustomed to it, and did it, I might almost say, with a sort of murderous glee.

About two o'clock we reached the ancient Hierapolis, now Membidge. The only remains of the place where the Emperor Julian with his victorious army crossed the Euphrates by a bridge, intent on subjugating the Persians, an enterprise, however, in which he met his death, are the ruins of the temple erected to the Dea Syra, a few palaces, the walls, and many aqueducts, which must have traversed the whole city. There is not a vestige of the bridge, and of the city itself, which Julian had made the metropolis of the Euphrates country and the chief seat of commerce, there are but few remains.

A hot wind was blowing which dried up the tongue and made the lips smart. The fresh water and the shade of the ruins was all the more grateful. In spite of our guide's admonitions to proceed, so that we might reach our still distant destination before dark, we took a long rest ; it was getting dusk before we reached the fertile and cultivated banks of the Sajur, still some distance from our night quarters.

Our way lay through undulating country, sometimes sloping gently to the river, sometimes high above it with steep descents. We had not gone far when loud human voices broke the stillness, and armed riders came in sight and fired at us. Lieutenant Lynch immediately ordered a halt. Our Turcomans, to whom the prospect of a skirmish did not seem at all agreeable, withdrew into the background, when Lieutenant Lynch requested them to turn back in a body, well aware that a doubtful friend is often more dangerous than an open foe. Accompanied by an attendant, he rode calmly up to the attacking party, who meanwhile had halted. The coolness, presence of mind, and superiority of Europeans makes a great impression on these children of nature, who act on impulse, not on calm consideration. A few words sufficed to explain the incident. Our numbers had alarmed the neighbouring tribes ; they feared an attack and had prepared for defence. After they were convinced, to their great satisfaction, of our peaceful intents, they conducted us with joyful demonstrations to their sheikh. He was an old acquaintance of Lieutenant Lynch, who enjoyed great popularity among the natives, because, knowing their tastes and weaknesses, he did not disdain to conform to them.

Before reaching our night quarters we had a most fatiguing march. The darkness had increased, and our way by the river went now through deep clefts, now over steep precipices, which made me giddy and obliged me to shut my eyes. I could scarcely get my tired horse along. But our young friend, Selim Khan, suffered most from the unwonted hardships. It was with the greatest difficulty that he had kept his seat, and he now declared that he could go no farther. We could not permit him to pass the night alone in the open air, so Helfer stayed behind, helping him on slowly with the aid of our servant.

A weary hour had passed, which seemed to me an eternity; at length a group of tents came in sight, magically illuminated by burning watch fires, the goal of our day's journey. The picturesque sight made me soon forget my fatigues. A fire was blazing before almost every door, by which the women were preparing supper; the children squatted round with eager eyes, the men lay near comfortably smoking their chibouks. A large space in the centre of the encampment was specially surrounded with fires for the protection of the flocks from wild beasts, particularly wolves, who are apt to come and carry off a good meal.

We were received here with more ceremonious politeness than genuine hospitality. In spite of every demonstration of respect a certain embarrassment was evident. Lieutenant Lynch soon got to the bottom of it, and his observations of an influence from high quarters adverse to the Expedition were confirmed. The English and the navigation of the Euphrates were a thorn in Ibrahim Pacha's side; he considered himself to be sole master of Syria, and here was a handful of foreigners about to dispute his possession. This was too much for his ambition. But, as he did not dare to oppose the English openly, he secretly put all possible difficulties in the way of their work. He privately countermanded his official orders to the subject tribes to furnish the Expedition with means of transport, labourers, and supplies. He even inspired the free tribes, who had shown themselves friendly to the English, with so much fear of his revenge that they drew back and refused to continue their aid. Lieutenant Lynch, however, again succeeded in restoring confidence.

The next morning we soon entered the land of the Euphrates, whose clear rapid waters wind through the landscape like a ribbon. With silent awe I greeted this witness and associate of the most ancient and memorable events in the history of the human race. It has for ages pursued its course unchanged, spreading blessings around, indifferent by whom, or whether by any, they have been enjoyed. Its shores are now inhabited by various half civilised tribes, partly agricultural, partly nomadic. The fertile soil repays a hundredfold the little pains bestowed upon it. Why should its owners aim at higher results? They only labour to satisfy the unbridled avarice of their oppressor or to be plundered by Bedouins.

A range of hills of pleasing forms skirted the river to our left, but the entire absence of wood creates a void, even in this fruitful district, in the eyes of the Northerner.

When we were near Port William, Lieutenant Lynch hastened on, probably to apprise the commander, Colonel Chesney, of our unexpected arrival. He received us very politely, and hoped we would make ourselves as comfortable as the encampment permitted, as it was too late to reach Bir (or Birejik) on the other side of the river that night.

I saw little more of the camp that evening than that it was surrounded by earthworks surmounted by a few guns. The commander lived in a flat-roofed house built of stamped mud, which barely kept out the sun, and with nothing but openings for windows; besides a few small rooms, it had a good sized mess room for the officers. Two tents were put up for us, in which we were very comfortable.

The next day being Sunday, we were invited to attend Divine service, which, in the absence of a clergyman, was performed by Dr. Staunton, the physician of the Expedition. I then understood but little English, and nothing of the sermon that was read; still the seriousness displayed by officers and men did not fail to induce an elevated frame of mind. Although there may be more of outward form and usage than inward

devotion in the English Church service, it has a greater
and more salutary influence than many will allow.   In
the most remote quarters of the globe, and under circumstances the most ·various, it is a bond of union
between every member of the English nation.

We spent the day of rest at Port William, and
Helfer took the opportunity of communicating to the
commander the objects of our journey and his desire to
explore the unknown interior of Asia. Whether it was
that Helfer's love of research met an answering vein
in the Colonel's mind, whether the perseverance with
which we had both pursued our aims enlisted his sympathy, and he thought Helfer likely to be useful to the
Expedition, or whatever it might be, when we were
preparing to start for Birejik, he invited us to remain,
proposing to us to give up the arduous land journey to
Basrah and to make the voyage by the steamer, provided that Helfer was willing to place his knowledge of
natural history during the voyage at the service of the
Expedition.   It was left to the Affghans either to perform the voyage as passengers or to go by land to
Basrah and meet us there.

Once more a momentous decision had to be made,
the consequences of which we could not foresee, but it
was to have signal results for our journey, and indeed
for our future lives.

The large steamer *Euphrates* was launched, although unfinished. In six weeks it was hoped she would
be ready. The members of the Expedition, highly educated, intelligent men, specially selected for the purpose,
inspired us with confidence and esteem.   Everything

promised an interesting voyage. How could we but congratulate ourselves on the prospect of making it, and escaping the hardships of a land journey, of which we had had a sufficient taste. We thankfully accepted the offer, and thenceforth considered ourselves as members of the Expedition.

Much as there was that was melancholy connected with this Expedition, by which even our lives were placed in jeopardy, the memory of it will ever dwell with me as an elevating and inspiriting episode in our travels.

It is to be hoped that in the course of time the Euphrates will be open to steam navigation, but a second voyage like the first ought never to be ventured on.

The two steamers, the *Euphrates* and *Tigris*, destined for the navigation of the Euphrates, had been sent in iron plates from England to Iskenderoun, the harbour in the Mediterranean nearest the Euphrates. Thence they had to be conveyed by land to Port William, about 110 English miles. In order to perform this difficult task, owing to the nature of the country and the entire absence of roads and means of transport, roads had to be made over mountains and through rocky defiles, wagons had to be built strong enough to carry boilers weighing from three to five tons, and draught horses, or oxen, and men for conducting these loads had to be hired.

For this purpose a line of transport was established from Suweidieh to Port William, taking advantage of the Orontes and the Lake of Antioch, and a staff of officers were allotted to each station, who were almost always on the march between them with their men. In the camp there was most diligent labour, carpentering and hammering in every workshop as in a great manufactory. Each one worked as if the completion of the enterprise depended upon him alone, and each looked eagerly forward to the time when his labours would be rewarded by smoothly gliding down the splendid river. But it was soon evident that the health of both officers and men would suffer from over exertion, the climate, bad and unusual diet, and frequent bivouacking in the open air. There were many sick to be tended as well as losses to be mourned. Intermittent fever and dysentery prevailed at every station, and the two medical officers of the Expedition, Dr. Staunton and his brother Mr. A. A. Staunton, the former of whom was ill himself, and could not leave the camp, were not sufficient to attend to the sick. Helfer was therefore very soon asked by the Colonel to render help in this department and to go immediately to Killis to attend Major Estcourt who was very ill. Not only the Major's position in the Expedition as third in rank, but still more his amiable character and gentlemanly bearing, which had inspired universal liking and esteem, induced Helfer at once to accede to the request, although he was very reluctant to leave me alone in camp.

Our Affghan friends were distant with the English, which I attributed to the political relations of their country with England. I was therefore not surprised when they told me that they were tired of waiting and should make an excursion to Orfah and Diabekr. They set out before Helfer returned, taking with them, by agreement, our Turkish money, which would be useless below Basrah, and giving me valuable jewels in exchange.

I was now quite alone in the camp. The study of English, reading, writing, and drawing, beguiled my time. Two trees, the only ones in the neighbourhood, were the limit of my daily walk; the kind consideration shown me by the Colonel in my painful situation lightened it as much as possible. I shall ever gratefully remember the delicate courtesy with which he almost always accompanied me in my walk. Although unwell himself and suffering from fever, and very much occupied, he found time and inclination for this attention.

Helfer found Major Estcourt in the delirium of a severe typhoid fever, and weeks passed before he could safely leave him. Meanwhile the rainy season set in, and not only increased the difficulties of the undertaking but the numbers of the sick. The works, which all had to be carried on in the open air, proceeded but slowly, for most of the workmen were in the lazaretto which had had to be erected. The rain often turned to snow storms, which made the camping ground rotten. My health succumbed to these deleterious influences, and I was attacked by a typhus fever which brought me to the brink of the grave. All that I remember of it is, that in the evening after the officers had left the mess room, my husband used to carry me into it, wrapped up in rugs, from our tent, which was covered with snow, as the only place protected from the weather; that he used to watch over me by night and carry me back before breakfast. Thanks to his nursing and my vigorous constitution I recovered, though very slowly, and not entirely until we took possession of our stern cabin in the *Euphrates.* I shall never forget the day on which I was able to appear again at table, and was greeted with sincere pleasure by all present. My emotion was at its height when a glass of old Rhenish wine was handed to me to support me, for which purpose the gentlemen had kept their last bottle. Wine had long disappeared from their table, and the thick water of the Euphrates was their only beverage. Moments like these are graven deep in the memory.

It was doubted by many whether it was possible to transport such heavy loads and to continue the works at this unfavourable time of year, and with the difficulties doubled by the opposition of the local authorities; they advised waiting until spring. But the Colonel, for whom the word 'impossible' did not exist, insisted with indomitable perseverance on the continuance of the works. There was the more necessity for this, as the funds granted for the Expedition were exhausted, and the officers were making advances from their own resources. At length, on the 9th of December, by dint of vast efforts, the last and heaviest load, the boiler, was brought by 104 oxen and 52 drivers through a triumphal arch into the camp, adorned with flags for the occasion, amidst loud acclamations and a salvo of guns. These sounds must have been very unwelcome to the Mutsellim of Birejik. He had hoped

and done his best to frustrate success. Not long before
he had induced the native labourers to leave the camp
and stopped the supplies of provisions. Thus the workmen of the Expedition were left to themselves after
eight of them had succumbed to the hardships they
had undergone. No one but a man like Colonel Chesney
could have carried such an undertaking through. His
own energy stimulated that of his subordinates. No
one would leave any task that he had begun unfinished,
for he knew that the commander considered that it
could be done, and he was looked up to and trusted by
every one. Once when he received intelligence that
the diving bell, weighing 55 cwt., was sunk in a swamp
far from solid ground, and that it was impossible to get
it out, though in a high fever, he got up from his bed,
began to dress, and ordered his horse, intending himself
to go and see that it was done. Remonstrances were
useless, and not until Mr. Hector, an equally energetic
character, promised to undertake the difficult task, did
the Colonel give way and lie down again on his sick
bed. He was so exclusively occupied with the Expedition that once when the hammering was stopped, not
to disturb him, as was supposed, when almost in a state
of unconsciousness from fever, he asked that it might
go on, as the noise was a satisfaction to him. He
seemed to regard all care and comfort as luxury and
effeminacy, unworthy of any one belonging to the
Expedition. Mr. Kilby, the English agent in Aleppo,
bought a cantar, 504 lbs., of potatoes, for a change of
diet for the Expedition, for the high price, certainly, of
£8. The Colonel was much incensed at this extrava-

gance, and desired that they should not be used, but distributed to the neighbouring people for seed. Nothing but the representation that a change of diet was really needful for the sick induced him to alter his purpose. Towards the end of December the cold at Port William was very severe, the thermometer stood at 25° Fahrenheit, and the windows of our little cabin were thickly frozen. We used all our wits to protect ourselves from the cold on the river within the iron walls, and succeeded better than others. One day the Colonel was pacing the deck shivering and shaking ; Helfer invited him into our cabin ; he honoured us with a visit, looked round, and said, ‘Why, you look quite comfortable here.’ Helfer showed him the windows stuffed with wadding and other contrivances; without another word he turned away and went up on deck again. Nevertheless he knew how to value the services of his officers and to procure for them the recognition they deserved.

Notwithstanding every effort, the completion of the steamer proceeded but slowly, and it was evident that she could not start before spring. Meanwhile we had heard from the Affghans. They had proceeded with a caravan, the last in the year, to Baghdad and Basrah, and would wait for us there. Impatient as we were to continue our journey and proceed onwards with them, every way but by the voyage down the Euphrates was now cut off, and we had to submit to the inevitable.

The Colonel resolved to employ the weary waiting time in an exploring expedition to the Taurus mountains ; but the heavy rains which in this variable climate had succeeded to frost, and his state of health, occasioned it to be put off from day to day. At length, on the 9th of January, after a bright frost had again put an end to the rains, the excursion was really to start. The wags of the Expedition, who, in spite of the gravity of the situation, had not lost their good humour, called it the hospital expedition.

Chesney set out at the head of his troop, accompanied by Lieutenant Murphy, the astronomer, an amiable and scientific man, but never ready, and therefore called Mr. Tardy, and by Mr. Ainsworth, who, animated by the same zeal for the Expedition as the Colonel himself, was his constant companion, and therefore called Tertius. All shivered with cold, and could scarcely conceal their weakness.

The stables also had had a bad time of it in camp, and many a lame *rosinante* was brought out. The Colonel, wrapped in his cloak, was assisted to mount, but without his servant's help he would have slipped over on the other side. The other gentlemen were not much better. Helfer could not refuse the Colonel's invitation to go, though for his objects there was not much to be looked for in snow a foot deep.

Melancholy as the sight of the sick Colonel was, and much as I feared that he would never come back, I could not forbear a smile, he reminded me so strongly of the knight of the rueful countenance. Nevertheless, after some weeks of arduous marching among the Taurus mountains, they did come back, fresh and in good preservation: a proof of what may be accomplished by resolute will, and of the value of change of air and scene in climatic fevers.

Helfer only accompanied them as far as Aintab ; the impossibility of finding anything among the snow-covered mountains, and anxiety about me, left alone at Port William, determined him to return. At Aintab he made the acquaintance of a fellow-countryman, Herr Comenus, a military surgeon, in the service of Ibrahim Pacha ; he invited us to pay him a long visit, and we resolved, to avoid staying at Port William at this unhealthy season, to go to Aintab, and thence to Aleppo, to our friends the Pochers. A few hours after Helfer's return we were ready to start. There were no dresses and adornments to pack, as in Europe, one great advantage at any rate.

Supplied with horses by the obliging Major Est-court, we reached Arul, though amidst heavy snow storms, the same day, and met with a kind reception in an Armenian family.

The ladies, who were in a separate room, invited me to take a seat at the tandour to warm myself. As I much needed warmth, I sat down at once in the space made for me at this novel contrivance. In the middle of the floor there was a circular opening about two feet deep ; in this was a large pan of coals ; over it a frame standing on four legs, on which was placed a wadded coverlet extending far beyond the opening. The ladies sat round this in a circle, their feet hanging inside, the upper part of the body bent forward, the arms up to the shoulders under the cover, so that their heads, bound up in thick handkerchiefs, and their backs, covered with fur jackets, were all that was to be seen of them. A hand ventured out now and then to guide the end of the nargileh into the mouth. This is how the women sit during the short but severe winter. The tandour is the only means of warming rooms without windows at a temperature of 26° Fahrenheit.

Much snow fell during the night; our horses sank up to their knees, and our guide told us melancholy stories of a troop of soldiers who had been attacked and torn to pieces by wolves on this road. Happily preserved, however, from a similar fate, we reached Aintab in safety.

Aintab is one of the most important towns of Armenia, and is finely situated at the foot of the Taurus mountains. Watered by the Sajur, and surrounded by fruit gardens, it has always been a centre of traffic between Antakia, Orfah, and Aleppo. The castle, built upon an isolated rock, like that of Aleppo, served as a strong fortress even during the time of the Egyptian Caliphates and the Crusades. It was now occupied as an outpost by Ibrahim Pacha's troops. Airy minarets pleasantly broke the uniformity of the mass of flat-roofed houses. The population was about 20,000 : two-thirds Mussulmans and one-third Armenian Christians.

Herr Comenus received us with exceptional politeness, but, as it seemed to me, with some embarrassment. Perhaps, I thought, his invitation was not sincerely meant, and was only a customary courtesy among fellow-countrymen in the East; at all events, he was evidently not at his ease. But when he apologised for the absence of his wife, an Armenian, on the pretext of a great wash, it was all explained, for among my beloved German housewives in such a case a visitor is unwelcome. At length she came in. Helfer had prepared me for finding her a small-minded, bashful person, rather the servant than companion of her husband. As to the smallness of her mind he was not mistaken, but it seemed to relieve her from any particular bashfulness. Her face would not have been ugly if the Aleppo carbuncle had not disfigured the left half of it, and made it so unlike the right that she might have represented two different persons. Her dress, even by the standard of the country, was not neat, but it had not been improved by the household occupation she had just been engaged in, for her sleeves were so wet that they clung to her arms. Making her salaam in the most phlegmatic manner, not a feature betraying the least sensation, she sat down by me on the sofa.

I did my utmost to make myself agreeable by friendly gestures and smiles, but my efforts were all thrown away, no change took place in her stolid countenance. I could do no more; we sat side by side in silence, and even her husband, who offered his services as interpreter and playfully suggested subjects, could not succeed in making her more animated. The only thing that could rouse her out of her apathy was anything relating to spending or making money; in all money matters she held sway. She was so indolent that she left the room unswept for days; one day, to put her to the test, I seized the broom myself, as if I were going to sweep it, but she looked quietly on as she sat on the sofa. I no longer troubled myself about her.

Aintab afforded me an interesting opportunity of making acquaintance with the family life of the Armenian Christians, which is little known to Europeans, and it is difficult for strangers to get access to them, as the women do not appear before men. The Armenians are about on a par with the Turks as to civilisation. Timid and reserved, they submit outwardly to the rulers, whom they secretly despise.

Chiefly and successfully occupied with trade, they often amass great wealth, but carefully conceal it; the most wealthy keep up an appearance of poverty, for which, owing to the rapacity of the Turkish government, they may have good reason. The habit of heaping up riches, which they neither spend nor enjoy, and the tendency to avarice is handed down from father to son, and clings to them wherever they go. They are scattered almost all over the East as wealthy merchants, but their characteristics are everywhere the same.

The Armenian women enjoy no better position than the Turkish; they are merely the servants of their husbands. Indeed, while the sensual Mussulman often becomes the slave of his slaves, the cold Armenian merchant is always the strict master of his wife. They perform the household duties as mere girls; they do not eat with their husbands, but wait upon them as their lords. They are unveiled indoors, but do not allow themselves to be seen by any strange man. When there is company, they keep in a place on purpose, a kind of box about five feet from the ground, in the great hall of the house, screened by latticework. From this they can look down upon the men at their feasting without being seen. It is the more to be regretted, as the screen often conceals a galaxy of beauties. At Aintab I really saw the much lauded Oriental beauties whom I had hitherto looked for in vain.

The relations and friends of my hostess came, as Oriental custom requires, to pay their respects to me ; I was as much an object of curiosity to them as they were to me. As they could only speak Armenian or Arabic, our conversation was limited, and could only be carried on with the help of Herr Comenus as interpreter. They expressed astonishment and regret that I had had to leave my mother and brothers and sisters, and shook their heads when told that I had accompanied my husband of my own free will. ‘ A husband,’ they said, with a contemptuous shrug of the shoulders, ‘ is not worth leaving one’s people for.’ They received my assurance with incredulity that I was ready to follow him wherever he chose to go, and of the pleasure of seeing the world they could form no more idea than of conjugal happiness, for they never leave their native place. Betrothed as mere children by parental authority, they see scarcely anything of their husbands before they are married, and afterwards the entire engrossment of the husband in money making and his despotic relations with his wife are not calculated to awaken affection. Affection for parents and brothers and sisters absorbs all the tenderness of the female heart, and a mother’s love often becomes a passion. After our visitors had been amply regaled with liqueurs and coffee, and had filled the room with the vapours of the nargileh, they departed to make way for others, for whom the entertainment was repeated.

As I have said before, I was greatly surprised, among the twenty women whom I saw that morning, to see at least eight classic beauties. The regular oval of the face, the finely formed nose, the large dark eyes shaded by long thick eyelashes, the brilliant complexions of these southerners form an incomparable whole; but they are destitute of the nobler charms added by mental culture and care of the person. Their dress shows an utter absence of good taste and eye for neatness; generally made of thick silk, torn and soiled, inherited perhaps from mother or grandmother, the coarsest and most untidy linen peeps from beneath it. The neck and arms, if not accidentally cleaned by a Turkish bath, look dusky, as they do not wash them in the house. The hands are fat and coarse, like those of a servant, and the inside and the nails coloured red. They place the highest value on jewellery, especially on the head dress, a high silver casket, the cover of which, made of ornamental Venetian open work, is hung round with gold coins. The number and size of the gold chains round the neck, and bracelets on the arms, announce the wealth and position of the wearer. But with all this they are not without natural grace, and are free from that awkwardness which often takes refuge in tasteless ornament amongst women whose education just suffices to make them feel the want of it.

The next morning I returned the visits of some of these ladies belonging to the well-to-do merchant class;

everywhere I found the same lack of comfort, the same appearance of poverty. In most of the large rooms the extreme cold is allowed to penetrate through un-glazed windows, closed with a shutter at night, and open doors, and the pan of coals affords but little protection against it. It is inconceivable how these people, accustomed to great heat in summer, can exist in such airy houses with two feet of snow on the ground. The theory that a store of warmth protects for a long time against cold seems to hold good here. In our northern climates no one could bear such cold indoors.

Among all these women I found only one distinguished by mental endowments. Tagu, a girl of fifteen, was the daughter of one of the richest Armenian merchants. She was of middle size, slender, and without the fulness of figure so admired by Asiatics. From under the close fitting tarbush flowed rich chestnut-coloured locks, richly adorned with gazi, Turkish gold coins. Her soft brown eyes, finely formed and shaded by long dark lashes, betrayed the awakened soul which her countrywomen lack; a sweet smile played about her lips, and gave her a child-like *naïveté* to which a sort of dignity was lent by the finely-arched nose. Her obliging manners, her efforts to make herself agreeable, confirmed the expression of her countenance. She listened attentively when Herr Comenus translated to her my descriptions of Europe and the life of women there; she clung to and caressed me, and entreated me to take her with me; she would wait upon and follow me, and be faithful and obedient. I had some difficulty in pacifying the lovely creature, and in explaining to her that she could not go with us, because we were not going to Europe, but still farther to foreign lands.

I sincerely and deeply regretted having to leave her to a father who cared for nothing but money-making, a bigoted mother, and a betrothed unworthy of her. In her seventh year she had been betrothed to a boy of nine, who was to be brought up as a gold-worker, and whose training turned out most unfortunately, for he took to idleness for his business, and to drinking for his pleasure; and poor Tagu was to be given to this good-for-nothing fellow! The Armenians consider betrothal as a sacred vow, from which they can only be released by priestly authority.

Nowhere, perhaps, is the influence of the priests greater than among the Armenians of the present day. Without the safeguard of salutary laws for the regulation of public and private life, subject to the arbitrary rule of the Turk, without any champions of their rights, they allow the priests full sway. Priests decide disputes as judges and law-givers, and when they cannot put a stop to earthly evils they offer pastoral consolation by referring the faithful to a future life and recompense hereafter. In short their influence is unbounded. But wherever power has been wielded by priests they have misused it; how could anything be expected from these rough and ignorant men but the spiritual despotism they impose upon this politically oppressed people?

Two of these gentlemen came to pay their respects to us. One was an elderly, well-fed, self-complaisant, smiling man, with a smooth, full-moon face and red nose; he needs no farther description; these people are only too well known, who, having no liking for castigations themselves, do not impose them on others, but live and let live. Spirituous liquors appeared to suit him; he nodded, well pleased, to our host, when he handed him a brimming glass and said, with an ironical smile, that the very Rev. Father was fond of a glass. 'Well,' said he, 'it's a human weakness,' and gulped down the spirits until he had taken his fill, and sauntered away to repeat the scene somewhere else. This is called here taking a bit of breakfast.

The other was a younger and thinner man, with a thin arched nose, eyes sanctimoniously kept on the ground, firmly compressed lips, and a physiognomy which would have done honour to a Tartuffe. He took his seat modestly and reverently on a cushion, and, carefully avoiding the posture of the infidel Turks, sat with his legs hanging straight down, wrapped in a most Christian manner in his gown, to the edification of all beholders. Being a secret worshipper of the green bottle he smiled bashfully when the glass was handed to him; but our host knew him well, and ostensibly pressing him, he filled one bumper after another, which he swallowed with averted face. This reverend father, with his soft sneaking manners, was, in consequence of the edifying discourses he delivered, the chief spiritual adviser of the Armenian fair ones.

Our host wished to ask a number of the ladies to dinner, and thus to give them an entertainment after European fashion. But this was an unusual thing, and it was necessary to obtain the priest's consent; he refused it, of course with all due gentleness and meekness. Herr Comenus then invited a party without ladies, when the reverend father gave us his company, and displayed an appetite truly astounding.

Tagu seemed as if she could not be separated from me; she came often, and brought her elder sister with her. Though not so pretty, her features were pleasing; but she was meanly dressed, and wore no ornaments; her hair, instead of hanging down in luxuriant braids, was concealed under a little tarbush. She took her place behind her sister, on whom she gazed with affectionate pleasure, and her sole desire seemed to be to anticipate the wants and wishes of others, and to wait upon everybody. I was naturally much struck with the contrast between the sisters, and asked the elder why she did not wear pearls and gazi on her head; whereupon she answered, with a blush, that she should never be married. I did not understand her meaning until I learnt afterwards, that, though the Armenians have no convents for women, many of their daughters take a voluntary vow never to marry, and then renounce all ornaments, and strictly practise religious observances, but consider it to be their chief duty to make themselves useful to their relatives. Considering the family relations I have described, in which the conjugal tie is not nearly so strong as that between brothers and sisters, the vow of celibacy can be no great sacrifice to a girl.

A Mr. Georg, gold-worker, schoolmaster, and painter of saints, chiefly, however, dealer in novelties, in a word, factotum of Aintab in the arts and sciences, had heard of our being in the place, and came to see us. Visits from European travellers in this part of the world are always important events, especially to a schoolmaster with a thirst for knowledge. Perhaps he thought that he should derive all kinds of wisdom from the mere sight of Europeans, and from breathing the same air, for there could be no special communications. Nevertheless he invited us to dinner. Not wishing to offend the man of learning, and to have an opportunity of seeing his wife, whose beauty, I had been told, was unequalled, we accepted the invitation on condition that his wife should dine with us, for we had heard that she was never visible, and extremely shy and retiring.

Completely frozen, and with wet feet, we arrived at our polite entertainer's house. I longed to be warmed, and hoped the learned gentleman would have made some progress in the amenities of life, and would have provided a warm room. But I was disappointed; I shall never forget the intolerable cold I suffered there. We were received in the great hall used on festive occasions, in which two doors and windows wide open exposed us mercilessly to the cold air. Often as in my own country I had had to pay with a headache for the close stove-heat at church festivals and christenings, I now devoutly longed for an old grandfatherly Dutch tile stove. We wrapped ourselves as well as we could in our shawls. I could not get the idea into my head that I was on Syria's sun-burnt steppes. What erroneous notions we have of distant lands when we only visit them on the map.

At last came dinner, by our express wish served according to the custom of the country. A mat was spread before us, and in the middle of it was placed a round tray, raised a few inches on feet; and on this a tin dish containing pilaw. A wooden spoon for helping it showed advanced civilisation. This, a dish with sauce, and another of cakes fried in oil, with a little glass of good liqueur, formed the whole dinner. We took our places on cushions in a circle, and helped ourselves with appetites sharpened by the cold. I had looked in vain for our pretty hostess; her husband excused her by saying she was engaged in the kitchen, and presented his mother instead, a kindly old lady. I was no better satisfied with the exchange than the gentlemen, and when the cooking was over, insisted on the appearance of the lady of the house. It was hard to make the Armenian understand that it was opposed to all the respect due to his wife to let her work in the kitchen while we sat at table: according to his notions it was quite in order. But when he saw that I was determined not to begin until she gave us her company, he went to fetch her. His long absence convinced me that it was not easy to induce her to come. At last, led in by him with evident reluctance, she appeared. Her face almost concealed by a handkerchief over the high casket, she approached us shyly and shamefacedly. After much pressing she took her place next to me, avoiding my searching glances as much as possible. But she could not be persuaded to partake of the meal. I almost forgot to eat myself, I was so engrossed with gazing at her.

It is impossible to imagine more lovely features than hers, and her complexion was of a dazzling, almost sickly transparence. A slight flush suffused her cheeks whenever our eyes were turned towards her, and her soft blue eyes shaded by dark lashes begged us with touching entreaty not to molest her with our gaze. Her modesty seemed to be deeply wounded by being an object of general admiration. There was something spiritual, I may almost say nun-like, about her which was as little as possible like one's idea of the busy wife of a schoolmaster.

I should have liked to include her, Tagu, and many other beauties whom I afterwards saw, among my specimens of natural history, and to have put them in a cabinet of curiosities at home; they would certainly have attracted many admirers.

I learnt afterwards that her romantically melancholy expression was caused by her having no children after five years of marriage; according to their ideas, childlessness is a disgrace and the greatest sorrow that can befall a woman. Hella and her husband had been betrothed as children of five and eight years, and had associated together as brother and sister, until Hella was twelve, when they were married. She had a sister with her, not nearly so beautiful, quietly dressed, and without ornaments; she seated herself at a respectful distance. They told me she was a widow, and as such it would be unbecoming for her to wear any kind of ornament, or to mix with those happy women whose husbands God had preserved to them. All that I saw and heard brought forcibly to my mind the great contrast between the position of Asiatic and European women.

My mamaluke costume enabled me to walk out in the streets of Aintab, which I could not have done in a woman's dress without exposing myself to insult. The Mussulmans were not yet accustomed to see women unveiled, nor man and wife walking arm in arm: in their eyes the greatest disgrace and degradation to a man.

The military occupation of the town made it much more lively than usual, with its comparatively small population. Still the streets, as in all Turkish towns, had a gloomy aspect, owing to the high court walls without windows; but the bazaar, with its buyers and sellers, was particularly lively, from the soldiers mingling with the people, making purchases for dinner, or crowding round the steaming eating booths where a sort of relishing cutlet was sold. In spite of Helfer's long beard, and our great endeavours to look like Orientals, we were at once recognised as Europeans, and not seldom heard the exclamation, 'Engliska Giaour!' For since the Euphrates Expedition had been in the neighbourhood, every foreigner was taken for an Englishman, and the insulting word Giaour, almost gone out of use among civilised Turks, was quite a customary expression in fanatical Aintab.

In our walks we met General Hamsa Bey, a very young man for his rank. It was Ibrahim Pacha's policy to fill many of the high posts in his army with young Georgian slaves, whose qualities, especially their cunning, adapted them for it, and on whose subservience he could rely. In the General's suite was the Governor of the fortress, a stout Egyptian with only one eye, and no longer young. Herr Comenus introduced us as his countrymen, two brothers, travelling together, whereupon the stout gentleman looked narrowly at me, and clapping Helfer on the back, said, 'A pretty brother that!' and went on with a laugh.

The next day we were surprised by a visit from the two gentlemen. Following close upon the heels of those who announced them they entered without ceremony, to the horror of our hostess, who saved herself by flight from the gaze of the strange men. Herr Comenus was also rather embarrassed, for he had never been honoured by a visit from these lofty gentlemen before. It was evident that the object of their call was to learn more about the hated Expedition, and to show their familiarity with European manners. We satisfied their curiosity so far as seemed good to us; we took care to represent the enterprise, the success of which we had ourselves begun to doubt, as undoubtedly approaching completion. In order to enliven conversation I showed them my sketch book; the eye of the Governor fell upon the portrait of a very pretty Englishwoman of fair complexion. He was enchanted with this, to him, new style of beauty; he was acquainted only with that of the south. He then passionately expressed a desire to our host that he would buy the lady for him—really and truly—let it cost what it would! We stared. He was really in earnest. After we had with much difficulty persuaded him of the impossibility of it, he exclaimed, much put out,

'Well, then I will at least have her picture?' This I could grant him and made him a present of it.

When the gentlemen took leave they invited me to visit their ladies; they did not speak of a harem.

We ascended to the citadel, whose massive walls have withstood the ravages of time, and which was now only occupied by soldiers. A guard received us, and without asking what we wanted, took us into a great hall. In the midst of the space was a mixed multitude, mostly belonging to the lower classes. Their faces betrayed the most various emotions, from rancour and arrogant self-assertion to servility and abject resignation. Others squatted round the walls, in miserable rags, hopelessly staring before them. They were country people bewailing their hard fate; but no one expressed his feelings; profound silence reigned.

We must have inspired the guard with respect; making way for us by cuffing and pushing, he conducted us to the upper end of the hall, separated by a barrier, where, to our astonishment, sitting comfortably on a cushion, was the Governor, presiding at a sort of public court. His officers sat beside him in a semicircle to the right and left, as well as some scribes, distinguishable by the writing implements in their girdles; they had to be at the service of his Excellency in intricate cases. On the ground was a large pan, from which was exhaled the pleasant perfume of the celebrated Latakieh tobacco; the long pipe of each one was passed through one of the holes round the edge, and thus they smoked together. The Governor looked very stern, but on seeing us a slight smile passed over his face, he made a sign to us to come nearer and take seats by him. Long gilt pipes, like that from which the smoke encircled the Governor's head, were handed to us. I could not smoke, but for the sake of appearance I blew hard into the pipe so that thick clouds rose up ; I also, though not without difficulty, crossed my feet under me, but preserved silence, for my voice had often betrayed me. Thus outward decorum was preserved, and none of the Mussulmans present seemed to detect a Christian lady in the unabashed mamaluke, especially as my presence was tolerated by the Governor. How had times changed, and how may they change yet? Perhaps I was the first woman who had ever sat by the judge in open court. Let us hope that still greater changes may take place in the East.

The proceedings were as summary as they were drastic. A plaintiff came forward ; silent as he had been before, he now poured forth a volley of accusations against the poor culprit, who was led or dragged in, and from whose rueful face and trembling limbs one could see that he knew the fate awaiting him. The indictment was brought forward, and a few words said to the accused, whereupon, in a pitiful voice, he protested that he was innocent. The Governor only seemed to lend half an ear to it all ; he considered for a few moments, and then with a stentorian voice pronounced sentence, and away went the poor sinners to the bastinado.

The scene was repulsive to us, and we availed ourselves of the first pause to rise ; with a respectful salutation to the Governor, as soon as Turkish dignity would permit, we left the assembly, glad to breathe the free air of heaven again, cold as it was.

We next paid a visit to the General. Like a finished Frank dandy he advanced to meet us in the inner court, which was filled with officers, gallantly offered me his arm, to the horror of his subordinates, and led me a few steps up into the interior apartments. Two young slaves, splendidly dressed, opened the door of a light, spacious room. The soft carpets on the floor, a great divan along the wall, and several pieces of European furniture scattered about, gave it an appearance of half Asiatic, half European luxury. Immediately on our entrance the door opposite opened, and a female form appeared, not strikingly beautiful, but very pleasing ; on her head the becoming fez, with a light gauze handkerchief round it embroidered with gold.

Her slight figure was shown to advantage by the close-fitting dress of a Turkish lady. My gallant host at once advanced to meet her, took her by the hand, and led her to me. This was the first and only time I ever saw a Mussulman in actual contact with a woman, as in the presence of others they maintain the strictest reserve. Shyly and with a blush she gave me her other hand, and with a gracious bend invited me to sit beside her on the divan, not after Turkish but European fashion. Her face was expressive, and her eyes soft and modest. I should have liked to talk long and much with her, and to discover what was in her mind, but unfortunately there was no interpreter at hand. Helfer had remained with the officers, and the few words of Turkish which I could speak, and the General's few French phrases, did not suffice for conversation. As usual, coffee and a variety of sweet fruits were offered me, but not a nargileh. I took leave with sincere regret that I could not converse better with this interesting lady.

The Governor's wife had also to be visited; Madame Comenus went with me, being sure of not finding any men there. My costume occasioned difficulties, the guards hesitating to allow me to enter; it was only after the repeated assurances of my companion that I really was a woman in disguise, that I was permitted to enter the inner apartment of the women. To my astonishment it was more like a gipsy's cave than the luxurious abode of a Turkish favourite. Although it was mid-day the low vaulted chamber was only sparingly lighted by a lamp, so that it was some time before I could see what it contained. Articles of dress, from worn-out rags to gold-embroidered tunics, all in heaps together, implements for cooking and eating, drums and cymbals, all alike dirty, lay and hung in the greatest confusion on the ground and on the walls. The room was filled by a large number of black women and girls, slaves or companions, squatting on the ground in a half circle round their mistress. She was a striking contrast to them. She reclined on a soft cushion of splendid material, under a canopy adorned with gold embroidery, enveloped in a transparent veil, and was apparently asleep. The noise occasioned by our entrance and the rising of the attendants awakened the sleeping beauty. She slowly rose, and with a careless movement removed the veil from her face, but let it fall immediately on seeing me, and extending one of the roundest, whitest arms I ever saw, she pointed with displeasure to the door, as a sign that I should at once withdraw. Madame Comenus, who was on friendly terms with her, now explained who I was, why I had adopted a man's dress, and that I had been pressingly invited by the Governor to come and see her. Upon this the veil, again thrown back, disclosed such dazzling beauty as is but rarely met with except in Oriental fairy tales. Much as it differed from European beauty it diverged almost as much from the usual Asiatic type. What might be the land of her birth? It was as if the good fairies had united the peculiar charms of all nations in her person. An alabaster whiteness and transparent purity of skin, which seemed as if derived from the far north, gave her something of the ethereal and spiritual, but the earthly asserted itself again in the luxuriant fulness of her figure. The fire of her dark eyes and her peculiarly glossy black hair showed her to be a daughter of the tropics, while an almost childish physiognomy, which reminded me of our *Mignon* faces, betrayed European blood. In fact she combined the characteristics of several parts of the world. I could learn nothing more of her ancestry than that she was an Egyptian slave, the child of slaves in Nubia. When it is considered that types of all nations are represented in the slave market at Cairo, such a mixture seems not impossible.

I stood long in astonishment before I took a seat near her, which, on account of its stationary inhabitants, was by no means inviting. Our conversation was limited to a few words of mutual greeting; but I was entirely taken up with the contemplation of her perfect loveliness.

Meanwhile, negro boys and girls, clad in most fantastic fashion, tumultuously arranged themselves for a dance; some of the old women seized the drums and cymbals, others prepared to sing, while a pretty negress handed coffee. The scene bore unmistakable evidence of Egyptian origin, and I was vividly reminded of our gipsy hordes and of Weber's 'Preciosa.' My neighbour would certainly have been the loveliest Preciosa ever seen on the stage; but she took no part in the merriment, she looked on with indifference at the oft-repeated mummery. She was not well; the flushes which came and went on her pale face betrayed how severe was the pain she was trying to conceal. She had been confined six weeks before, and was suffering from a bad breast. Comenus, her physician, if I may call him so, had never been allowed to see her without her veil, and her deeply-rooted prejudices would not permit him to examine the affected part. He was not a little perplexed, as the anxious Governor daily urged him to cure his beautiful wife, and had asked me to give him an exact description of her state. But neither could I induce her to let me see her breast; she turned her dark pensive eyes on me at the suggestion, and more suspiciously than before she eyed my dress, and my, to Asiatic women, unusual height. So to my sincere regret I had to leave her to her sufferings without relief.

After Aintab had gratified my desire, beyond my expectations, to see Eastern beauties, there was nothing farther to interest me. We left it after a stay of some weeks, when the weather became milder, in order to accept the invitation of our good friend and countryman Pocher to spend the rest of the winter season, until the steamers should start, at his house at Aleppo.

We were heartily welcomed by our friends, and I gave myself up to the enjoyments of which I had so long been deprived, the comforts of a well-ordered home, and intercourse with educated people.

Herr Klinger too, had looked forward to our coming; he could now complete his musical productions; all forces were united, and our evenings enlivened by many a successful concert.

Spring comes in warm and early after the short severe winter; by the end of February the air was mild, and all nature was reviving. Helfer could then no longer endure to be within the city walls; he longed to be in the open air, to renew his explorations, and to collect specimens for the benefit of the Expedition.

Here follow the notes from Helfer's diary verbatim, which, with a few other scanty remains of his papers, were saved from destruction.

CHAPTER VI.

EXCURSION TO THE SALT LAKE EL-MALAK.[1]

(From Dr. Helfer's Diary.)

ON the 24th of February my wife and I, Herr Klinger
and Herr Franz Hübner, who accompanied us from
fellow feeling as countrymen, set out to visit the Salt
Lake El-Malak, which supplies a great part of Syria
with salt ; also the chain of basaltic mountains which
traverses the middle of the plain, and to collect orni-
thological, entomological, and botanical specimens for
the Expedition.

Leaving behind the olive and fig gardens, which
extend for two or three miles from Aleppo in a
southerly direction, by degrees all trees disappeared,
and even the brushwood came to an end. We passed
through a gradually rising rocky district, and then
descended into the plain, which was lost in the
distant horizon.   The singular uniformity was only
broken by three or four of the low, conical hills so
frequent in Syria.   The lowest part of this plain, about

---

[1] A report of this excursion appears in Chesney's 'Narrative of the
Euphrates Expedition' (Appendix VI. p. 439), but with variations. All
personal particulars are omitted, and it bears internal evidence of having
been written in English by Dr. Helfer himself.—TR.

thirteen miles from Aleppo, is formed by the Salt Lake
El-Malak.

In the village of Sfri we met with an unexpectedly
good reception in the house of an old woman whose
son was a hunter. Her house was clean, and so were
the beds which she prepared for us on mats, and a
stewed pilaw was very good. The villagers, agricultural Arabs, had made remarkable progress in civilisation. Their houses are made of stamped earth, and
resemble beehives; the door, placed opposite to the
prevailing wind, gives light and air. These conical
round houses are very small; when the family increases
they are not enlarged, but new ones built as they are
wanted, so that four or five of them, close together, often
belong to one family. The women go about unveiled,
and the arrangements of the dwellings and mode of
living indicated, as far as I could see, a monogamic
rather than a polygamic family life. The men diligently
cultivated the ground, and even young mulberry plantations were to be seen. They said that they willingly
payed tribute to the government in Aleppo to be protected from being plundered by the wandering Arab
tribes, who, before Ibrahim Pacha's rigid rule, advanced
even to the city walls. This Arab village afforded
pleasing evidence that culture and civilisation might
easily be introduced here under due protection and
encouragement.

The son of our old hostess and another powerful
Arab were persuaded to accompany us. The next
morning we started before daybreak for the salt lake,
about two miles southwards from the village, and at this

season much larger than in summer. A rivulet rises
northward from Sfri, and flows into the lake. Owing
to the slight fall it forms numerous swamps, which had
been increased by the winter floods, and large tracts of
land were turned into marshes. The oases among
them were filled with *Juncaceæ*, but were quite destitute of long grass, as was also the shore of the lake
itself, which presented a most monotonous appearance.
About a mile off we saw several small inlets; but we
were prevented from examining the lake more closely
by the impassable morass and want of boats.

A large number of water-fowl of various kinds
frequent the lake and its shores, but nowhere have I
found them so shy. Even when we were a long way
off thousands of wild ducks, geese, and other water-
fowl rose up on our approach with a noise like distant
thunder, and took refuge in the middle of the lake,
where they looked like dark, moving islands. In spite
of the difficulties we pursued the game with great zest,
and were rewarded by considerable booty, for which
we were chiefly indebted to our Arab hunter, who did
not hesitate to go into the water up to his neck, and
incited two excellent dogs to fetch the birds.

I cannot determine the extent of the lake, as it now
exceeds its usual boundaries by over one half: according to our guides, at this season it would take a
day and a half to walk round it. The water is somewhat bitter, and does not at present contain much salt.
The method of obtaining it is very simple. During
the summer heat the water evaporates and retires,
leaving in the deeper parts the pure crystals of salt,

which are collected and carried on the backs of camels
to the various districts of Syria. In my opinion a
great part of the vast plains, generally but erroneously
called the Arabian desert, was once covered with sea
water; after the subsidence of the water the low dried-
up surfaces were for centuries saturated with saline
particles. This is the case with the Lakes El-Malak,
Geboul, and others less known. The accumulation of
water in winter dissolves some of the salt in the soil,
and again evaporates. This, at least, appears to me
the simplest and most natural way of accounting for
this mode of obtaining salt.

We returned to our hostess late in the evening in
order early the next morning to make an excursion in
a south-easterly direction to the basaltic mountains
about ten miles off. A fine, fruitful plain extends in
this direction, but not far from Sfri cultivation ceases,
and numerous ruins of villages afford evidence that
the country was in much better condition not very long
ago. Vegetation had just begun to appear; numberless bulbs, of whose existence a few weeks before one
would not have had the least idea, were peeping forth,
but not a single specimen belonging to the class
Phanerogamia was yet in bloom.

A complete system of basaltic rocks has been
formed here, no doubt by one of those volcanic erup-
tions which have so often taken place in Syria from
the earliest historical period to the present day. Like
all basaltic formations it is based upon limestone, and
forms narrow perpendicular valleys with clefts in all
directions. Blocks of stone of all sizes lay scattered

about in every direction. The entire absence of water produced such a wilderness as I have never seen. Not a shrub, not a blade of grass was to be seen, and even the black rock was but rarely covered with *Leconora* or *Parietaria.*

On the summit of the chain there is a broad table-land, in some places six or seven miles in extent; the only inhabitants of this desolate region are yellow hyenas, one of which we shot, and numerous wild boars. The existence of these animals, which generally prefer woods and morasses, may at first sight appear singular, but they find suitable food in the bulbous plants which are nowhere so abundant as here. The soil in many places is literally ploughed up by these creatures in search of food, though we saw but few of them. A rather heavy spring rain set in, very beneficial to nature, but very unpleasant to us; we might have suffered from it, as we were unprovided against it, had not our hunter taken us to a cave which hospitably received us all. I was extremely surprised to find in this cave, about thirty feet below the surface, a roomy, neatly arranged habitation. On one side was a raised place for sitting, on the other a fireplace, with an opening for the smoke; on the third, a part partitioned off for sleeping-rooms, and another large room, apparently intended for animals. There was comfortable room for us all, and a separate sleeping-place could be arranged for me and my wife. Our horses could also be taken in; the only difficulty being to lead them down the steep descent into it, but it was accomplished, for the beasts of burden here are used to difficult passages.

While the fire was crackling, and a kettle of rice being boiled, our hunter told us many anecdotes of his sporting adventures, which Herr Klinger, who perfectly understood Arabic, interpreted. Among the many curiosities of the neighbourhood, he mentioned a large town in ruins, which, though not far off, had never yet been visited by Franks, and which he himself had never ventured to go to for fear of the Aniza Arabs who pitch their tents there, until the previous summer, when he and another of his tribe had been there to search for wild potatoes (*Lycoperdon?*), and had seen nothing of the Anizas. This account greatly interested me, and we resolved to visit the place. It was very difficult to persuade the man to guide us, but no Arab can withstand the promise of a good backsheesh, and he consented. Before starting next day, I examined the neighbourhood more particularly, and found, to my great surprise, that many such caves like that in which we had passed the night existed, forming a troglodyte village of over fifty habitations, exactly alike, lying close together, and sufficient to accommodate over one thousand persons. We explored many of them thoroughly, but could find nothing which afforded any clue to the period of their origin; they probably date from the earliest times, and served the people who ruled and displaced each other in turn here for dwellings for generations.

Our way led over the high table-land formed by the basaltic hills. It was interesting to observe in this desolate region traces of a former high state of civilisation. We could plainly distinguish terraces cut in the hills; spaces scarcely twenty feet wide had been cleared of stones, and long walls, with towers, pillars, and pyramids had been constructed with them; the further we went the greater was the number of these monuments. It was evident that this chain must once have been a considerable border fortress.

Having traversed the plateau for about two hours, we again descended into the plain, which was surrounded by part of the mountain range, in the form of a horse-shoe. On its open side the guide pointed out a little hill, under which the town lay; according to him it was of greater extent than Aleppo, and all that I saw as we approached convinced me of the former importance of the place.

From the basaltic hills I had observed scattered traces of an ancient military road, which in the plain was quite distinct and in good preservation, extending for about two miles from the hills to the town. The bed of a deep canal, now dry, ran alongside of it. Where the water could formerly have come from it is difficult to say; but these dry canals are frequent in Syria.

On approaching the place I saw something like ruins, and soon found myself in the midst of a formerly large town, called by our Arab Belet-Chan-Asra, which he said had never been visited by Europeans. It was completely in ruins. Probably demolished in .very early times, it has been left untouched, and has not served for the site of Roman temples or mosques, like Hierapolis, out of which the Mahometans have built

Membidge, and which exhibits traces of every age. That is not the case here, the plan of the whole town, even of every house, may be recognised. The buildings are curiously constructed of wedge-shaped basaltic stones, with the broad side outwards, the inside being filled with small stones.

The city was surrounded by a wall, but there were many buildings and temples beyond it. The traces of square towers, fifty feet apart, and with sharp projecting corners, are distinctly visible. I observed only two entrance gates, connected by a straight street more than two miles long. Part of one of the gates is still standing; it is formed of enormous blocks, and the angles can still be discerned. The opposite gate has fallen in; on one side I found the following Greek inscription:—

      . . . ΑΒΙΗΕΝΟϹΙΡ . . . .
      . . . ΤΟΔΕΤΟΤΙ : : ΟϹΑΝΗΓΕΙΡΕΝ . . . . .

and on the other side—

          . . . . ΤΟΝΕΥϹΕΒΕϹ . .
      ΕΥΕΡΓΕΤΗΝΚΑΙΝΙΚΗΓF . .
      ΒΑϹΙΛΕΑΚΥΡΙΕϹDΥΔΑΒ

Two buildings only are preserved, but their form is so singular that I cannot explain what may have been their purpose. One is a large vaulted hall, with an arched entrance and windows opposite; there are no traces of any other apartments. The other appears to have been divided into many small rooms, and may perhaps have been a bath. An inscription which I copied may afford an explanation; it is on a square tablet in the wall, but is unfortunately only partially legible :—

☩ΔωβΑΙΙΑ   ΤΡΙΚΑΙΟΙΟΥ
ΚΑΙΑΓΙΙΙΥ⅂   Ε
VΟΙΚΑΙΝΤΝ   ΚΑ
                  Α

Near the wall with this inscription is a well-preserved sarcophagus.

Both these buildings lie at the south end of the city, near the gate. Not far from them is a long colonnade, some hundred feet long, but so filled up with sand that I could not advance many steps along it. At the extreme southern extremity, within the walls, there is one of those hills peculiar to Syria, probably at one time surmounted by a castle or temple. The ramparts were particularly strong, and occupied a considerable space; the front towards the town partially remains; in this there is a huge square gate surmounted by a strong block of basalt; it bears an inscription, of which I was able to copy the following fragments :—

ΦΡ
ΑΙΑΔ
ΥϹΡΓΕΤ
ΗΙΚΟΥϹΔΕϹ
ΥΙΙΑΙΧΟΥϹΙΙΡΑΙ
ΔΥ ∷ ΗϹΕΙΙΙϹΚΟΙΙΟΙ
ΟΡΤΙΒ⅃ΓΟΥϨωΕΙΟΙ

On wandering further among the extensive ruins I discovered the following inscriptions. On a bas-relief which may have belonged to a temple :—

ΑΤΟϹΟϹ
ΤΑΥΙ
ΗΤΟϹΗΝω

Over the door of a private house :—

. . . . OIKEHΛIΠCΛM( )HKA
IROHΘOCKдΦO( )BHΘ

I refrain from all conjecture as to the age of this doubtless once important city, but will observe that in two places I found the Maltese cross, which plainly indicates a temporary settlement of Christians. Among sundry ruins which we saw on our return by another route, were those of a large villa in the midst of a melancholy solitude, but surrounded by picturesque hills, from which there was a splendid view over the immense plain. Besides these, I discovered the foundations of two large buildings, which might have been temples.

On asking whether there were not other ruins in the neighbourhood, I learnt that about half a day's journey off, in the direction of Palmyra, which it was said would be reached in twenty-four hours from Belet-Chan-Asra, other and still more extensive ruins existed. Tempting as a visit to them was, we had to give it up. Our provisions were exhausted and our little company was not in a plight to go farther alone; moreover our guide decidedly declined to accompany us. He left us here, as we decided to return by a shorter route than through Sfri, where he lived.

We passed the night here and spent a good part of the next morning in exploring this interesting spot, but hoped to reach Aleppo before dark by going direct towards it. Knowing in which direction it lay I could rely upon my compass. We set out in good spirits and urged on our steeds as much as we could. But they were poor over-worked beasts, and during the last two or three days had had but scanty feed, and continually relapsed into a slower and slower pace. Spurs and whips were of no avail, and we made but little progress. Evening came on, but not a trace of the extensive suburbs of Aleppo was visible; we then perceived alongside of us, a long dark line, moving in the same direction as ourselves. We halted to watch the surprising apparition more closely, and, if possible, to get some good out of it, as we had given up all hope of reaching Aleppo.

On approaching, we recognised a tribe of wandering Arabs, who, with wives, children, household effects, and cattle, had left their encampment to find fresh pasture. It was a most curious and picturesque sight. The vanguard was formed by a troop of mounted and well-armed men; they were followed by a number of camels meditatively stalking onwards, with their heads elevated, and their eyes having a patient and gentle expression, as if they were conscious that they bore their masters' greatest treasures, for high upon their backs women were enthroned with sucklings in their arms and naked children by their sides. Then came a confused mass of heavily-laden asses, men, women, and children, each loaded with some of his or her property. Last came flocks of sheep, oxen, young camels and horses; the number and quality of the flocks, are, as is well known, the criterion of the wealth of the tribe. Armed men on foot and horseback closed the procession.

On our, to them, doubtless, strange appearance, the

foremost stopped, and two of them rode up to us to ask 'Who?' and 'Whither?' Herr Klinger gave a satisfactory account, and did not fail to introduce me as an officer of the mighty English on the Euphrates, who was travelling through the country under Ibrahim Pacha's protection, and wished to return this evening to Aleppo. They then introduced themselves as belonging to the tribe of Gekim Arabs, whose great sheikh was called Omar. After they had returned to their people and made their report, the sheikh himself came to us with a larger retinue. The usual ceremonious greetings and assurances of friendship having been exchanged, he said that it would be impossible for us to reach Aleppo that day, and hospitably invited us to pass the night in his tent, which he would have pitched near. We thankfully accepted the invitation without hesitation, as otherwise we should have had to camp out in the open air. They had selected for their new dwelling-place a spot not far from where we were, behind a low range of hills; it offered protection and pasture for their numerous flocks.

It was very interesting to observe the dexterity and skill with which these people unpacked, pitched their tents, and furnished them at once with every convenience, while the women busied themselves with the preparation of the evening meal. The sheikh, a tall, handsome man of dark complexion, in the prime of life, asked us to be seated near him; coffee and pipes were handed to us; when my wife declined the pipe, the sheikh looked at her as if surprised at this want of good manners; he gazed at her with increasing scrutiny which resolved itself into admiration and astonishment. At last he exclaimed, 'A woman!' on which I said, with emphasis, 'My *wife*!' However, he paid no heed to this, but lost in gazing at her, said, 'What a pity her lips are not blue! but that could be remedied.' The Arab women, as is well known, colour their underlips with an indelible, caustic blue dye, by which they are swollen and frightfully disfigured.

He now began to negotiate; he asked me what sum I demanded for my wife, and commissioned Herr Klinger to tell her that she should be his chief wife, should have a tent to herself, and have his other wives for her attendants. I took the matter as a joke, laughed at it, and told him it was not our custom to sell wives. But he seemed unable to comprehend this, and became more and more importunate, told us how rich he was, and it was evident that his passion was increasing. I began to feel alarmed, and gave Herr Franz a hint to go and get the horses ready. The sheikh then brought out a bag of gold and offered it to me for my wife; I pretended to be half won over, but signified to him, through Herr Klinger, that a transaction so strictly forbidden as the sale of a wife demanded serious consideration; in order that I might discuss with her and my companions how it was to be done without incurring the penalties of the law, he must allow us time to talk it over undisturbed. Suspecting nothing, he nodded assent; he was certain that I could no more withstand a bag of gold than an Arab. We left the tent and the encampment, found Herr Franz with the horses, mounted them without delay, and rode off, at first at a walking pace to avoid any noise, and then at full gallop. I was seized with an indescribable terror; I fancied that all the wild horde were pursuing us, until after two hours' flight, ourselves and our beasts ready to die of exhaustion, we reached the first gardens outside Aleppo, and felt ourselves safe, for the Arabs do not now venture to the gates of the city with intent to plunder. Did they really pursue us, or was it only the effect of my heated imagination? I cannot say. The probability is that a violent abduction before the gates of Aleppo, where Ibrahim Pacha's court was very severe against all evil-doers, appeared to the sheikh too perilous, and that this consideration sufficed to cool his passion. For if he had thought fit to pursue us with his swift steeds, the little advantage we had gained in starting could not have saved us from his hands. We thanked God for this escape, and after an unrefreshing night in a gardener's hut, reached Aleppo early next morning.

Meanwhile, news had arrived that the steamers were nearly completed, and that the *Euphrates* would soon start from Birejik; this determined us to set off immediately.

At the same time, to my great delight, we received intelligence from Colonel Taylor, the English resident at Baghdad, that Messrs. Hunter and Brown, our Affghans, were on their way thither.

Thank God, they are alive! I have not the slight est doubt of their trustworthiness.

CHAPTER VII.

WITH THE ENGLISH EUPHRATES EXPEDITION, UNDER COLONEL CHESNEY.

(From Dr. Helfer's Diary.)

March 14, 1836.—When we reached the Euphrates, after a pleasant journey of two days, we found everything at Port William in busy confusion. The great steamer *Euphrates* was ready, except her bulwarks, on which they were diligently at work, while a rail served for a provisional substitute. For the rest, in putting the separate parts of the vessel together, much attention had not been paid to elegance; everything was still of its natural colour. The second smaller boat, the *Tigris*, had not been taken in hand at all below deck; her machinery was but half finished; nevertheless, hundreds of things were stowed away in her; she was merely to float down the river with the stream without steam power. A flat boat, roughly built by native workmen, was to be attached to the large steamer, laden with coal, iron work, &c.; it was a wretched transport, leaky to begin with. Two boats for the diving bells were to be built under the supervision of Mr. Hector, and sent on afterwards. Turks and Christians were seen everywhere, laden with the most various things, and all in such haste, as if the magazines had been on fire. Anvils, bellows, iron rods, screws, guns, mortars, gun carriages, wheels, cylinders, sacks of cotton wool, trunks and chests, astronomical instruments and tent poles, and an immense quantity of planks lay scattered about, and it looked as if the Aniza Arabs were in the midst of one of the plundering exploits they conduct in so masterly a style. To us, however, it was a pleasant sight, for it held out a prospect of an early start from this dismal spot, where we have been the greater part of five months.

My wife lent a helping hand in arranging the ship's library in the space allotted to it. Looking through these select works—the English classics especially, with which she is as yet unacquainted—affords her much pleasure. The English have made admirable provision, not only of technical literature, but of reading of every sort. No well known author in their rich national literature is wanting. To Pauline, as she says, it opens up a new world; she has at once asked for a selection of books, among which are Addison, Johnson, Shakspeare, Gibbon, and a few humourists, which she has placed upon the drawing room table, that they may be always at hand. She revels in the idea of gliding safely and comfortably down the glorious river, well provided with food for the mind, and passing the noble monuments of bygone ages on its classic shores. This alone is sufficient to make up to her for all the hardships she has undergone. I am rejoiced to see her so happy. May it always remain so.

March 15.—I have to-day, it is to be hoped for

the last time, visited that gloomy place Birejik. It is
built like an amphitheatre. The difficulties put in the
way of the Expedition by Sultan Mahmoud, his petty
tool, Reschid Pacha, and the present Mutsellim of
Birejik, the desolate, unpicturesque forms and white
hue of the Mesopotamian hills, the extreme monotony
of the country hereabouts, of which I knew every inch,
made me dislike this place extremely.

Lieutenant Murphy went to fix points for the
survey of the river; I went with him to botanise.

It is curious that vegetation is full a week more
forward on the Mesopotamian than on the Syrian side.

The curious voyage to-day on board the native
boat was really dangerous. The clumsy craft was so
crammed full of asses, goats, sheep and people, that,
as like a Roman triumphal car it is open behind, the
water came in. The Turks began to pray their Aia-
alla-hillulla. The stream carried us far beyond the
town; this was all right for us, but inconvenient for
the poor people with their beasts, who had to go back
half a mile.

March 16.—To-day all was commotion in the
camp, for, after nearly a year's labour, the steamer was
to float on the Euphrates for the first time; a novel
sight for the world around.

After breakfast the crew were summoned on deck
by the ship's bell for divine service. When it was
over, the firman of King William IV. of England was
read, by virtue of which, in order to establish communication between the Asiatic possessions of Great Britain
and the mother country, his Majesty had concluded a

treaty with his dear and powerful ally, the Sublime Porte, permitting him to build steamers &c. within the Asiatic states of the last named empire. This, and a long list of engagements and customary expectations were read, and finally a set of rules for the conduct of members of the Expedition.

1. All to rise and breakfast at daybreak, and each man then to go to his allotted task, which, chiefly of a scientific nature, consists in surveying the bed of the river to Basrah.

2. Dinner at 5.30, and tea to follow soon after, in order to afford time for noting down the events of the day, and that all may retire early.

3. No one to go ashore except well armed (pious wish !), but use is only to be made of weapons in the greatest extremity.

4. After 9.30 lights to be extinguished in all private cabins.

5. Smoking not allowed (to my regret) below deck.

The Mutsellim and chief magistrate of Birejik were invited to the solemn commencement of the voyage. They came, with their numerous suites, a great deal too early, and were in the way, as we were still very busy packing. I undertook to entertain them by showing them the splendid edition of ' Parry's North Pole Expedition,' the plates in which really interested them. When they saw the Eskimos, they laughed, and said they were Arabs in winter costume. More distant friends also, even from Aintab and Aleppo, had arrived ; the shore was thronged with people, who had collected together when they saw the smoke issuing from the chimney and heard the noise. At length, about noon, the preparations were complete. The members of the Expedition were seized with enthusiasm as the bridge was withdrawn and the cables were loosed ; even the rigid muscles of the Colonel's face betrayed his emotion by a slight quiver when the inevitable ' Hip, hip, hurrah ! ' of the sailors was heard, and the steamer was for the first time in motion. The last difficulty, however, was not yet overcome.

It was decided to go up stream past Birejik. But the main stream forms a sort of cataract over rocky ground near the village of Kafrin, about a gunshot from Port William. It was thought that this could be avoided by steering through a second smaller branch, which, where it falls into the main stream, is about 1,000 feet wide. The current at the outflow was very strong ; we could not stand against it, and, to avoid being carried away, we cast anchor. But neither anchor nor engine sufficed ; the cable broke, and we ran upon a sandbank. ' Mash Allah ! ' exclaimed the Turks on board, ' what will become of us ? '

With great difficulty we got off and tried to over-come the force of the current ; but, despite all our forces, scarcely any progress was visible up stream. I was then informed that the chief cabin was full of water, and that my plants under the table were soaked. The paddles turned up the water with so much force that it rushed in through the cabin windows.

While I was putting the plants with all haste into fresh blotting paper, I heard the vessel grating on the pebbles in the bed of the river. I felt that she stood still for a moment, and then, swift as an arrow, turned round. Before I got up we were in the main stream. A disaster had just occurred ; the man at the helm had been thrown with great violence against the bulwarks, and had his thumb crushed.

The steamer could not withstand the current with all the power of her engines, and we were obliged to cast anchor about twenty minutes below Port William.

This was a melancholy end to our sanguine expectations. But the Turks were glad to have escaped with nothing but a fright, for they had never felt safe for a moment in the iron monster, as they called it, and inwardly triumphed over the failure of the enterprise. For the Colonel and all the rest it was a severe blow ; I could estimate the depth of their discouragement by my own. We landed in silence and walked back to Port William, telling those who had remained there that the boat could not withstand the current. Towards evening we returned much out of spirits to the steamer to retire to rest.

March 17.—But all who were acquainted with the perseverance of our chief knew very well that he would not rest satisfied with the first unsuccessful attempt to go up stream. In fact, he at once gave orders to lighten the boat, by the removal of everything not absolutely necessary ; to take off the covering of the paddle wheels, because the water spurting back from it struck the wheels and obstructed their force, and to make other alterations in the machinery.

The steam was got up early, the boat turned up stream, and her movements watched with anxious suspense. She moved, the paddles laboured powerfully against the current, the white foam was thrown up, she glided firmly onwards in the right course, answering well to the helm, and in a few minutes arrived at Port William amidst the shouts of the assembled multitude. But the commander was not satisfied with this success; yesterday's fiasco must be fully atoned for; faith in the invincibleness of the steamer must be restored. Soundings were once more taken above Port William, the boat again set in motion, and in a few minutes she was at the dangerous spot.

The water rushed in mighty waves over the hidden rocks; but close to the right bank there was a clear passage, for which they steered with all their might; the boat, only yielding for one moment, glided majestically over the whirling waters. Loud acclamations from the multitude, and the 'passed over' of the English announced the victory. The fine vessel now proceeded onwards to salute the town. The banner, with the crescent, moon and stars on red ground, was unfurled beside the British flag, and a salute of twenty-four guns was fired in honour of the Grand Seignior, which resounded through the rocky shores of Mesopotamia, and no doubt gave the Turks a great idea of the defensive powers of our ship. The whole shore, the roofs of the houses of the amphitheatre-shaped town, even the minarets, were crowded with people; a special place had even been reserved for the women, that they too might witness what seemed so incredible, that iron could float and even go up stream. But now that they saw the work accomplished with their own eyes, they were seized with terror; they thought it must be the result of supernatural powers, and the black clouds which issued from the funnel confirmed them in the notion that the English must be in league with the devil. And when one child fell on another from a minaret, and neither was hurt, they attributed it to some devilish spell. Nevertheless, the mother came veiled in thick cloths to ask for a backsheesh, because the English had occasioned her child to fall from a minaret. The love of backsheesh then, was greater than fear of the devil. The only gun left in the castle, which was destroyed in the earthquake of 1822, was fired off in answer to our salute. It was badly executed by a company of irregular soldiers, and if it induced the governor, who was leaning out of a pavilion in the castle, and nodded his approval, to make comparisons, he must have been compelled to place less confidence in the security in which he had been lulling himself. Many of the Turks had said, ' Well, we have them ' (the English) ' here; we shall have to see how to get rid of them.'

The steamer altered her course above the castle, and in seven minutes was alongside of the sister boat, the *Tigris.* This successful manœuvre gave us all confidence.

March 18.—Several articles having been taken on board, including Lieutenant Murphy's astronomic-magnetic and pendulum instruments, which required the greatest care, the voyage began again. With a renewed ' Hip, hip, hurrah ! ' we took our last leave of Port William, and in a few minutes were at our yesterday's moorings. After the first unsuccessful experiment, a number of things had been landed here, and had now to be taken in again, which prevented our continuing our voyage to-day.

A pretty little encampment of tents was pitched on the shore, for which Mr. William Estcourt, brother of our Captain Estcourt, furnished the requisites, which he carried with him on his tour through Egypt and Syria; he was come to pay his brother a visit, and to accompany him to Beles.

As usual, the inhabitants of the shores of the river, men, women, and children, assembled in great numbers, and sat immovably for hours staring at the ' monster.'

I made another excursion to the chalk cliff called ' The Cave,' because it contains a not inconsiderable cavern. The pleasant spring air and the bright hues of the virgin green were a foretaste of the pleasures awaiting us a week later a degree further south.

Of the Expedition corps the following gentlemen were allotted to the *Euphrates*:—The Colonel as commander, Captain Estcourt, Lieutenant Cleaveland, Mr. Charlewood, and Mr. Fitzjames, Lieutenant Murphy, Mr. W. Ainsworth, Mr. Rassam and Seyd Ali as interpreters, Mr. Thomas Hurst, engineer, twenty-five English sailors in their various capacities, three native sailors, and my wife and I as passengers.

For the *Tigris*, not yet finished, the following were left behind in Port William:—Lieutenant H. B. Lynch as second commander, Mr. Eden, Lieutenant B. Cockburn, the two brothers Staunton, Mr. Thomson, Messrs. Elliot and Sader as interpreters, Mr. Clegg, engineer, eighteen English sailors, the baggage, and four natives. Lieutenant R. B. Lynch, of the Indian army, accompanied his brother as passenger, to return by this route to India.

March 19.—We remained here to-day also. I made an excursion to the southern, that is, extreme point of the range of chalk hills, where the river makes a bend to the westward; on the other side of this a plain extends, through which the Kersin flows before it joins the Euphrates. Beyond this point you can no longer see Birejik—a time I have been long looking forward to.

I went up hill and down botanising and entomologising, while Lieutenant Cleaveland and Mr. Charlewood went down stream in two boats to take soundings. Even these boats were a wonderful sight to the natives. I afterwards met several dirty Arab women, also going down stream to collect rubbish washed up by the river for fuel. They called out to me, laughing at the distant boats, and exclaiming, 'Fock! Fock!' (far! far!) meaning that I should not be able to overtake them.

On the extreme point there was a flag belonging to Murphy's trigonometrical survey. It was untouched. The people really behave very well; they have not as yet stolen even any of the wooden pegs, and, considering the scarcity of wood, it is much to their credit; they have a great respect for everything that belongs to the English. The fear of offending those who may some day be their masters may have something to do with it.

The heat to-day was as great as with us in June, if not greater. The shortness of spring here is very remarkable ; in some places the tender grass is already getting burnt up.

On my return I met a man armed with a musket. I took no notice of him ; but as I went on he made signs of hostility, such as threats with the stock, and he pointed to the south, meaning, 'If you go down you will be killed.' He could easily have attacked me, as I was unarmed. The security which we have enjoyed in the whole country has made me careless. This is the only hostile demonstration I have met with in the six months.

March 20.—After a few more preparations in the morning we followed our course southwards. I cannot tell how glad my wife and I were as we stood on deck, to see the steamer push off and glide swiftly down the river. Our speed was so great that some gentlemen who wished to accompany us by land could not keep up with us at full gallop.

For one quarter of an hour we went on in pleasurable excitement, when, with a noise like thunder, we struck upon a sandbank, and came completely to a standstill. Every effort to move backwards or forwards, with the whole power of the engine, was in vain. The steamer would not move. We were stuck fast.

It is now evening, and to my great chagrin I must write that we are still immovable on the sandbank. All efforts to float the steamer have been fruitless. With the help of the coal transport, which had meanwhile arrived, an anchor was cast ashore, the water emptied out of the boiler, and the vessel thus raised about four inches. In vain; she was and is immovable. The pebbles rattle incessantly against her iron walls with a peculiar and, to my ears, by no means agreeable music. Shall we have to wait till the water rises? To-day it is falling. Although after the heat of yesterday the temperature is fallen to 35° Fahrenheit, and there is a heavy downpour of rain, the water will scarcely rise, for in the Taurus and the Armenian mountains the snow still lies hard and firm.

Lieutenant Murphy and I were put ashore, and as there was nothing for me to do in my naturalist's department, I helped him in taking triangles. The Arabs came as usual, and watched our manipulations with eager but unobtrusive interest. Nothing astonishes them so much as a telescope directed to some object they know, or a magnetic needle which follows the movements of an iron instrument. We almost daily hear the exclamation, ' Frengi Kibir ! ' (the Franks are great).

If we meet with the same sentiments everywhere, more friendly people cannot be imagined. Among the lower classes I have not met with any religious intolerance ; at most, only pride of the privilege of being followers of the great prophet, and pity for unbelievers.

March 22.—After two days the rain had at length melted the snow on the mountains, and so swollen the river that the steamer began to rise. Yesterday evening the usually clear water became thick and yellow, and some slight movements indicated that she was rising. But it was too late to get up the steam, and so we had to pass the night in the same place between hope and fear.

At five o'clock the steam began to blow off. A few provisions having been taken on board, the moorings were loosed, and the engine began to work, at first only at half power. The sounding chart in hand, Lieutenant Cleaveland could now guide the steamer with tolerable certainty. Our voyage to-day was a successful one ; the boat did indeed glide over a sandbank, but we did not stick, and made seventeen knots in an hour and a half.

The country here is picturesque, and with more cultivation and wood might be called charming. The forms of the mountains are rather pleasing than grand. On the banks we saw many ruins of buildings, but so crumbled away by the decay of centuries that their original form is no longer distinguishable.

The country reminds me of the Rhine; Colonel Chesney may be right in comparing the upper part of the Euphrates with the Rhine, the middle with the Danube, the lower part with the Nile.

We landed at the Turcoman tent village of Gourlou, where Captain Estcourt, who had preceded us for the survey of the river, was waiting for us. Here, too, the people were obliging and unobtrusive ; the men came on board without fear, to examine the novel monster. 'Only God,' they said, 'can possess such wisdom.' The sheikh brought a lamb as a token of friendship.

The river here forces its way through a narrow rocky channel, and falling over almost perpendicular rocks, forms the Gourlou whirlpool. We had looked forward with anxiety to this dangerous point; but owing to a previous examination by Mr. Charlewood, and the directions of Captain Estcourt, who stood on shore, we happily passed over it, amidst the acclamations of the multitude. There is a legend that Mahomet drove forty swine into the river here, and as a reward God granted to the faithful a safe passage over the rapids; but that unbelievers should pass them safely was considered an extraordinary miracle.

The rain had brought with it a chilly damp atmosphere, like gales and rain with us in March. Nevertheless, I went ashore as soon as I could and took my way alone southwards, as it was said that about five miles distant there were ruins of a large town. For the first time I was armed with a dagger and pistols, but with the perpetual stooping which the pursuits of a naturalist require, they were a great burden to me. It was, however, dictated by prudence on a distant excursion alone.

The natives came near me without fear. When they saw me digging up plants (*Leontodon tuberosum*), and I told them in answer to their questions that it was for medicine, they laughed, dug some up themselves and ate them, and said, 'That is not medicine, it produces neither vomiting nor purging.' They examined my weapons with curiosity, and asked me whether it was true that the pistols would kill five persons at once without firelock, and when I told them that they would kill many more, they timidly withdrew.

The two Estcourts afterwards overtook me, also the

gentlemen from the sounding boat, Messrs. Eden, Charlewood, and Fitzjames, and at length the Colonel himself with Mr. Ainsworth the geologist, so that the greater number of the officers assembled at the ruins of Jerabolis.

The ruins were quite worth the long walk. They are, doubtless, the remains of a strongly fortified castle of moderate extent.

A hill about 150 feet high extends some way along the river; on the plain on the other side of it we observed remains of earthworks and ramparts. The hill is artificially divided into two parts; fragments of massive walls lay about, which, still furrowed in some parts, probably bore bas-reliefs.

The sounding boat proceeded further. Captain Estcourt followed it on horseback. The rest of us returned to the steamer, which we reached at nightfall.

We could not find any information about the ruins of Jerabolis in the ship's ample library, for the notices about the upper course of the Euphrates in the sources of ancient history are more scanty than of the middle.

March 23.—To-day was such an uninteresting and unpleasant one that I hope we shall not have many like it on our voyage. A strong east wind made it piercingly cold; torrents of driving rain and storms hindered our progress. The sounding expedition did not return till late, quite wet through and half frozen, having gone as far as the mouth of the Sajur. They found a good depth of water the whole way, so that we can go on to-morrow.

March 24.—If we go on at this rate it will be at least six weeks before we reach Babylon. It was

planned to start early, but a coaling transport, which
was to have been brought by horses yesterday, did not
arrive, and so we had to wait for it this morning. The
flat boat, the *impedimentum ex malitia* of the Colonel,
which was in advance of us, was to precede us under
command of Fitzjames; but when the cable by which
she was fastened was loosed it appeared that the water
had fallen, and the clumsy, heavily-laden boat stuck fast.

During this delay I made another little exploring
excursion, for the weather was warmer and brighter;
the snow-capped Taurus chain was plainly visible at a
distance of about 45 miles. Our interpreter, a Chaldean
from Mosul, named Antoni Rassam, went with me. He
had been employed in translating Arabic MSS. at the
College at Malta,[1] and had spent several years there in
almost monastic seclusion, until he was attached to the
Euphrates Expedition as interpreter. His appearance
was very remarkable; his striking height, his dark
complexion, and the child-like, kindly expression of his
face formed a singular whole. He was, in fact, a child
in artlessness and amiable ignorance of the world. He
expressed his satisfaction at being set free from the
strict rule of the pious folk at Malta with all the sim-
plicity of a child, but he never abused his liberty. He
was an excellent chess player, there was no match
for him on board. It may here be observed how

---

[1] Dr. Helfer says that he had been 'a pupil of the Bible Society at
Malta,' which is obviously a mistake. The above statement is taken
from the 'Narrative of the Euphrates Expedition,' by Col. Chesney
Appendix XII. p. 555.—Tr.

universal chess is in the East, and what masters of it are found even among wild Arabs.

The coaling transport arrived at two o'clock and we started; but when we had overtaken the flat boat and tried to stop, our anchor would not hold against the current, and we were compelled to cast anchor on the Mesopotamian side. Again a great loss of time, for there could be no thought of going further to-day. We have so many little mishaps—if only greater ones do not follow!

Still my impatience is hardly justifiable. Considering the numerous difficulties of the navigation of this river, in utter ignorance of its course, the sudden rise and fall of the water, the numerous shallows, and the want of sufficient fuel, a rapid voyage is not to be expected.

Equipped with my naturalist's implements, I intended to ascend a range of hills extending along the shore, but found myself unexpectedly on an island. Two artificial channels about fifteen feet wide and perhaps as deep, separated the alluvial land from the foot of the hills. When and by whom were these channels made? Their purpose was undoubtedly to drain the fruitful soil. They can scarcely be the work of a Mussulman government.

For the first time I saw the natives armed with slings, which they use partly as a means of defence and partly for killing birds; large flocks of these had collected to devour the newly sown durra (maize).

While I and my wife were walking along one of the canals, we observed that the whole population of a picturesque village of tents on the heights were hastening towards our steamer; on arriving at the canal, they at once took off their clothes, put them on their heads, and waded through the water up to their breasts. They seemed peacefully inclined, regarded us with respectful curiosity, and promised to bring eggs and milk to-morrow. On board they readily lent a hand to drag the flat boat to land; but none of them could be induced to go with us to fill up the gaps caused by some workmen having left us, their fear of the smoking monster is too great. They also prophesy that the whole crew will be eaten up by savage Arabs lower down.

March 25.—Again to-day we had a difficult voyage. We started at eight, and all went well till we were opposite the ruins of Jerabolis; but there we went aground; all efforts with the engine were in vain, and had to be discontinued. I was afraid the fate of last Saturday was to be repeated, but a strong current floated us, twice however to drive us on to shallows again, but happily only for a short time.

Fruitful plains extend here on both sides; the mountains recede from view; only a few of the conical hills, so frequent in Syria, are to be seen, as if placed there on purpose as points for taking triangles. The country is certainly something like that of the Middle Nile. The river has not only made a broad bed for itself in the plain, but has cut a number of arms in the alluvial soil. This has made the navigable channel very shallow, and in consequence we stuck fast again in a narrow, apparently impassable channel, unable to move backwards or forwards. By a dexterous manœuvre of Lieutenant Cleaveland's, however, we got off, and happily reached our destination about half a mile above the mouth of the Sajur.

Not only human beings were amazed at the strange apparition of our steamer, but horses left their pasture and came galloping up to get a nearer view of the novel monster, and even a jackal stood for a time quite bewildered, with ears pricked up, on the banks. In default of other means of crossing the stream the natives here use inflated sheep or pig skins, which they place under the body, carrying their scanty garments in a bundle on their heads, and, pushing back the water with their feet, men, women, and children swim fearlessly over the rushing stream.

No sooner were we along shore than I set out on an excursion. I crossed the chalk range which commands the river, to explore the ruins on the other side. Traces of ancient civilisation, man's handiworks, are everywhere met with. In many places the rocks are cut through; on the highest point there was probably a fort, connected with the present ruins by a broad road running along the ridge of hills; on the farther side of these, gallery-like excavations are visible and caves in the rocks. The ruins themselves lie about two miles from the mouth of the Sajur. near the nomadic village of Seraset.

The whole appears to have been a strongly fortified place, but except some foundations and weather-worn stones scattered about there is little to be found but a ruined entrance through the rock, and a round cistern, into which the clear and excellent water of a little brook flows. An Arab family, who were just sowing a little patch of land with hemp, had taken up their abode in a cave under this cistern. Some of our antiquarians take these ruins for those of the ancient Europus; they appear to me more likely to be those of Ciciliano.

Near the landing place at the mouth of the Sajur, I observed a hermit's grotto, partly fallen into decay, cut in the top of the chalk cliff, probably of modern date. A cross on the summit induced the conjecture that some Christian anchorite may have found shelter here, though on the other hand a rough Arabic inscription, which I could not decipher, pointed to a Mussulman.

Lieutenant Cleaveland and Charlewood are gone on with the boat to take soundings. Major Estcourt and his brother have finished mapping the river; they were waiting for us here.

March 26.—To-day Colonel Chesney and all his officers made an excursion to the ancient Hierapolis, the present Membidge, about nine miles distant. I did not join the party, as I had explored the place five months before on my journey from Aleppo to Port William with Lieutenant Lynch. It offers nothing more than what is everywhere to be seen in Syria, fallen greatness, ruin, and desolation where advanced culture and civilisation once existed.

The gentlemen of the sounding boat have returned to-day with the report that they have found a wide paved road all along the shore from Sajur to Kala.

I made two excursions from here; one to the place where the Sajur, divided into two branches, empties itself almost imperceptibly into the Euphrates, the other on the opposite side, among the chalk cliffs, which are curiously tossed about. Neither afforded me much booty.

March 28.—The smoke from the funnel announced that we were to proceed this morning. There is no certainty to be got from questions, nor answers, nor intentions, as circumstances may change at any moment; but if the steam is up we know that we really are going on. My wife and I took advantage of the interval to mount the neighbouring hills once more. We found, quite near, considerable ruins of a fort, to which a paved and cemented road led up ; there was probably another fort opposite to it, surrounded by an arm of the Euphrates. Grain is now grown in the dry bed.

When we started the natives were standing anxiously waiting on the shore; the clouds of black smoke frightened them, and when the steam escaped with a roaring noise, the women and children ran off and the men exclaimed, 'God save us from this danger!'

Our voyage to-day in very shallow water might have been dangerous; but it was a very pleasant one, and in thirty-three minutes we made two or three miles, till we reached the Castle of Kalat-en-Nejm. We were aground four times, but thanks to the continual sounding on both sides of the steamer, we did not stick.

For two or three miles more the river is wide, full of green islands and sand-banks as far as the mouth of the Sajur; it is then narrowed by a mountain ridge and has in places a depth of seven fathoms. The scenery is varied and beautiful. The glorious river, now bounded by lofty cliffs, now widening to a broad expanse, the verdant islets, the blue mountains in the distance, form very pleasing pictures. Further on the country becomes wilder. On both sides of the river there are lofty mountain ranges of chalk formation, the strata lying arched and curved over each other. The regularity of the layers looks like the work of man, while their vastness bears witness to a greater than human power.

A few wretched nomad tents, and long-eared black goats, grazing here and there, were the only traces of life we saw, and this in a country where at every step you meet with evidences of a former flourishing state of civilisation.

March 29.—We landed below the Castle of Kalat-en-Nejm, which stands upon an isolated rock commanding the river. Although the place is very remarkable, it was not marked on the map, and we could find but scanty notices of its history. The probability is that the Arabs in their time of prosperity raised the fine buildings on Greek or Roman foundations, and that for a long period it was in good condition, until about fifteen years ago, when an Arab tribe, having refused to pay tribute to the Turkish government, were pursued by the pacha's soldiers, took refuge in the fortress, were besieged and conquered, and a wide breach was made in one side of the ramparts. It is said that in the times of the Romans there was a bridge over the river here and a tunnel under it to the Mesopotamian side.

We all betook ourselves to this castle, each following his bent and giving himself up to his own reflections.   Lieutenant Murphy ascertained the length and breadth of the place by astronomical means; Mr. Ainsworth tried to determine the age of the buildings; my wife and I collected plants and insects; the Colonel and Mr. Charlewood, provided with lights and ropes, and guided by an Arab, proceeded to explore the tunnel.   In this I joined them; we descended 200 stone steps interspersed with slopes, and by removing some loose stones opened a wide subterranean passage, but, on account of the dangerous state of the roof, further progress into it had to be given up.   Probably these spaces served as dungeons or sally ports.

These vaults are inhabited by vast numbers of large bats (*Rhinolophus*).   They continually put the lights out, hovered round our heads, and flew in our faces, giving us smart boxes on the ear.   Their excrement gives an idea of their numbers, for in some places it was five feet deep, dried to dust, and emitted such a horrible smell that it was impossible to stay long.   What a treasure of insects lies here metamorphosed, and I cannot get at them!

The castle is one of the most magnificent erections of the sort that I have seen, and must have been built during the Saracenic dominion.   All those portions spared by the storming above mentioned are still standing, and in good preservation.   The great halls, the flight of steps at the entrance, several corridors and small apartments, as well as a little chapel with a sort of chancel, quite in European style, are distinctly recognisable. Wild pigeons, red-legged partridges, bats, and lizards haunt the forsaken walls in large numbers. The whole neighbourhood is covered with ruins, among them many remains of mosques. It is a melancholy panorama, only enlivened by the majestic river.

Our voyage seems now to be planned systematically; we remain a day at each station, while the boats precede us to take soundings; then we follow them for about eight hours. Lieutenant Cleaveland returned to-day from his exploration. For the first time he had met with resistance and thieving propensities among the natives. An Englishman who had remained on shore alone to take care of the horses, was attacked and robbed by six Arabs, who swam over from the other side. I am afraid this will happen to us lower down, if we ramble about alone as we have done.

To-day we went over to the Mesopotamian side, to investigate whether the old Roman road from Hierapolis to Carrhæ (Harran) led across the river here. Opinions differ about it. Major Rennel maintains that it must have been at the mouth of the Sajur, which is very improbable, on account of the breadth of the river there. Here, on the contrary, the bed of the river is narrow, and the remains of a quay, built of large blocks of stone, about half a mile long and defended by little forts, facing those on the Syrian shore. plainly point to former communication between the two sides. That considerable buildings once stood here is indicated by extensive quarries, something like those of Syracuse. The most important thing for us, however, was the discovery of the Roman road to Harran, in some parts in good preservation.

Our station to-day was animated and interesting.

Not only the natives on the Syrian, but those of the other shore came to gaze at us. They swam across without effort, and brought goat's milk and eggs on their heads. Among the rest, we observed eleven Bedouins, who came fully armed on horseback, tarried awhile on the bank, then entirely stripped, fastened their clothes, arms, and other baggage to sheepskins bound together, and had them pushed before them by two men swimming sideways. They drove their horses into the water, and held fast to their tails, encouraging them in very loud, falsetto voices. Thus they all reached the opposite shore in safety. How little these children of nature want to satisfy their requirements.

March 30.—I am to-day quite unwell and confined to our cabin. I went out with only the white under-cap and tarbush on my head without the turban, although the sun was rather hot, and got a sun stroke. My head burns sadly, but I am not losing much to-day, for after a short voyage we went aground again. It was of no use to pump the water out of the boiler to lighten the vessel; we could not get off, and I am at leisure to dream of a better future. The natives are become much wilder. The inhabitants of the two shores are carrying on a war of mutual extermination. A Syrian told us it was his greatest desire to drink the blood of his enemies. Lieutenant Murphy was to-day, during his astronomical survey, attacked by forty Arabs, armed with guns, swords, clubs, and bows and arrows; but so great is their fear of the enchantments of the Franks that they did not venture to lay hands on the three Englishmen; but if once we lose our prestige all safety will be at an end.

March 31.—Another standstill to record; it seems likely to be the chief event of every day. We started early; the river was splendid, the channel deep, the shores pleasing, in parts romantic, though bare of wood except on a few islands. My eyes are now used to the dazzling whiteness of the chalk cliffs. The narrow passage through which the river makes way for itself was already in sight, and I was eagerly looking for the change of formation and products on the other side. Only six miles to our halting place, the ruins of Kara Bambūge, when the steamer made an unlucky turn, we stuck fast, and could not get off.

April 1.—No hope of soon getting off. The current sends the steamer higher up on the sandbank. We are in want of the cables, anchors, and provisions daily expected from Alexandretta.

In order to fill up the time, Messrs. Charlewood and Hector and Rassam were sent to take soundings as far as Beles. Although still tormented with headache, I went an excursion with my wife, the Colonel, Lieutenant Murphy, and Mr. Ainsworth. All were well armed as usual, since Mr. Hector had what was happily a comic rather than a tragic adventure, though it might easily have turned out to be a serious one. An audacious Arab, with the politest air in the world, proposed to take off his silk neck-handkerchief; when Hector contemptuously pushed the fellow off, he opened his mantle and showed that he was armed with sword and gun. Hector, without showing the least fear, coolly held his double-barrelled pistol to the man's head, whereupon, with a profound obeisance, he withdrew. Mr. Hector took part in the Niger Expedition.

We went to the tent village of Bambūge, whose sheikh, an enlightened man amongst his people, was looked upon as the ruler of the whole district. He had been invited by Ibrahim Pacha to the late festivities at Aleppo, and had brought back the news, as a great state secret, that the English were secretly in the Pacha's service, and that the steamers were intended for the transport of Egyptian soldiers for the capture of Baghdad.

It is very troublesome here to be known as a doctor. People who have been suffering for years from incurable diseases hope to obtain help which it is impossible to give. My search for plants at once betrayed me as a hakim bashi, a character, however, to which I owe much kindness.

The heat was great; when we reached the village we asked for milk, but could not get any; my head was in a burning heat, which increased the tormenting thirst. Once more I asked for halik (milk), when a blue-lipped Hecate seized me mysteriously by the arm, took me into another tent, and showed me a vessel full of sheep's milk, but would not give me any until I had felt the pulse and gently touched the wound of a young man lying there, badly wounded in the head. She was then satisfied, and sure that her patient would recover; so great is the faith of Orientals in European power and knowledge. I moistened my burning lips with a draught.

Vegetation is very forward here ; we returned well laden with treasures.

April 2.—On the days when we are stuck fast we occupy ourselves with reading, and the ship's classical library provides a good selection. We have read Gibbon with profit, parts of Herodotus and Ammianus Marcellus. Ancient history is so much more interesting here, where every moment recalls stupendous events.

Towards evening we were agreeably surprised by the sight of the flat boat. The clumsy craft is difficult to turn, and the strong current would certainly have carried it beyond us, if it had not run upon a sandbank not far from the steamer.

The brave Fitzjames at once came on board, and gave us a humorous and picturesque description of his Argonaut voyage without a rudder.

For six days the boat had been fast upon sandbanks, different ones, but always at least one a day. It had struck upon rocks, sprung leaks, which had to be stopped with earth and cotton, and had twice been attacked by Arabs in mid river, who, however, had not courage to stand English shot. The crew had had to endure hunger, heat, cold, and wet, and now at last they had to stick fast with us.

April 3.—Although it is Easter Monday, officers and crew have had a laborious day. Every effort was made to float the steamer, but just as she began to move the hawser snapped in two, and we were hurled firmer than ever on the wretched sandbank. O blessed patience, how severely art thou tried! But I am ashamed of this exclamation when I look around me and see how inevitable difficulties and adversities only call forth greater courage, energy, and endurance in my comrades, and reflect that no murmurs are ever heard. I will follow their example, and in future write no more about being stuck fast, but only make three crosses at the most.

A caravan of fourteen camels brought us to-day the things we want and the long lacking provisions. But they were unladen at Bambūge, so that we could only enjoy them in anticipation. Another trial of patience, after being restricted for a month to Euphrates water, particularly hard for the English crew, who miss the rum to which they are accustomed.

A serious incident occurred to-day in consequence of the feud between two Arab tribes. Sheikh Hassan, of the tribe of Beni Seid, could not wait to see the wonder (Merkeb Inglis) until our steamer reached his village. He therefore crossed the river on an inflated sheepskin, and was hospitably received on board the steamer. After he had been shown over it, he said with great gravity as a compliment, ' The English are people of higher descent than the Arabs.' He is a flat-nosed, brown, thick-set, elderly man, with a scanty beard, but a person of consequence in this corner of the world. His tribe are attached to him, and have gone through many a bloody struggle for him. There is a feud between him and his neighbours the Fachals, a wild, powerful tribe on the Mesopotamian side, who have killed two of his children. This has so increased the enmity between them, that they thirst for vengeance and drink each other's blood. The feud originated in a usurpation. When Sheikh Hassan's father, who had enjoyed great consideration among his people, died, during his son's minority, his brother was sheikh, but he still usurped the office after his nephews were of age. Indignant at this, the eldest, Hassan, with his brothers and a great part of the tribe, went off and formed another tribe—whether with or without bloodshed and violence we could not discover, as we could not hear the other side. At all events, the feud must have been very fierce, as three of Hassan's sons have fallen victims to it. He related his murderous deeds and plans for future bloodshed with the greatest coolness ; it appears to me that he would be quite as ready to plunder us as he is to assure us of his friendship, if he could. His people boast that he is a capital horse stealer. Although his tribe is not so strong as the Fachals, their craftiness keeps the balance true.

We wanted to get to the Syrian shore with our little boat, for each of us to go about his business, and to take back the sheikh. But, as we were fast in the middle of the river, and there was an island between us and the main land, orders were given to steer first for the Mesopotamian side, to follow it for a little way up stream, and then to let the boat float down to the intended landing place.

The sheikh expressed great alarm at having to land on the side where his mortal foes lived, but was pacified on being assured that he was quite safe with the English, and that we should cross over at once to the other side without stopping.

The Colonel and Murphy intended to take some

bearings, for which Corporal Greenhill carried the instruments. Mr. Hector was to return to Port William to conduct the *Tigris*, now ready, through the channels ; these four, myself, Rassam, who was to buy sheep, eggs, &c., in the village, and the boat's crew formed the party ; it happened that we were all unarmed. After we had landed, the Colonel and Murphy went off, while the rest lingered near the boat, I busy botanising.

On the shore stood five men, who, as soon as they recognised the sheikh, made signs of hostility by lifting their feet and striking the soles. He saw that he must fly as fast as possible, begged urgently to be put across that instant, and hastily loaded a fowling piece, which he had just received as a present from the Colonel. I looked about to discover what had so scared the man, and saw a hundred Arabs running towards us from the next tent village. But Hector, trusting to the influence of the mighty English, took no steps for having the sheikh put across. A serious combat seemed to me inevitable, and I hastened to get the help of the Colorel and Murphy, but before we could reach them the hostile Arabs had reached the shore, and had begun to fire upon the sheikh in the boat. Two of the most daring leaped into the water; the sheikh fired off his gun and shattered the arm of one of them ; he then cowered down in the boat, the bulwark of which protected him from the sword thrusts now aimed at him. Just then the loud crash of a 9-pounder, loaded with blank cartridge, was heard from the steamer, and the tribe were scattered like spray. Our friends on board had observed the transaction and given timely aid. All this was the work of a few minutes. The sheikh was quickly taken on board. It was a miracle that none of the balls which had pierced the boat had struck him.

The rest of us marched in a line to the shore, without showing any fear, to meet the Arabs, who were again collecting, but they were not disposed to attack us, and retired to their village. Rassam now also returned; during the action he had been in danger of his life, and had only saved himself by giving out that he was an officer under Ibrahim Pacha, commissioned to make peace between the hostile tribes; he had even persuaded the people to give him back the sheikh's fowling piece, which they had taken from him and were carrying about the village as a trophy.

How rough and bloodthirsty these people are, and yet so childish and simple. They have good natural abilities, and much might be done with them if it were set about in the right way.

April 5.—In spite of all our endeavours, three crosses again.

Lieutenant Murphy, his assistant Greenhill, Seid Ali, as interpreter, and I made an excursion on the Mesopotamian side to the highest chalk hill, 1,000 feet above the level of the river, about five miles off. We used to see it looking down from Port William. Lieutenant Murphy wished to take some bearings, and I promised myself a rich booty in plants and beetles. We reached the summit without difficulty; it is crowned by the ruins of a most ancient watch tower. A great extent of country lay spread out before us, forming a pleasing picture towards the south. Towards the north the ranges of hills tumbled about looked like colossal ruins—a wild and desolate scene only enlivened by the far-gleaming waters of the river.

There is no cultivated land, except a few patches sown with wheat on some of the islands. The sand and mud is turned about a little with a pitchfork, and the seed is then thrown in.

While we were busy with our affairs a crowd of armed Arabs assembled. With bare arms and legs and their tarbushes ornamented with tufts of tulips, they looked very much like Indians. Keeping our arms in readiness we retired into the ruins of the tower. Seid Ali pretended not to understand Arabic, partly to avoid their importunity, partly to overhear their conversation. 'See, there are four of the foreign dogs whom we should so like to plunder! If only they had not the devil inside them, who has his seat in the fire-ship!' They sat down and followed our movements with the greatest interest, but if any of them ventured to touch any of our things we gave them a stern reprimand. It does not do here to relax the dignity of a master for a moment.

Meanwhile more Arabs came up. They carried a wild pig which they had killed, and excused themselves for touching the unclean beast by saying that Rassam had ordered them to do it. We left the place; Murphy took further observations. I was successful in collecting, and we did not get back till late in the evening.

April 6.—Nothing but crosses to put down! The

water is continually falling; we are upon dry ground. The Colonel is very unwell, he has had continued attacks of fever.

April 15.—Still upon dry land. It cannot be helped. How could I think of gently gliding down during the exploration of the river. We must think ourselves happy that, at any rate, the British mother country takes good care to provide the children she sends out into the world with news from home, and food for the mind, and so keeps them in constant intercourse with herself. It is incredible what a mass of daily papers comes by every steamer by way of Malta and Alexandretta, or from Constantinople; it is impossible to get through them all. Besides these we have the chief periodicals, such as the ' Transactions of the Royal Geographical, Mineralogical, Geological, and Astronomical Societies,' the ' Quarterly ' and ' Edin-burgh ' Reviews, the ' Athenæum,' ' Literary Gazette,' ' Penny Cyclopædia,' ' Sporting Magazine,' ' Asiatic Journal,' ' United Service,' ' Blackwood,' ' The Nautical Magazine.'

Thus we are kept informed of what goes on in Europe; I also learn something of the latest German literature, by means of English translations, and the criticisms of our productions interest me very much. So well provided with reading we can well bear the long delay.

We are on a very friendly footing with the Arabs about here. They bring us every day, leben (sour milk and mustard), truffles, wild garlic, a root something like chicory, sometimes eggs, and even wild pigs, besides the everlasting sheep, which are our chief diet.

Like all half savage races they are ignorant of the value of money, and will not take it; but exchange is carried on all the more eagerly and profitably by our people, who brought all sorts of manufactures with them. Orange-coloured cotton handkerchiefs are great favourites. During the last week we have seen the natives wearing boots and orange-coloured turbans.

These friendly relations enable me to pursue my rambles lightly armed, that is, with only dagger and pistols, a great comfort with the increasing heat and the various apparatus I have to carry.

Two horse stealers were caught to-day, an Arab and a negro, just as they were about to make off with some of our transport animals, which were grazing on shore. They were brought bound on board and shut up in the dark coal-hole. The Colonel was at first inclined to send them as examples to Ismail Bey at Aleppo, where they would have been beheaded as notorious thieves. Their friends did not concern themselves in the least about them, but only laughed at them for their want of alertness in being caught. The culprits themselves, thinking the Franks would eat them, only prayed to be killed off hand, before the great bad spirit below in the dark ship strangled them. The poor devils escaped with only a fright; after a slight chastisement they were let go.

April 18.—Thank God, after being stuck fast for nine days on one spot, we are afloat again. Yesterday morning, to our unspeakable delight, the water began to rise at the rate of an inch an hour. We sat the whole day on deck, watching the Euphratometer, manufactured by ourselves, and calling it out to one another as every inch on the scale disappeared in the water. About seven o'clock we heard the first low, and to us now musical sound of the rattling of the pebbles under the steamer. At the same moment, however, the strong, double anchor cable broke. Quick as lightning she turned round, and as there was no steam on she ran half a mile into another channel and was again set fast between sand-banks. To our great joy the water rose unusually high during the night, and at six a.m., with full steam on, we regained the right channel; the steamer obeyed the smallest movement of the helm and behaved very well.

We lay to near shore to take in the coal, heavy tackle, &c., which had been unladen. In this the Arabs, who had come running up, were very helpful; amidst frightful yells, they drew along the chain cables, leaped into the water, and worked well, naked as they were, for over an hour. Just as we were about moving off our brave Fitzjames and his crew arrived on foot; he brought the bad news that the flat boat had got stranded and had sunk. The clumsy craft had not been able to withstand the current near Kara Bambūge. The river there, in winding between the last high chalk cliffs, forms a remarkable pass, which is important for physical geography; the land is more level further down and the hills are of a different formation; the current dashes on the rocky shore, and sets with great force on the opposite side. Every effort to guide the craft in this dangerous pass was fruitless, with a loud crash it dashed upon the rocks, so that the crew had scarcely time to save themselves, first by means of the cotton bags and then in the boat. The Expedition sustains a great loss by this misfortune. Fifteen tons of coal, the life-blood of our engine; barrels of flour, provisions, and weapons of all sorts, clothing, &c., have sunk in seven fathoms of water, and nothing will be able to be saved, even by the aid of our diving bell. The gentlemen think much less of their own losses ; Major Estcourt, who lost a considerable part of his baggage, said laconically, 'One must be prepared for such disasters beforehand.'

To cheer us up, soon afterwards, black clouds of smoke announced the arrival of the long-expected *Tigris*; she came down the river with extraordinary speed, and cast anchor near us. We all hastened on board to welcome the new arrival. She had shared our fate and had been thirteen days on a sand-bank.

The *Tigris* was at once ordered to proceed to the place where the raft was wrecked, and to save what could be saved. We were delighted with her majestic appearance as she glided past us up stream, stemming the current, and sitting on the water like a nymph. I comprehend the awe and fear with which this wonder inspires the Arabs. We felt the same ourselves forty years ago, and now rejoice that man's genius has curbed the elements and employs their force for his own ends.

A violent storm, like the tropical tornadoes, in the evening, endangered our being cut adrift and driven again upon the bank, which lay before our eyes. The waves tossed and foamed and beat with fearful force against our ship's sides, and made her creak and tremble; but the danger happily passed over, and we went to bed relieved from anxiety.

April 19.—We were ready to start at six. The water, which had risen over eight feet, presented a grand expanse. The quantity of foam, and the dirty reddish colour, were signs of a still further rise. It was more difficult to steer than usual, owing to the many banks covered with water. The only warnings against shallows were the tops of the tamarisks, of which there is a scanty growth among the pebbles. We have not seen a trace of the '*forêt immense*,' which Geoffray marks on his map of the Pachalic of Aleppo, above and below Beles, for a distance of eighty leagues.

On the left shore there was a large settlement of the Fachal Arabs; nearly 1,000 tents were pitched in the plain. Large herds of camels, horned cattle, horses, and sheep were grazing within the camp, while the whole population assembled on the shore to stare at the steamer. They invited us to stop, and when we went past, swift as an arrow, some of the men tried to follow us on their fleet horses, but in vain, for we were making eleven and a half knots an hour.

In an hour and a half we reached Beles. We anchored near a meadow with grass up to the knees, a picturesque spot with extensive distant views, and what appeared like considerable ruins in sight, about three miles off. This may have been the ancient harbour of Aleppo, as this is the point of the river nearest to the city, and the country is favourable for communication.

We have now made 100 English miles in thirty-four days—not a great result, but still satisfactory, considering the difficulties and labour of a trial trip like this.   How long will the remaining 1400 take?

As soon as we had breakfasted everyone hastened to land to turn the stay to account after his own fashion.   Mr. Tardy was first this time; he wanted to take a survey of Barbalissus before noon.   Estcourt wished to make a sketch; Ainsworth, our antiquary, to search for the hunting park of the kings of Syria; and I, as lord and master of the animal and vegetable creation, to seek out and greet my subjects here.   Cleaveland and Charlewood are to set up a workshop on shore, as the steamer is to be cleaned and painted.   We intend to stay several days here, as we expect provisions from Aleppo.   I hope they will come.

Tired and exhausted by the heat, for it was 86° Fahrenheit in thé shade, we returned at sundown, and interchanged our observations at dinner.   Our cook, an American negro, is unfortunately not skilled in his art, or the conversation might have been more lively.

April 20.—The scum which has come up with the rubbish and settled between the vessel and the shore has brought a multitude of insects with it.   It literally swarms with them, and I find some very interesting specimens which I have been wishing to possess for years. For instance, *Scaritidæ, Polyphemus,* with *Cicindelidæ* and *Tanymecus* united, and other species which are new to me. The crown of all, however, was *Megacephale Euphratica Oliv.,* which I have been looking forward to ever since I have been on the Euphrates. The whole day occupied with entomology.

April 21.—To-day, like yesterday, sought for and preserved new treasures. My Pauline and I were quite dexterous in spying out and capturing the most minute creatures, hardly visible to the naked eye. No one on board enters into it, and they laugh at the importance we attach to these invisible things. So various are men's tastes.

Decomposition takes place so rapidly in this climate, and our people are so weakened by repeated attacks of illness, and so susceptible of miasmatic influences, that the exhalations from the decaying vegetable matter accumulated round the steamer have produced five cases of severe intermittent fever in scarcely twenty-four hours. The poor Colonel suffers from it more than anyone. I fear, unless he takes more care of himself, he will not live to carry out his undertaking.

Besides the large wrecked raft, four pontoon rafts have been built. They form a considerable fleet, intended for the transport of various articles, including the diving bell, weighing three tons. We heard to-day that one of them, under command of Sarder, and manned only by Arabs, had been attacked and robbed by Bedouins. The *Tigris* was at once despatched to the spot to demand compensation from the delinquents. She was scarcely off when we saw Sarder coming down, seated on the diving bell as on a throne. A desire to oblige the English, and perhaps also to get a backsheesh, had induced a troop of Arabs to attack and drive away the Arab crew. Sarder tried in vain to restore peace. The shots were whistling round his head, and he had to jump into the water and swim to shore.   Thence he threatened to fetch the fire-spitting ship; which would kill them all. This electrified them; they came and kissed his shoulders, and fell at his feet, until he forgave them, and could continue his voyage in peace.

April 22.—To-day Pauline and I took a walk to the distant ruins, accompanied only by Rassam, our learned Chaldean.   The nearer we get to the Aniza Arabs the more cautious we ought to be, but our conscious superiority makes us careless, and I fear something unpleasant may happen.   Perhaps I, on my solitary rambles, shall have to pay the first ransom.

While my wife, seated on a height near the grave of a sheikh, was taking a sketch, I had time to inspect the ruins carefully; they are the first I have seen in this country built of burnt bricks. They are flat square bricks, joined together by a thick cement, an excellent binding material.

The whole district, an extensive undulating tract of country, covered with luxuriant vegetation, is strewn with rubbish, fragments of bricks and potsherds, indicating the site of a town.   The bricks are evidence of its Assyrian origin.   On these ruins Romans and Saracens have built again, which is obvious from numerous foundations, although but few ruins remain which indicate what they were.   Among these is a Roman castle, probably the palace of Barbalissus, a huge, thick, square tower with small windows.   Most of the buildings are of the Saracenic period; there are several rather rough mosques, in one of which two sarcophagi are found. A well preserved minaret, eighty-two feet high, is a real ornament to the neighbourhood. A winding stair of 112 steps leads to the top, from which you enjoy an unlimited panoramic view. The elegant structure is adorned with Arabic inscriptions and sentences from the Koran. Unfortunately it will not long rear its form aloft, for its foundations are very much undermined, apparently on purpose.

The subterranean vaults are inhabited by jackals, foxes, and hyænas. The lion is also said to be found in the bushy marshland of the river. I have not seen one myself, nor yet crocodïles, but Mr. Ainsworth and several of the crew maintain that they have seen them. It appears to me highly improbable that they should exist so high up the river, and if they did the Arabs could hardly swim in it so carelessly. But I can confirm the existence of the beaver, as we had the good fortune to capture one ; it is destined for the Zoological Gardens in London.

April 23.—There was a slight skirmish to-day. Corporal Greenhill was busy driving in a station flag for the survey, not above 200 yards from the *Tigris*, when several Arabs rushed upon him, pointed their long lances at his throat, and made signs to him to take off his coat. Being so near the steamer he was unarmed and could not defend himself. The thieves took off his blue coat, and eagerly cut off the brass buttons with their sabres, no doubt taking them for gold. They then made him a polite bow, jeeringly handed him back his mutilated swallow-tail, and made off as fast as they had come. This insult was too much for a Briton. Breathless, and trembling with rage,

Greenhill came back to the steamer, and, pointing to his coat, disfigured by holes instead of adorned with buttons, he demanded satisfaction for the insulted honour of England. In order to avenge him, and still more to inspire the Arabs, who were getting too bold, with proper respect, a detachment of well-armed men was quickly despatched, under command of Major Estcourt, to pursue and, if possible, capture the thieves. Lieutenant Cleaveland climbed the nearest hill to see which direction they had taken, and at about eighty paces off he saw a troop of Arabs approaching. Without thinking he fired at them. They were startled and stood still; but when Cleaveland, who is near-sighted, took out the long telescope which he always carries with him, to see that his shot had taken effect, they beat a hasty retreat, probably taking the telescope for a powerful rifle. Several of us, myself among the rest, hastened to his assistance. We rallied round his awe-inspiring tube, as if it had been the green banner of the Prophet, and it was borne by Sergeant Quin before us in triumph. Thus we joined Major Estcourt. He had seen spies on all the hills, and numerous hordes of Arabs, probably Aniza, in the distance, but none of them ventured nearer. As it was not our purpose to pursue them farther, after we had occupied the hill for an hour in pouring rain (a phenomenon at this time of year), he allowed the men to march back in two columns in military order. Corporal Greenhill was of course very much put out.

In spite of this peaceful termination of the affair, we had a man severely wounded. The brave Fitzjames fell down the slippery descent, and broke his leg just above the ankle. He was carried back to the steamer unconscious. Happily he is of such a cheerful temperament that when he was hardly come to himself, and only just informed of what had happened, he began to arrange his toilet, even while his leg was being set, in order, as he said, that he might be fit to receive visitors.

April 28.—My daily and often distant excursions afford me the opportunity of thoroughly inspecting the country and convincing myself of its great fertility. The statement that the interior of Syria is not fruitful from want of water and high temperature applies only to some parts, and even in these, the olive, fig, and vine could be successfully cultivated. The whole way from Biroæ to Babylon was once planted with trees; and what might not be done by cultivation considering the extraordinary fertilising properties of the alluvial soil of the Euphrates!

Here, near Beles, corn, a sort of *Hordeum*, grows wild among the hills, and in many places the grass is so thick that you cannot get through it. A footway, which was made a few years ago, is impenetrably grown over by a species of *Antonatum*. Each different plant chooses a spot for itself of from 20 to 200 feet square, which it occupies exclusively. Oats, bromus, centaury, camomile, viola, wormwood, aconite, and other species are interspersed, each covering a separate field, producing a mosaic on a grand scale.

We are to-day very busy packing and writing. Reports and collections are to be despatched to the mother country in a few days to show that her sons are not spending time and money for nothing. I am reluctant to part with my collections before I have had time to classify them, for in this the naturalist in distant lands finds his reward and delight; but, on the other hand, I am glad to show that there is some use in my accompanying the Expedition.

Our adventurous Elliot was sent as an ambassador of peace, on foot, and in a garment of camel's hair, such as the dervishes wear, to the distant camp of the Aniza Arabs, the scourges and worst plunderers of the country. They proudly style themselves 'Sons of Ishmael' and 'Princes of the Desert.'

In the clear evening light we saw a dark moving mass in the horizon, and hoped that it might be the much needed provisions from Aleppo, which are likely enough to be plundered by wandering Bedouins. We followed the moving line with eager suspense, for in a solitude like this, where the only living thing you see is a wild pig, an owl, or a crow, and you hear nothing but your own voice and the howl of jackals and wolves, every new sight is an object of the greatest interest. Slowly, far too slowly, the mass drew nearer. We now recognised the long lances, adorned with ostrich feathers, of a procession of Arabs. In measured and solemn march the dromedaries bore their riders, one in front of the hump, the other behind. The chiefs, however, were mounted on splendid horses, and when they perceived us they gave them the reins to display their agility.

When about 200 paces off, the men alighted, stuck

their plumed lances into the ground, and sat down in a semi-circle. Before long our dervish Elliot came prancing up on a spirited little horse to announce the arrival of the 'Princes of the Desert,' whereupon the necessary arrangements were made to give them a good meal after their long march. A number of sheep were sent, with the proper quantity of rice; the viands prepared for us would scarcely have satisfied their keen appetites.

To pitch their camp, kill the sheep, skin and tear them in pieces, and make an excellent pilaw was but the work of a few minutes. We looked on at a distance, as etiquette forbade our going nearer. Having satisfied their hunger, and the chiefs having reassumed their dignity, three of the most eminent came on board, accompanied by Rassam and Elliot. Their physiognomies were different from those we had seen before, and two of them might be called very handsome. Although their complexions were dark brown, their long curly hair, long narrow faces, with rather an expression of suffering, and their soft but sparkling eyes, reminded me of representations of the Crusaders. They were received by the Colonel, surrounded by the officers, in the grand saloon, with the utmost ceremony, and the customary assurances of friendship having been exchanged, and the pipes of peace smoked, they were conducted to the tent erected for the night. On shore the spectacle of some Congreve rockets awaited them, which astonished them greatly. They asked if the stars went beyond the moon and remained suspended there.

April 29.—Our guests came on board again in the morning with the same solemnity as before. Although longing for a nearer inspection of the marvels, they did not betray their curiosity in the least.

It was thought well to acquaint them with the power of the ship's guns. They were first shown guns with bayonets, and the firing of them with a match seemed to them like magic. They had never seen cannon, and the effect produced on them by some discharges of canister from two 9-pounders into the water was tremendous. They were terrified, and said, ' Who can resist you? you kill 1,000 men with one shot!' They were then shown the armoury, at the sight of which they exclaimed, ' Why so many weapons? One shot from the great gun would drive away all the Arabs!' But the machinery, the great beams, the piston and cylinders excited their greatest astonishment. ' How,' they asked, ' can you work iron like that? it is cut as fine as cheese.' They saw Fitzjames in passing, stretched upon his couch, and expressed polite regrets at his accident. They recommended eating lamb as the best means of curing a broken bone.

They were much struck with the library in the saloon. ' See,' said one, ' that is where they get their wisdom from! How costly these books must be; they are even gold outside,' pointing as he spoke to the gilt lettering on the binding.

Meanwhile Pauline was sketching one of them in her book; he observed it, took the book, and in turning over the leaves he saw a sketch of a Turkish lady on horseback, and exclaimed, ' How can the Franks do

it ? In such a little space, the woman, the horse, and
actually saddle, bridle, and bit, all just as it is ! '

Our guests were invited to dine with us to-day,
but they satisfied their appetites beforehand in camp
with an excellent pilaw. They had never before sat
on chairs at a table, but dexterously took the places
assigned to them. Having never handled spoons,
knives, and forks, they watched their neighbours, and
imitated them so well, that one might have thought
they had often been guests at European tables. They
made their remarks with dignity and without constraint. ' What do you want these instruments for ? '
they asked, pointing to the forks. ' Has not God given
you fingers ? ' When pork was put on table, a delicacy
to us after the everlasting mutton, they did not touch
it, but made the sensible remark, that ' everyone must
obey his precepts.' They took no wine, but were not
surprised that we drank what was forbidden to them.
The transparency of glass was new to them ; they
wished to pour out water for themselves, but could
not tell whether the glasses were full or empty.

In the afternoon a solemn deputation came to enter
into an eternal treaty of peace with our great sheikh,
and to receive a written firman to that effect. This
was Colonel Chesney's wish. Rassam was commissioned
to draw up the articles in Arabic, and they were at
once accepted and ratified on both sides without any
diplomatic subterfuges. The Colonel then said, ' We
are come as friends ; we will bring you all the manufactures that you want and take your wool in exchange.'
' Taib, Taib ! ' (Good) they exclaimed with emphasis.

'But,' continued the Colonel, 'we desire to live in
peace and friendship, not with you only, but with all
the tribes. You are in perpetual enmity with the
Shamar; make peace with them! Want of unity
divides and weakens you; union will make you strong.'
They listened to him calmly, then the eldest answered,
'Peace is good, but there must be war too ; without it
there would be no men. Our fathers and forefathers
made war with the Shamars, and we must and will do
so too. It is enjoined by our laws.' It was vain to.
argue against this.

May 1.—The officers and crew who were sent to
take soundings as far as Ja'ber returned to-day greatly
exhausted, having walked thirty miles through thorns
and briars in the burning heat.

Our amiable Estcourt has a severe attack of fever
again, and, out of regard for the English doctors, has
to allow himself to be treated after the English fashion,
which means to be everlastingly taking calomel. Only
the English constitution could survive such treatment.

May 2.—The *Tigris* is going on to Ja'ber to send
the sounding boat from there to Racca. We, unfortunately, have still to wait for the caravan of provisions
from Aleppo.

Locusts have appeared in that neighbourhood in immense numbers, but, although it is only thirty-six miles
off, they have not come as far as this, and Ibrahim
Pacha has adopted such vigorous measures against
them that further devastation is averted. He sent the
whole garrison out, 12,000 strong, to collect locusts,
and pays a private person four piastres for a bushel of

them ; the people found this a pleasant way of earning money; they shut up their bazaars, and so it is difficult to get a pair of boots, a tarbush, or even provisions.

May 3.—This is a fine place for sportsmen; it swarms with wild pigs, who, however, are so tame that you can kill them with clubs. The antiquaries tried to make out that they are descendants of those in the celebrated zoological gardens of the Syrian satraps, and to find traces of the park of Belisarius, a difficult task, as there was not a tree to be found. On the edge of the river, however, the gnarled roots of a liquorice tree were laid bare, so these gentlemen thought they had discovered the site of the old forest. The multiplication of wild swine appears perfectly natural to me, without the hypothesis of a zoological garden, for their food is abundant, and they are protected by religious prejudices. Mr. Charlewood and I were lucky enough to kill a boar weighing $2\frac{1}{2}$ cwt. On an island near we saw a whole family of them, who regarded us with curiosity. Three were killed. The Colonel started eleven in one place. They are a different variety from ours; the young are striped like a zebra; the old ones reddish brown and very large. The Arabs have not such a horror of these unclean beasts as the Turks. Some of those on board are even ready to eat their flesh. It is with insignificant things of this sort that civilisation sometimes begins.

May 6.—Inch Allah! The goods are come. To-morrow we leave this spot, which promises to be of great importance as the first English settlement and the harbour of Aleppo. I no longer feel any interest in this monotonous country, its scenery, or products. The everlasting white chalk fatigues the eye; the conglomerate lying upon it, here mixed with flint, only gives it a reddish hue; the narrow strips of spring green begin to be bleached; summer is beginning, but it looks like winter here. It is far too near Europe and its products for me; I sigh for the tropics.

May 7.—The time lost at Beles is to be made up, and the steamer is to go straight on to Racca, a distance of seventy miles. Our voyage to-day was more agreeable and interesting than any before. The shores, at first covered with tamarisk bushes, were soon clothed with trees of larger growth, which, with the underwood, formed impenetrable thickets. Thousands of birds, some of them new to me, sung and twittered in this safe retreat, and nightingales warbled their love songs. I have never heard such a chorus of birds, and perhaps it will be the last time for a long while, as the tropical birds have splendid plumage but no song.

The people will scarcely venture on these islands, on which the lion is said to be occasionally found.

Two or three miles below Beles the river divides into several branches, which, when the water is high, unite and form a vast lake. There was a great inundation here a fortnight ago; in many places the water reached the tops of the tamarisks. Nothing remains of it now but a few ponds, larger or smaller. The banks have a washed look, and now and then a high bank which has been undermined, falls in.

This part of the country seems more thickly inhabited. The Waldi Arabs live here, a tribe directly subject to the Aniza, and indirectly to Ibrahim Pacha. The men go half naked, but look more to be trusted than the Fachals and Beni-Seids. They grow corn and practise a sort of primitive irrigation. An apparatus of wood, not unlike a draw well, is placed perpendicularly in the river; ox-hides are filled with the water thus drawn up; these are fixed on rollers, drawn over the land by oxen, and the contents emptied on the fields. In other places we saw water-courses made of clay on a wooden foundation.

The crowds on shore greeted us with the usual 'Mash Allah!' Some tried in vain to keep pace with us on horseback.

We got safely along to-day, though the reports of the soundings—six feet—five feet—did not sound reassuring. Opposite Castle Ja'ber we struck, but were afloat again directly. This ancient castle, celebrated even in the time of Alexander, called the Giant Castle, is a desolate ruin, like everything else once grand and beautiful on the shores of the Euphrates. In the background is Tell Marabbou, the Holy Hill. Alexander the Great crossed the river here on his way to Thapsacus. Benjamin of Tudela, found the castle, which is built of bricks, a strong place in his time. A lofty minaret rises out of the ruins and serves as a landmark in the desert.

We found the *Tigris* anchored on the shore near Ja'ber, and lay to near her. While the tamarisk wood brought by the Arabs was being taken in, I made a hasty excursion to a cornfield, where there were myriads of sulphur-coloured *cistelides*. We then went on, the *Tigris* ahead of us. The shores are becoming flatter, the chalk cliffs, mere breccia, disappear. A sort of aspen grows along with the tamarisk, which here and there reaches a considerable height.

Our course was almost direct north; the river, divided into three branches, makes a great bend. We changed our course, but got into a bog, and were stuck fast for ten minutes. The *Tigris* came to our aid, and the woodwork intended for bulwarks having been unshipped, and the boiler emptied, so that the boat was raised five inches, we got off. The day was lost though.

May 8.—It was fixed to stay here to-day too, to replace the loss of coal by the wood on an island near. We must turn what the country affords to account. It was not lost time to me, as it was an interesting field for my observations.

On one side of the island the vegetation consisted of slender tamarisks, brambles, and aspens of a species new to me, with scarcely any growth on the sandy soil beneath. But the other side was grown over with high grass and large aspens. Wild swine, jackals, and foxes abound. The sparrows are very bold. They build their nests in the brambles and grass, six or more, one above another. They do not seem to be acquainted with man, for they stared at me without fear, like birds do at an owl, and did not fly away.

Our magpies and starlings are also at home here, and I heard a few nightingales. On examining a deserted nest I discovered one of the *Buprestis* family and some other species I have long been seeking.

May 9.—This morning there was a scene which reminded me of the primeval forests of America. The crews of both steamers were sent to cut wood on the island, and had to cut their way through the thicket. The Arabs seem to have felled timber here at one time, for many half-rotted trees were lying about. Indeed, they set so little value on it, that they have burnt patches of wood for no purpose.

By noon enough had been taken in, but being green it gave out so little heat that we did not get off till five o'clock.

The short course to Racca was very pleasant. The undulating outline of the hills on the Syrian side looked picturesque in the afternoon light. The river, which hitherto has never kept the same course for a thousand yards, is now straight for some distance, and there is a fine view over the broad expanse. We passed several important ruins in this district so memorable in history, Susa, for instance, next to Palmyra, the chief town of this country, but there are very few remains of it. We were also so fortunate as to make out with tolerable certainty the doubtful site of Thapsacus, the present Hamman. A dam built of stone along the river, still traceable, marks the spot where Alexander and his army crossed, and this agrees with the account of the situation given by Xenophon.

The extensive but ruined walls of Racca, the ancient Nicephorium, were illumined by the last rays of the sun as we drew near. We lay to near the town on a low, swampy shore.

May 10.—The Arabs here, of the Effadee tribe,

look like a set of thieves, and are doubtless very sorry they cannot plunder us. But they are timid: only two of them ventured to come near us this morning, bringing milk in little wooden vessels. Rassam went and spoke to them in a friendly way, and then they brought things for sale, but made the shameless demand of half a gazi (a florin) for a little milk. Several then came, each one bringing something— leben (curds with mustard), butter, fat extracted from boiled sheep's tails, and live sheep. Competition lowered their demands, and at last they offered their goods for a few yellow handkerchiefs.

Their tents stood about a mile east of Racca. Most of them wore nothing but a shirt. Some of them had a rusty sabre in their girdles, while others were only armed with a staff with a ball at the end.

They soon became very bold. One tried to take my gun out of my hand; another the pistols out of my wife's girdle, as backsheesh; a third drew a rusty sword because our servant Mahomed prevented him from coming too near the steamer; but he decamped fast enough when Rassam intervened, unarmed, and threatened to cut his head off. Another stole a hammer, but was found out, and sent off after a bastinado. Nevertheless, friendship was sworn with the sheikh, who thought himself highly favoured to be allowed to come on board and see the wonders.

The women showed themselves too. They were uglier, if possible, than those we have seen before. Recognising my wife as one of their sex, they exclaimed in astonishment, 'Marra! marra!' and said what a great pity her lips were not blue.

My attempt to reach Racca on foot failed. I got into deep mud, then to a broad ditch full of water, and had to ask an Arab to take me over. For a considerable reward he took me over on his back, the water reaching to his waist, and the ground was so slippery that I was in danger of taking a bath against my will.

I went on, but soon came to a second impassable ditch, which had evidently belonged to former fortifications, with a few mulberry trees on the banks. So I had to turn back, and was glad to find my Arab again, who had evidently been waiting for me, hoping to extort a still larger backsheesh. I afterwards went to the town in a boat with Murphy, who had to take trigonometrical measurements. I never saw more scanty and miserable remains of a once famous place. There is nothing but the wall, crumbled to mud and clay, to give any idea of the size of ancient Nicephorium. Shapeless mounds mark the site where Haroun-el-Raschid, after leaving Baghdad, built himself a palace, and then an observatory for his son El-Mamun, from which the astronomer, El-Bathene, measured the first meridian line. Here, and in a minaret of later date still standing, Lieutenant Murphy took his astronomical observations—the first, perhaps, for a thousand years.

Dr. Rauwolf, of Nuremberg, who visited the Euphrates in 1573, describes Racca as still a considerable place. Now the harsh clacking of storks is heard there as they stand meditatively on the walls. The black ibis builds its nest by thousands in the ramparts, and troops of jackals and foxes come forth by day from their subterranean haunts.

For the first time to-day I saw a swarm of locusts cross the water. They formed a broad, compact mass. The stronger jumped upon the weaker ones, who had to support them, and so passed over. If many perished, myriads reached the opposite shore, and alighted inside the walls. But there their greatest enemy, the green merops, was awaiting them, the only bird here with a pleasant voice.

May 11.—We were under weigh at six, but cast anchor in half an hour near Amram, not far from a wood of the same name, which, on account of the wild beasts which infest it, is in evil repute with the Arabs. We had to lay in a fresh stock of wood. My first attempt to penetrate the thicket failed. When the crew had cut a way through it, I came to a place covered with tamarisk trees, and should not have got so far if wild pigs, who swarm here, had not trodden down the ground. Brambles, rank asparagus, clematis, sarsaparilla, and other creepers made farther progress impossible.

Swarms of large mosquitos made the place intolerable. Still the day passed quickly and pleasantly to me, as it always does when I can listen undisturbed to Nature's voice. I seem to hear it more clearly and to love it better than that of any human being, except my Pauline's.

When at night the jackals, attracted by the

remains of the sheep we had consumed, came prowling about, and began their soprano concert, they howled me to sleep.

Friendship was sworn here with the Weldah Arabs by Rassam on his head and beard. They greedily ate up the piece of bread given them as a token of friendship, when a sudden noise frightened them. The Effadee Arabs meanwhile came swimming on inflated skins over the river, and, as if they had been ordered to do it by the Franks, tried to drive away the Weldah's cattle. They thought we had betrayed them, and Rassam had some difficulty in regaining their confidence. Under the powerful protection of the foreigners, they shouted out curses and challenges to their enemies.

May 12.—In the afternoon I was put over to the other side—an undulating, treeless, arid plain, on the edge of which is a range of low hills lying east and west. The plain was quite uncultivated, but numerous beds of ancient canals and rough Arab watercourses, showed that it had been, and perhaps is now sometimes, cultivated by the Arabs about here.

A violent storm, with a fog which made it almost dark, prevented me from exploring. I thought these atmospheric phenomena portended an earthquake, but all remained quiet, and the evening was fine.

May 13.—We went on to-day in a perhaps adventurous way, without, as before, sending on a boat to take soundings. The *Tigris*, commanded by Lieutenant Lynch, went first. The fear of getting aground made me nervous; but as the water was always from two to three fathoms deep, I took courage and enjoyed the scenery. After a pleasant course of three hours and a half we landed at a well-wooded spot on the Mesopotamian side, as the *Tigris* has to take in wood again.

Three Arabs on horseback, almost naked, came up to us, cautiously asking if we were friendly to them. They would willingly be subject to the Franks, and pay tribute, if they would protect them from their enemies. After our assurances of friendship, they galloped off, but soon came again with a large retinue. They belong to the Afadel tribe, are fine men, but behaved quite like savages. They asked nothing for the sheep which Rassam bought of them but a piece of bread, which they divided amongst them, for they looked upon it as a token of friendship of which they all wished to partake.

When the twelve o'clock bell was rung on board, they ran away in a fright, taking it for a hostile sound, and only took courage to return after many assurances of friendship; but then they were more importunate.

May 14.—We proceeded to-day in the same way, the *Tigris* ahead. The river is favourable to navigation here, being deep and three hundred yards wide; but to our surprise it took a sudden turn southwards towards the mountains.

A layer of basalt lies on the top of a layer of flints. The top is a black mass, and loose, black stones fall over the naked precipice, which appears to shut in the river.

The grandeur of the scenery increased the nearer we approached the passage of the Euphrates through the rocks. This is the third rocky barrier since Birejik, and is called the dark precipice. After going on for a quarter of an hour we lay to near the ruins of a castle, opposite Zelebi, our most picturesque landing-place on the whole voyage. We hastened to land, I with doubly pleasant anticipations, from my love of nature as well as interest in antiquities.

About a mile lower down are the ruins of a castle, which must have been very strong at one time, built of blocks of gypsum, filled up with basalt. On the land side a portion of wall with three arched openings is left standing; on the river side it has fallen into the water. Not only time, and the hand of man, but earthquakes have conduced to the destruction here, as is shown by the deep clefts and rents in the walls.

Myriads of locusts were devouring the remains of herbage; they are of a different species from those we saw at Racca.

May 15.—To-day, Sunday, which when possible the Colonel strictly observes, there was time to visit Zelebi, the summer palace of Zenobia. She built it when Queen of Palmyra, after the death of her husband, and it was from here, on her flight after the conquest of Palmyra by Aurelian, that she was taken prisoner to Rome. Her name still lives among the Arabs, who call the ruins 'the marble palace.' They consist of glittering laminated gypsum, and are in parts in such good preservation that one wonders how they came to be deserted centuries ago. The town is in the form of a triangle, the angles being marked by three hills, and in the middle is the Acropolis. The walls are flanked with towers, twelve on one side and eight on the other. Towards the river they are further apart than on the rest of the walls. Perhaps there was a high road through here from Palmyra to Assyria, for there are traces of a bridge on both sides of the river. Raumer, in his travels, says that the city was at that time completely in ruins.

May 16.—The third day's course, without any obstacle, brought us to-day to El-Deir. The sheikh sent one of his vassals to welcome the foreigners, and to ask their protection ; as this man was accustomed to conduct rafts of wood to El-Deir and Anah, he served as a pilot. Besides, thanks to Lieutenant Lynch's skill, we passed safely over the shallows, only six or seven feet deep, though we floated over a flooded cornfield.

The course of the river is very winding here, between cliffs of chalk and conglomerate. Not far from El-Deir we got into such a narrow side channel, that in making a turn we struck the shore. Fortunately it was only alluvial soil, so that no harm was done, except that a quantity of mud came in at the cabin windows. The city, if I may call it so, is built like an amphitheatre on a height, and looks pleasant. On approaching, our steamer hoisted the English and Turkish flags, and fired a salute.

We cast anchor on an island opposite the town, to avoid being exposed to the throngs of curious people. But it was of little use, for the river soon swarmed with them. Old and young came swimming on inflated skins, the strong ones bore the weak, the parents their children on their backs. They felt the steamer's sides, and they called out to one another: 'Iron, all iron!'

El Deir is 309 miles from Birejik, and is the first place with settled dwelling-houses. Up to this time we have seen nothing but tents and ruins.

May 17.—The steamers were hauled over to the other side of the river, as we had to take in wood and coal.

The interior of the town by no means accords with its outward aspect. The houses are more like mud hovels than human habitations, and so dirty and close that they must be unhealthy. The inhabitants, a dirty and beggarly set, very unlike the nomadic sons of the desert, combine the vices of savages with those of a town-bred proletariat, without the benefits of civilisation. I saw many countenances of a Jewish cast, with more brilliant colour than we have seen amongst the Arabs.

We had some trouble in ridding ourselves of their importunity. They had to be prevented from climbing up the vessel by pointing bayonets at them.

A few gardens, enclosed by mud walls, contained fig, pomegranate, and mulberry trees. Six forlorn looking date palms also, were enclosed by a hedge, probably the most northerly on the Euphrates. Melancholy as they looked, Pauline and I hailed them as precursors of the land of our desires. On low lying spots, liable to inundation, melons, maize, and cotton are planted, but not till June.

From an elevated spot, near El Deir, I took a view over the boundless, silent plain, and its monotonous vegetation.   A species of *Adonis* grows luxuriantly here and there, intermixed with other desert plants, *Gnaphalium*, *Artemisa*, and *Carlinea*.   I saw no sand, particularly no sand drift.   The soil consists of crumbled conglomerate and masses of loose stones, and it is this formation which occasions the desolation, for it greedily soaks up every drop of water, and the brooks and springs, from six to fifteen feet below, never come to the surface.

May 18.—El Deir was hailed by us as the beginning of settled habitations and cultivation, though of a very poor sort.

We left it to-day, and after surmounting some difficulties near a mill, got happily out of a side channel into the main stream.   The water is still rising, and in many places overflows both banks.   Little fields of corn, provided with rough means of irrigation, without which nothing can thrive here, and enclosures, in which the nomadic tribes take up their winter quarters, and guard their cattle from wild beasts, give the land a somewhat cultivated look.

After a course of two hours and a half we came to Karkin, the ancient Circesium, which seems to contain many ancient remains.   Near here is the mouth of the Khábúr, the ancient Araxes, an important river in the history of these lands, by which the Emperor Julian shipped his fleet into the Tigris.

In going up it our *Tigris* got into shallows, from which, however, she soon extricated herself.   But it was not thought advisable for our boat, which draws more water, to attempt it; so we cast anchor two miles lower down, on the Mesopotamian side, where we passed a dreadful evening and worse night. Scarcely had the sailors and I landed, they to make the anchor fast, and I to botanise, than we were enveloped in clouds of large mosquitos, and although we sprang on board again directly, our hands and faces were entirely covered by the blood-thirsty creatures, and we could hardly open our eyes. The plague spread to the steamer; all windows and doors were closed, but the vermin got through the smallest chink. Neither anointing ourselves with vinegar, oil, or even tar, which the sailors tried, was of any use; there was nothing to be done but to go to bed and get under the clothes, which made the heat intolerable.

Pauline made a number of bags out of my insect-net gauze, which, stretched on wire and put over the head, enabled us to go about and to see. Everyone thought himself fortunate who had one.

May 19.—Our station to-day was overgrown with tamarisks : a good place for collecting. But the mosquitos made it impossible to stay on shore.

The *Tigris*, which went ten miles up the Khábúr, and found the river deep, but narrow, came back about one o'clock; we went on together to Máden, the first Turkish town, where Ibrahim Pacha's rule is at an end. It appears that he has not thought it worth while to take possession of it; it could not have offered the least resistance.

The Colonel fired a salute of four guns here, to the terror of the inhabitants, who, although they live in perpetual feuds, had never heard the sound of cannon before.   Our wood was exhausted, and, as there were no trees, the people furnished us with fuel at the expense of their buildings.   They rapidly demolished stables and other structures, pulled the beams out of the rubbish, and sold them to us for yellow handkerchiefs.   On the whole they are obliging and civilised, if the word can be applied to Arabs at all.

Meanwhile we paid a visit to the ruins of Rahabeh, about five miles off, in a southerly direction.   The Colonel takes it for Rehoboth [1] of the Ammonites, in the times when the Israelites possessed the river from Racca to Anah.   The oldest structures, however, are of conglomerate, which easily crumbles away, and the more recent are of brick.   Completely in ruins it looks desolate enough.

There are said by the inhabitants to have been extensive vaults underground, which were still accessible a few years ago.   But we found the entrance quite closed up with rubbish.

The ruins stand upon an isolated hill, the advance post of a range, 150 feet high.   A boundless table land, called the Syrian desert, extends to the west.

From here all the way to the river there are remains of walls and brickwork, which have formed mounds in their decay, some of them grown over with corn, now just getting green.

Máden must once have been a considerable town between the river and the desert.

May 20.—To my great satisfaction, we go on to-day.   We are now rapidly approaching Baghdad, the

---

[1] Genesis xxxvi. 37.

object of my wishes just now, for there I shall hear from our friends, the Affghans. I hope to find letters from them, and to learn more particulars of our future plans of travel.

We went on at full speed, but did not make much progress in a straight line, as the river winds so much. The shores, monotonous as before; on the left a boundless flat, on the Syrian side a range of mountains, now some way off, now near the shore.

We wanted to get on as far as El Kaim, the place where the Colonel first navigated the Euphrates, but want of fuel obliged us to cast anchor at a place where there were tamarisks. While the crew were felling wood, we went, the indefatigable Colonel at our head, to see the ruins of a castle on the Syrian shore. We were not a little surprised to find, behind a castle of oblong form on a precipice, isolated by a ditch, the fortified walls of a large town, which, as well as a gate, are still standing; they are built of gypsum. The interior is a mass of brickbats and *débris*, except the foundations of a few large buildings.

It is difficult to say to what period this remarkable place belongs. The regular form of the defences, as well as the arches, the construction of which was not known till the Roman period, points to that time. But the entire destruction of the masonry inside indicates an earlier time. We find no mention of these ruins, and conclude that they have not been discovered by any explorers. The natives call them Salahyeh.

To-morrow we are to make 130 miles to Anah; the Colonel wants to make up for lost time.

May 21.—How vain are man's calculations! how useless to build on human power and wisdom in a contest with the elements! How powerless we are when opposed by those forces of nature, which we think to chain and bend to our will.   And how terrible to see valued friends perish before our eyes in the unequal contest.

I never thought it possible that I should have to record events like those of to-day. We seemed so fully justified in considering the favourable issue of the Expedition as secure. With two new, carefully constructed steamers, commanded by intelligent men, manned by skilful and willing crews, treated everywhere by the natives with respect, steaming on the peaceful river— who would not have looked forward with confidence to this first navigation of it?   And yet in the course of a few minutes we saw the *Tigris* go down hopelessly before our eyes, and only escaped a like fate ourselves by a happy accident.

We started in good time, and made a rapid course for four hours, when, our fuel being exhausted, at eleven o'clock, we lay to on the left shore, where a quantity of wood, which the Arabs readily sold, was taken in. During the interval I landed for entomological purposes. The sun was unusually clear, but the air very sultry, though the temperature was only 23° Reaumur (84° Fahrenheit).

At 1.20 all was ready, and both steamers went on. A few minutes afterwards we observed black clouds in the north-west, but nothing to alarm us, as it only betokened a heavy thunderstorm, such as, unlike this climate in general, often occurs about every other day at this season, ending in torrents of rain. It did not seem either as if the clouds were going in our direction. A light breeze arose, which caused us to take down the awning. Meanwhile the clouds increased every moment till the whole sky was darkened. We still hoped to outrun the storm; but the ominous clouds advanced with lightning speed, with a most portentous aspect. Out of the blue black background, little detached yellow clouds arose, changing their form every instant, and forming a semi-transparent vapour in the cloudless southern sky. The range of hills in that quarter, brightly illumined by the sun, made the darkness on the other side all the more conspicuous.

It was a strange and fearful sight, and we gazed at it with awe. But I had no idea that it was the simoom of the desert, which often buries whole caravans in sand, and that we were in danger of our lives. The mass came nearer every moment, and we could plainly see the yellow sand of the desert whirling in the air.

The steamers were steered towards shore, in order if possible, to cast anchor. But it was too late! The hurricane broke over our heads more quickly than the words can be spoken, and the clouds of sand wrapped us in total darkness. The engines were worked to their utmost power. But what is steam power against a hurricane? The *Tigris* was driven helplessly past us at lightning speed, while we were hurled with such force by a favouring gust on to the shore four feet high, that our timbers creaked and the light planks, intended for bulwarks, split like chips. We must have been lost if the brave officers and crew had not taken advantage of the moment, and with incredible exertions cast anchor, and secured the steamer in the bay.

I was standing on deck with my wife who, silent and motionless, held fast to the mast, when some one called out from below, 'Water in the stern cabin!'

I rushed down stairs, and saw the water streaming in at a window shutter, which had been driven in; I contrived to close it by leaning my back against it and putting my feet against the wall opposite, until a carpenter made it fast. All this occupied but a moment, and I hastened on deck again, where I found my wife in the same place.

The waves dashed over our heads and far in on shore. During a moment when the storm parted the clouds of sand, we saw the *Tigris*, scarcely ten minutes ahead, apparently standing still, but with her funnel bent on one side. Fresh torrents of rain, clouds, and mist hid her from us again directly, never to be seen more—she was engulfed in the furious waves, leaving not a trace behind! It was all the work of a very few minutes. The tornado subsided as quickly as it had come on, and bright sunshine lighted up the landscape which had just been wrapped in darkness. Our boat had shipped a foot of water, and the pumps were worked hard to get rid of it.

As soon as possible Mr. Charlewood, Mr. Ainsworth, and I jumped on shore; Pauline followed; who could stay behind when it was a question of saving life? We ran in the direction in which we had last seen the *Tigris*.

Some way off we saw the Colonel, who had that

day been on board the *Tigris*, with Lieutenant H. B. Lynch and Mr. Eden, coming towards us with tottering steps; we hastened to support our friends, who were dripping wet.

The sight of us induced a rapid change in the Colonel's countenance; he was dreadfully exhausted, and still more distressed in mind. He thought that the *Euphrates* and all on board were lost too, and as the sight of us assured him to the contrary, and he did not then know how many of his party had perished in the *Tigris*, he gave himself up to an ecstasy of joy, which, unfortunately, was of very short duration.

Mr. Ainsworth took charge of the exhausted men, while we hurried on to find the missing ones. On the way we met Mr. Staunton, hardly able to drag himself along with the help of some of the English sailors. Near the fatal spot we found Dr. Staunton, lying in a field of corn, whither he had been hurled by wind and waves; he was still unconscious, and did not know what had happened to him.

In vain we sought for Lieutenants Cockburn and R. B. Lynch; these two, the interpreter, Yussuf Sader, fifteen English sailors, and four natives had found a watery grave!

, The hurricane had struck the *Tigris* on her broadside, and disabled her machinery; waves, four or five feet high, came through the windows into the cabins, and no efforts could keep the water out. When the fore part of the deck was under water, and they were only eight yards from shore, Lieutenant Lynch declared that the vessel was sinking, and gave the word for the crew to save themselves by swimming. The nearness to the shore may have given rise to the hope that they might get still nearer, and have caused delay. But, meanwhile, the boat went down. A minute before the shore could be seen, but now there was total darkness, so that they could not see which direction to take. Only the Colonel, Lieutenant Lynch, and those before mentioned were so happy as to reach land.

Scarcely eight minutes elapsed between the time when the *Tigris* neared the shore till she began to sink, and in less than three minutes more she entirely disappeared.

In the hope that some of the missing might still be alive and struggling with the waves, boats were sent out in all directions, and far along the shore; they returned without success. Even the exact spot where the *Tigris* went down could not be discovered; not a vestige of her was to be seen.

How shall I describe the feelings of the company assembled on the evening of that dreadful day in the saloon of the *Euphrates*. I am not ashamed of the tears which I and all the rest shed over our lost friends. The sudden and violent death of so many who had become endeared to us, whom we had seen just before in the prime of life and strength, brought forcibly before our minds our own powerlessness in conflict with the decrees of fate. I had special reason for reverent thankfulness to Providence for so manifestly protecting me and my wife. For on this day we were to have lunched on board the *Tigris*, and to have gone on with her; we frequently did so, and it was a change as agreeable to us as to the officers of the *Tigris*. But, owing to the hurry in taking in wood, the men had not found time to bring the boat for us, and, for the same reason, Lieutenant Cockburn had missed the opportunity of asking leave to make the voyage to-day on board the *Euphrates*. This insignificant circumstance saved our lives, but cost him his. He was the only one of the officers who could not swim, and he had, in consequence, a great aversion to the water. A little while before, in a moment of ill-humour, he resolved to leave the Expedition. Pauline, to whom he mentioned his intention, represented to him that it would be very inopportune, and persuaded him to remain; she was therefore all the more grieved at his death.

May 22.—The grief that had no words yesterday, found some expression to-day. Staunton said in a scarcely audible voice: 'My poor Cockburn.' Lieutenant Lynch was heard saying to himself: 'How was it possible that my brother, who was such a good swimmer, could be drowned?' Mr. Eden muttered: 'Poor *Tigris*! so that was to be her fate.' And the Colonel said, with a forced smile: 'Wasn't she a pretty boat? But not even a frigate could have stood against a storm like that.'

Besides the loss of life, we all suffer more or less from the wreck of the *Tigris*. Everything not in immediate use, and all the stores were on board her. Many have lost all their luggage and money, and we have but little left but what we had on.

Lieutenant Lynch is the greatest sufferer. His position as commander of the steamer, for the loss of which he is responsible, is very painful; his pride is deeply wounded, his heart is smarting for the loss of his brother, and he loses, besides, a considerable sum from his private fortune.

The river and shore have again been searched, without finding any trace of the missing men ; there is scarcely a bit of floating wood to mark the scene of the disaster. At a depth of from three to five fathoms, we have not once touched the hull of the steamer with the lead.

To-day there was a funeral service for the lost, and thanksgiving for the saved, at which no one was unmoved.

May 23.—The Arabs behave very well; if they had any hostile intentions the last day or two would have given them a good opportunity of showing them, and even of taking possession of the steamer with all its treasures, for several of our crew are away, and the rest would not be a match for them. But they not only show no hostility, but behave better than Europeans on our coasts, who take advantage of the customary wreck laws. They bring spars, planks, casks, empty boxes, books, and many other things they have found, and only ask a backsheesh, which they take in the shape of yellow handkerchiefs. One of them told us there was a cask he could not lift. The crew hoped that it contained rum, but it turned out to be only vinegar. Poor fellows, they have now to dispense with this luxury.

May 24.—The hurricane which raged here, only extended to a comparatively short distance. Mr.

Hector, who was taking soundings ten miles lower down, saw nothing of it. The Arabs tell us that such storms occur but seldom. But we have had thunder and hail storms to-day, when there were hailstones on deck an inch and a half in diameter. All natural phenomena here seem to assume a violent aspect. We were painfully reminded of the hurricane to-day, when two corpses floated down the stream ; they were brought to land and buried with military honours. Now that all hope is over of finding anyone alive, we search for the dead, in order to pay them the last tribute of respect.

The proverb that ' misfortunes never come single,' unfortunately holds good in our case. The Colonel assembled all the officers to-day, and informed them that, when at El Deir, he had received orders from Government to close the Expedition on July 31. (Motives of economy were assigned for it; but probably some change had taken place in the political constellations of Europe, so that the connection with India by means of the Euphrates no longer appeared necessary to the Government, otherwise an expenditure of 20,000*l.* would scarcely have been thought so much of.) He had not thought it advisable to communicate this depressing order to his comrades, and to damp their ardour, just as they were making successful progress, and had therefore kept it to himself. (How heavily this secret must have weighed upon his mind.)

But now, the Colonel continued, after the loss of the *Tigris*, a great part of her crew, and the money on board her, he felt bound to inform them of it, and to take the opinion of the officers as to whether they should continue the voyage or turn back at once.

As was to be expected from these energetic men, actuated by patriotic ambition, they were all for going on, and even renounced their pay to lessen the expenses of the Expedition! On the other hand it was determined that the remnant of the crew of the 'Tigris' should at once return to England, to satisfy the economical intentions of the Government.

This incensed me, though it was certainly in accordance with the instructions received. These poor men, after patiently enduring hard work, privation, and sickness, having lost everything and gained nothing, and barely escaped with their lives, are to undertake an arduous journey through the desert, exposed to all sorts of hardships, at this hot season of the year, before the end is attained!

The rest of the day was occupied in writing reports of what has happened. I also wrote mine.

*   *   *   *   *

Here ends Helfer's journal of the voyage, so far as it escaped destruction; it falls to my share to add the rest.

Through Baghdad and Babylon to Basrah.

We reached Anah without any further disaster. The town, once strongly fortified, but now quite open, extends for about four miles along the river, and is surrounded by gardens, in which figs, apricots, pomegranates, and plums flourish luxuriantly, and even the date palm reaches a considerable height.

Three or four hundred paces from the town the cultivated ground ceases, and a range of chalk hills begins, which forms the boundary of the desert.   In the middle of the river, on a fertile island, there are the ruins of a fortress, destroyed by Julian, and rebuilt by the Arabs.   After the barrenness along the upper part of the course of the river, the trees and beginning of regular cultivation were a welcome sight.

After the *Euphrates*, which had sustained great injuries, had been repaired, on the 31st of May we continued our voyage to Hadisa and Jibba.   On both sides the banks are well wooded and the land carefully irrigated.   There is a good depth of water.

Near Hit we visited the celebrated bitumen springs, which are thrown up with extraordinary force, and seem to be inexhaustible, as they have been known and used from the earliest times.   By the Colonel's orders the bitumen was used as fuel for our engine, as with a mixture of earth it forms a solid mass.

Under other circumstances, the sulphur mines and warm mineral springs might be very profitable to the natives.   They now make a living chiefly by building boats, in which they have attained great celebrity.

We reached Felujah without obstacle.   The heat here began to be intolerable. Neither a double awning, nor any precautions, sufficed to protect us from it on deck, and below, the confined air was so heated that sleep was impossible.

The opportunity, therefore, of leaving the steamer for a few days was all the more welcome.   Major Estcourt was to go to Baghdad to receive money from the English resident there, and asked us to accompany him. The journey was represented to me as very arduous, but it was by no means refreshing on board, and my curiosity to see Baghdad, the city of so many wondrous tales, overcame all hesitation.

The party consisted of Major Estcourt, Lieutenant Murphy, Messrs. Charlewood and Fitzjames, Helfer, and myself, with servants and an Arab escort. We set out at sunset, badly mounted, for the saddles had no stirrups, in order to avail ourselves of the cool of the night, hoping to reach Baghdad at daybreak.

After spending over seven weeks on board ship the ride in the moonlight night, with so interesting an end in view, seemed like a party of pleasure. Childish reminiscences of the fairy tales concerning the city of the Khaliphs, about ministering spirits, dwarfs, and enchanted princesses, afforded subject of conversation till far into the night. Each looked forward to investigating the points which interested him most, and to comparing reality with fantastic fables.

But fatigue gradually stole over us, and we went on our way in silence, till we were revived by the dawning light. The hope of catching sight of the golden cupolas of the great mosque made us increase our speed. But when the sun at length lighted up the landscape there were no golden cupolas nor slender minarets in sight, but an immense marsh lay before us as far as the eye could reach. The Tigris had overflowed its banks and flooded the country for miles, and when it subsided it left it a swamp, out of which there was but a narrow line of little hillocks distinguishable above the rest.

Our anticipations were not a little damped by this prospect; and as, after the long ride, the stomach began imperiously to assert its claims, and there was no prospect of breakfast, even English stoicism gave way. I had taken care of Helfer and myself by taking provisions with me; taught by experience I never went an excursion without, in spite of the comments of the English gentlemen, who, however, after a scanty meal at table, had often thoroughly relished an Austrian 'Jausen'[1] in my cabin.

The English are so accustomed to their regular meals that they think it unseemly to take a bit of anything between. Now, however, to my great satisfaction, one after another of the gentlemen came up to me with, 'Mrs. Helfer, havn't you an egg left?' And before long the demands made upon my saddle-bag, the dimensions of which might have made Sancho Panza laugh, had completely emptied it.

It was soon evident that our exhausted steeds could not carry us through the bog; we had to dismount and proceed on foot, jumping, rather than walking, from hillock to hillock, and not seldom over the ankles in mud. We did not catch sight of Baghdad, on the other side of the Tigris, till noon.

From a little elevation we could see the river, and perceived that the ferry-boat, which connects the right bank with the city, was just pushing off. In vain we made signs that we wanted to cross; the more our Arabs called out to the ferry-men, the more haste they

---

[1] The term used in Austria for afternoon coffee; Vesperbrod, in North Germany, a slight meal, equivalent to 5 o'clock tea.—TR.

made to get away, and did not moderate their pace till they were in the middle of the river. As this was the last ferry for the day, there was nothing for it but to seek out the driest spot in the soaked ground for the night, and do the best we could. So we had to spend the night, sleepless and famished, in sight of the wondrous city.

Early next morning an angel of deliverance appeared. Colonel Taylor, the English Resident at Baghdad, had been told by one of the ferry-men that they had seen Europeans in the troop on the other side of the river, though we were all in mamaluke costume; and he at once conjectured that they must be members of the Expedition who intended visiting Baghdad, for he was aware of the approach of the *Euphrates.* But it was already evening; the gates are not opened after sunset; besides, the ceremonial customs to which the English are obliged, for the honour of their country, to conform, would not have permitted us to enter Baghdad on foot and at night. This was why we were not fetched till morning. At the gates we mounted splendid horses, ready saddled from the consular stables, and with a numerous escort, headed by a kawass with the silver staff, we made our solemn entry into the palace.

It was certainly calculated to give us a foretaste of the glories of the city of the Khaliphs.

We were most kindly received by Colonel and Mrs. Taylor in their palace. In accordance with Eastern custom, a bath was immediately prepared for everyone, for thus to refresh the weary traveller, after the dust and heat of the desert, is considered the first duty of hospitality, a virtue of which Homer sounds the praises. Thus revived, we were conducted to the breakfast table, spread with delicacies that we had not tasted for a long time. But, after two sleepless nights and a sixteen hours' ride, I could not keep my eyes open even while I was eating, and I found it difficult to adjust the rival claims of hunger and fatigue until our amiable hostess kindly took charge of me, and gave me a cool and quiet chamber where I could rest.

My slumbers must have been long and deep, for when Helfer awoke me the sun had long passed the meridian.

He, on the contrary, seemed scarcely to have rested at all. His eyes were fixed upon me with an expression of distress. I exclaimed in alarm, ' What *is* the matter? Whatever has troubled you so?' He turned away, and answered with faltering voice, ' I can't conceal it from you—I have to tell you that our friends, the Affghans, are ——— rogues!'

I started up as if stung by an adder. ' For God's sake don't say so! What has happened?' ' You shall hear,' he said, ' and then judge for yourself. This is what I have just learnt from Colonel Taylor. On their way to Basrah they passed through Baghdad; they applied to him for money, and in an unseemly way for princes of Lahore; but although he did not feel much confidence in them he complied with their request. A few days ago a banker at Mosul informed him that he had advanced a sum of money to the Affghan princes, travelling incognito, on the Resident's credit, and requested payment. Even this,' continued Helfer, 'did not shake my faith in our friends, for their funds might have been exhausted. I then thought of the jewels, which they left us in pledge for our money ' (and of which we had brought a few stones with us for the purchase of clothing). 'I quickly fetched them, and Colonel Taylor, doubting their genuineness, sent for a trustworthy jeweller, who, after careful examination, pronounced them a clever imitation, by which even connoisseurs might have been deceived ! '

The pledging of these jewels was then a preconceived device of these impostors to get possession of our money; it was impossible to doubt any longer.

Here we were then in remote Baghdad, deprived of all our means by the loss of the *Tigris*, and but scantily provided with clothing.

I did not venture to try to divine from Helfer's face what was passing in his mind. I knew how sincerely he liked both these men, and how he had built his hopes on them, and we bore the painful disappointment together in silence. But it was not a time for indolently giving way to our feelings. Our situation made it necessary that we should come to some decision at once, and act upon it.

Once more, here was a momentous crisis. Betrayed and left in the lurch by those in reliance on whom we had undertaken this long journey, should we proceed farther eastward, trusting in ourselves alone, or should we turn back half-way, a course alike repugnant to our characters and inclinations? We were both so averse to this, our courage and confidence had been so much

strengthened by the good and evil fortune that had befallen us, that we resolved to go on. Helfer thought it
would be best to go first to Persia; thence, he thought,
we should find some means of getting on to the lofty
mountain regions of Asia.

We wished also to take the advice of our experienced
friends, and joined the company in Mrs. Taylor's drawing room. Colonel Taylor listened to Helfer's new
plans, and then said that Persia might serve as a temporary station, but would never do as a residence for a
European doctor, as, though the Persians were ready
enough to avail themselves of his advice, they were not
in the habit of paying for it. 'First of all, however,'
he said, 'you want money. If £100 would be sufficient,
I shall be happy to place it at your disposal.' Helfer
was extremely surprised, and accepted this unlooked
for and generous offer with warm thanks. On the sum
being handed to him he was about to give a promissory
note. Colonel Taylor, however, said that he did not
wish any written acknowledgment. 'If you are a man
of honour,' he added, 'I do not want your note; if you
are not, it will be of no use. I will also give you a
letter of introduction to Captain Hennell, our Resident
at Bushire; you can talk over your residence in Persia
with him.'

So the die was cast once more, and we resolved to
go on by the *Euphrates* to Basrah, and thence to
Bushire, in Persia.

The evening having been pleasantly spent in relating our various adventures, to which each one contributed his share, we were conducted to rest, not in confined bedrooms, but on the flat roof of the house, where there were open sleeping apartments divided by partitions. Up there, in sight of the stars, in the cool night air after the heat of the day, (30° Reaumur, 99° Fahrenheit), and its many excitements, we slept deliciously. Consoled as to the future, we yielded ourselves to repose.

Of the city as it was in the time of the Khaliphates, with its splendid edifices, its palaces, mosques, minarets, schools, convents, immense wealth, its extensive khans, the famous observatory, the monuments of the saints, when learning and chivalry flourished, but little has come down to our days.

Since the dominion of the Khaliphs was overturned by Halagu Khan in 1258, the population of Baghdad, then estimated at 1,000,000, has sunk to 100,000. And this devastation and depopulation has been brought about, not only by the horrible butchery of the various conquerors, that of Timur, for example, in 1401, who burnt down the city, and ordered each of his 90,000 soldiers to bring him the head of an inhabitant of Baghdad, on pain of losing his own, but by pestilence and famine, as well as inundations, occasioned by neglect of the canals. In 1773, a very large number died of the plague. In the absence of registers the number could only be estimated by the quantity of linen used for winding-sheets. One merchant alone is said to have sold 20,000 piastres' worth.

Its advantageous situation between east and west, its numerous products, and flourishing trade, have always given the city of the Khaliphs, great political as well as mercantile importance, and have made it a coveted prize to every Asiatic conqueror; and for the same reasons it has raised its head again after every disaster.

Baghdad fell by turns into the hands of the Persians and the Osmans, until in 1638, under Sultan Murad IV. the Turks gained permanent possession of it, and it fell under the despotic rule of a pacha. The fate of the city and surrounding territory now depended on the good or bad qualities of these satraps. The necessity of defending themselves against attacks from Persia, and internal rebellion, compelled the pachas to maintain a large military force, while the great distance from Constantinople made them almost independent of the Sublime Porte.

The legitimate revenues of the wealthy pachalic are very considerable, but have been greatly increased by arbitrary exactions; yet they have often not sufficed for war expenses, and the luxurious extravagance of the rulers; and when some of the neighbouring Arab tribes have refused to pay tribute, and have had to be compelled to obedience, the governors have often been obliged to borrow money of the wealthy merchants.

But, in spite of injustice and extortions, the trade of Baghdad has greatly increased during the last few years; after the East India Company established a consulate there, the exports by way of Basrah to India became very considerable. The English consuls took the rank of Asiatic princes, and soon gained an influence equal to that of the reigning pacha, and their opinion was so much valued on all matters of importance, that the Turkish officials did not deem it advisable to undertake anything without a previous understanding with them. To maintain this influence and the dignity of the British nation the East India Company expended large sums.

The consul's residence is on the most magnificent scale. It comprises two courts, a large number of splendid apartments, massively built terraces for sleeping in the open air serdaps (vaulted chambers half below and half above ground, with galleries on the river side, used in the hot season), government offices, stables, and domestic offices. It houses a numerous retinue of servants, each one, after Indian fashion, having one special duty to perform, and presenting a curious medley of nations and languages—secretaries, interpreters, medical men, janissaries, and a company of sepoys, as a body-guard, who go on duty with military music and honours, and accompany the Resident on all ceremonial occasions. An elegant yacht, manned by Indian sailors, lies always in readiness at the palace quay, and the stables contain splendid horses. All this splendour, however, though at first it dazzles the eye and pleases the fancy, is rather oppressive to the stranger; the palace, with all its luxury, seems to him like a prison, from which the sooner he can make his escape the better.

The dignity of the British nation does not permit her sons to soil their feet with the dust of Baghdad, nor to show themselves in public without appropriate state. This precluded our perambulating the city and seeing its sights in tourist fashion.

It was only from the highest pinnacle of the house that there was a view over the city and its suburbs. The extent of the walls still standing, and the number of fine buildings in ruins, gave us an idea of its former greatness and grandeur.

Nothing now remains of the luxuriant gardens on the shores of the Tigris, with their palm-groves, pomegranate, apricot, peach, mulberry, and lemon trees, and handsome flowering shrubs, nor of the fields of wheat, rice, and maize, which once made Baghdad one of the most favoured spots on earth. All this is replaced by a swampy waste. The interior of the city has nothing to show but dirty, narrow, winding streets, with high, gloomy, windowless houses.

The ladies of Baghdad pay frequent visits to the baths, mounted on proud white palfreys, or modest asses, according to their rank and wealth. The baths are the sole places of amusement for Asiatic women, and there the richest attire is displayed and the gossip of the city discussed. They parade the streets with a stately retinue, muffled up in thick white shawls, which only permit their dark eyes and yellow slippers to be seen; or they pay visits on the roofs of the houses, which are reached by little staircases permitting free communication, and it is said that they are also used by the male inhabitants for secret assignations.

Mrs. Taylor offered to take me to the Pacha's seraglio, and to introduce me to his two lawful wives.

Equipped with the customary state, we reached the palace, and were received with all the ceremonial due to the consul's wife. We were conducted through a suite of large rooms, all richly adorned with gilding and carpets, but anything but clean, to a smaller apartment more in European style. A lady, about forty years of age, whose face still bore traces of former beauty, was lying on a sofa with side rests. Her eyebrows, lashes, and lids were blackened, her finger nails dyed red ; neck and bosom were enveloped in a costly shawl, and she was adorned with gold chains, rings, and bracelets. I should not have thought it possible that anyone would adopt the position she assumed while receiving a call, if I had not seen it with my own eyes. As she lay upon the couch her legs from the knees dangled over the side. Whether it was the correct mode of receiving company, or was done for exercise, I could not discover. Mrs. Taylor seemed to be used to it, and took no notice of it ; it was maintained while, with friendly nods, she gave this lady her hand, and while, with all due form, I was introduced. The princess was prepared for our call and for my disguise, only vouchsafed me a scrutinising glance, and then entered into lively discourse with Mrs. Taylor about the events of the day and the mysteries of the seraglio, which unfortunately was all unintelligible to me. Having assumed, according to our notions, a more decent attitude, and coffee having, as usual, been handed, she asked us to go and see her beautiful daughter. We went at once, and a charming creature she was, a rosebud in the first blush of beauty; she had a delicate complexion, timid blue eyes, light brown hair, and a sweet simple expression of countenance, quite a contrast to the Armenian beauties with their set and regular features. She reminded me more of a pretty European girl than any other Asiatic I had seen.

She advanced pleasantly to meet us; but on seeing me, she blushed deeply and cast her eyes on the ground. Mrs. Taylor hastened to explain; she then cast timid glances at me, and it was only by degrees that she took courage to look at me openly, to give me her hand and lead me to the soft cushions of the divan.

The princess was surrounded by ten companions, mostly Circassians, all more or less beautiful. The black hair of some of them was dyed red, which is considered very handsome here, and there is certainly something piquant in the gold shimmer on the dark ground. There was also a blonde beauty among them, with an almost German physiognomy, who seemed to be a general favourite.

While the princess sat on the divan, her youthful companions danced before us, in picturesque figures, to the music of a tambourine, and displayed much grace and agility; it was rather a variety of pantomimic attitudes than a dance. Before long, one of them, apparently tired, sat down at her mistress's feet, a second followed, and laid her head on the other's lap, who took down her long thick hair and arranged it anew; then both sprang up and rejoined the rest, giving a new turn to the game.

This, I was told, is about the only occupation, daily repeated, of young girls, until they are given to husbands unknown and unloved.

We could not linger long over this pretty sight, as

Mrs. Taylor wished also to call on the Pacha's younger
wife. She was quite young, a brunette, neither beautiful nor ugly, with rather strongly marked features,
much *embonpoint*, and a determined expression. She
was energetically rocking a covered cradle when we
entered. She seemed much honoured by Mrs. Taylor's
visit, and out of respect for my companion paid more
attention to me. In the course of conversation, Mrs.
Taylor mentioned that we had just seen the princess,
and that I thought her very beautiful. She hastily
withdrew the cover of the cradle, and exhibiting her
baby of a few months old, exclaimed eagerly: 'Say if
this one will not be much more beautiful!' Of course
we pacified her by solemn assurances of her daughter's
future incomparable beauty: another instance of the
predominance of maternal love over every other feeling
among Asiatic women.

We all assembled for the social tea hour in the
cool and spacious serdap of the consular palace. Each
one narrated some interesting episode from his life. Our
hospitable host and hostess gave us an account of what
they had gone through a few years before, during the
prevalence of the plague, drought, and famine, in
1830–31. The plague broke out, in the autumn of
1830, in the villages round, and, like a destroying angel,
drew nearer and nearer to the city, striking down
everyone by the way. The Mollahs set themselves
against all measures to arrest it, as being opposed to
the Koran. Colonel Taylor used all his influence with
the fatalistic Daoud Pacha to induce him to establish
quarantine, but in vain. He received the true Turkish

answer : 'He who is to die will die, and he who is to live will live.' The daily deaths were soon reckoned, not by units, but by hundreds and thousands. The consulate did not escape, though strictly isolated, for if infection was not brought by human beings, domestic animals, especially cats, carried it from house to house.

At the same time the Tigris overflowed its banks, broke all the dams, flooded the lowlands, destroyed several thousand houses, and all prospects of a good harvest, so that a fearful famine ensued.

By the spring of 1831 the number of deaths was estimated at from fifty to sixty thousand. Children who had lost or were forsaken by their parents lay about the streets in a state of starvation ; all family ties were loosened, all who could do so fled, without thought of those whom they left to perish.

To crown all these troubles wild hordes of Arabs took advantage of the defenceless state of the city to plunder it. The scenes of horror that ensued are best left untold. Let us rather linger over a ray of light in the darkness. This is afforded by the Christian heroism and self-sacrifice of Mr. Groves, the superintendent of the English mission, who, actuated by motives of duty and philanthropy, devoted himself to nursing the sick and comforting the neglected and perishing.

Colonel Taylor for a long time courageously braved the danger ; but when his palace was flooded he resolved to leave Baghdad and to go down the river in his yacht to his country house at Basrah. In vain he tried to persuade Mr. Groves and his family to accompany him. He would not neglect his Christian mission for a moment, and, besides his wife and children, several teachers, and Christian servants, remained in the sorely tried city, intent on feeding the hungry and caring for orphan children, as far as was in their power. He succeeded in rescuing many of the most destitute, many others were at least helped and consoled. He hoped that his family might be spared to him, as the pestilence was abating ; but at last it entered his house and snatched away his wife and children and faithful assistants. When Colonel Taylor returned to the city, after health was restored to it, he found Mr. Groves, who was left alone of all his family, mourning over their graves.

Priestly fanaticism, and the avarice, ignorance, and indolence of the people, had all combined to produce this state of things.

Helfer was very glad that the departure of a Tatar in the evening for Constantinople enabled him to commission his lawyer in Prague to repay Colonel Taylor's loan through a London banker ; for we had to leave the hospitable palace very early next morning on our return.

Fine horses from the palace stables were placed at our disposal : a splendid white creature, with flowing mane and tail, was brought out for me, and he pawed the ground impatiently till we should start. I feared that I should not be able to manage so spirited an animal, and asked for another. But Colonel Taylor himself encouraged me to mount, and said that then it would be all right ; and I was scarcely in the saddle when he became as gentle as a lamb, and obeyed the least movement of the bridle, so that the long ride was a real pleasure. This is the peculiarity of Arab horses, from growing up with human beings as playmates.

Owing to Colonel Chesney's haste to reach Basrah, the end of the voyage, we were unable to visit the ruins of Tak-i-Kesra and the ancient Seleucia, about eleven miles below Baghdad, on the Tigris. From their extent and magnificence they were taken by earlier travellers for the ruins of Babylon. The castle of Tak-i-Kesra, as the Arabs call it, is said to be equal to any of the Oriental edifices in size and splendour. Its façade, 360 feet in length, and its splendid portico, is said to exceed even the famous gate of the palace at Delhi, and Ali Kaper at Ispahan.

When Abu-Giafar-al-Mansor, the second of the Khaliphs, in 775, wanted to build a palace in the centre of his empire, he chose the province of Chaldea, and the spot on the Tigris, on which the descendants of Nimrod and Nushirwan, the wife of Kosroes, had built a sanctuary, called the heart of the earth, the key of the East, and the path of light. He used the edifices of Seleucia as materials for building his capital, Baghdad. Fortunately for the preservation of these ancient monuments, it proved that the expense of demolishing them and removing the materials would exceed their value, and so they were suffered to stand.

We had to take the shortest way to the ruins of Babylon, as Colonel Chesney, with the steamer, was to await us there.

When the extensive gardens and plantations of date palms on the west side of Baghdad are left behind, an uncultivated plain opens before you, generally affording firm footing, but now wet and marshy in places A road leads across it, chiefly frequented by the Shiites on their pilgrimages to the grave of Imam Hussein. The pilgrims not only perform their devotions at the shrine of their saint, but bury their dead, who are special objects of affection, in the consecrated ground there, for which they pay a high price. On this road, therefore, large caravans of wealthy Persians are often met with, accompanied by their closely veiled women, and a numerous retinue of their dead, enclosed in coffins, and borne on mules to the place of holy sepulture. Although the bodies are embalmed, they emit odours in the glowing heat as disgusting as they are injurious. But the hope of securing everlasting happiness for their beloved departed friends, by laying their bones in the consecrated ground of the followers of Ali, encourages the pilgrims to brave every difficulty and danger.

Along the whole route there are scattered remains of ruined brick buildings, melancholy evidence that at one time, between Baghdad and ' Babylon, the glory of kingdoms, the beauty of the Chaldees' excellency,' as it is called by Isaiah,[1] there was an unbroken line of habitations, villages, and palaces. Now there is nothing to be seen but a few wells and isolated khans. The latter have been mostly built by wealthy Persian families for the benefit of pilgrims, some of them like castles, as if for defence ; they afford the traveller comfortable shelter, and a good meal of fowls, eggs, dates, bread, and sweet lemons.

Late in the evening of the first day we reached the Iskenderiyah Khan, and, after another long day's ride,

---

[1] Isaiah xiii. 19.

the Mahawit Khan, where we took up our night quarters, in order to reach the ruins of Babylon early on the third day, which we were to be allowed a day to visit.

The nearer we approached to the Euphrates the more luxuriant grew the grass, so that it was often up to the horses' knees. Horses, herds of sheep and oxen were grazing on the plain, and the black tents of the Arabs were seen in all directions. A line of waving date palms in the distance marked the winding course of the river. The loneliness we had felt in passing through this desolate region now gave way to the consciousness that we were nearing the habitations of men.

Near the former boundaries of mighty Babylon we had to cross several of the ancient canals which intersected the country, and served both to irrigate the fields, which they rendered very fruitful, and as part of the system of fortification of the city : they were for the most part navigable. Their beds are now mostly dry, while the river has made the land a marsh far and wide. There was, however, so much water in two of them that the horses had to swim over with us, which gave me fresh occasion to admire my steed.

We were now at the foot of the Mujellebeh, the ancient impregnable citadel of Babylon, now an extensive bare hill 150 feet high. It forms the beginning of a scene of desolation, extending further than the eye can reach.

We went round the Mujellebeh in order to ascend the Kasr in the centre, the royal palace, with the hanging gardens of Semiramis. From the summit you can see the whole extent of the city, built in the form of a square, the four sides together forming an extent of thirty-four miles, and enclosing a space of seventy-two square miles.

Towards the south lies the hill called Amran, the lowest but most extensive of all, bounded on the south by the date gardens of Hillah; towards the north-east is the conical shaped mound of ruins called Tabaia, about seven miles from Hillah; towards the east the lofty and apparently isolated Al Huisrer.

The traveller's admiration is not called forth here by magnificent ruins of splendid edifices, such as Palmyra and Nineveh can show. It is the immensity of the destruction which fills the mind with awe.

What colossal structures must have stood here, if their fall could produce such masses of ruins. For all these hills, from top to bottom, consist of nothing but bricks, many of which, after the lapse of 4,000 years, retain a blue glaze and inscriptions or imprints of flowers.

Far to the south-west, almost on the edge of the desert, nine miles from the river, is Birs Nimrod, the most ancient and venerable ruin in the world; seen from the King's hill, it rises like a needle's point out of the ruins around.

In the midst of all this weird desolation the broad river pursues its course unchanged. A few stunted willows, descendants of those beneath whose shade the children of Israel sang their laments, stand mourning by the shore.

Overpowered by the spectacle and the recollections

of past ages, we lingered long on the spot where Semiramis wandered in her palace gardens forming fresh schemes for the aggrandisement of her empire, and the defence of the proud city; where Judah languished in captivity, and bewailed his hard fate; where Alexander, after conquering the world, and intoxicated with victory, defied the gods by beginning to rebuild the tower of Belus, which had been destroyed by fire from heaven, and where, not long after, he was overtaken by sickness, and succumbed to the lot of mortals in the midst of his bold projects.

This spot is said to be condemned by a wrathful God to eternal desolation and sterility. But not so; the Lord does not thus curse the ground and keep his anger for ever. Nothing has happened here but one of those vicissitudes to which all earthly things are subject. Nations, having reached the degree of civilisation of which they were capable, have perished; the measure of it to which they had attained was transferred to other nations, who brought it to greater perfection, and again transmitted it to others.

The ground is not condemned to sterility; luxuriant grass springs up, having been manured with refuse, and affords pasture for numerous flocks. The works of man have indeed been the victims of man's passions; but what man has destroyed man can rebuild, better and more in accord with the spirit of the age. And here, on the shores of the fructifying Euphrates, civilisation will flourish anew; no second Babylon will be built, but perhaps a seat of culture, peaceful intercourse and prosperity may be. This rich country is too near over-peopled Europe, the desire among the followers of Mahomet themselves to revise their political and social life is too strong for it long to remain closed against European civilisation.

Were we not justified in entertaining these hopes, when we behold the British flag, which has conferred the blessings of civilisation on so many nations, floating over the river? How could we fail to see the dawn of a day of promise in this first attempt to navigate the Euphrates by steam power? Could we fail to hope that the memory of the men whose lives were sacrificed in it will one day be blessed by nations whom it has delivered from the cruel bondage of ignorance?

We descended in silence from the King's hill, each of us given up to his own reflections. It is easy to philosophise over the instability of all earthly things when surrounded by fresh and blooming life ; but it is otherwise when there is nought but death and destruction before your eyes. You are struck dumb, and cast your eyes upon the ground with a profound feeling of your own insignificance. All your hopes and fears, your toil and endeavour, your loves and hatreds, your pride and ambition, dwindle into nothingness in view of such awful destruction.

The shades of evening were closing round us when we went on board the steamer and received a joyous welcome from our fellow voyagers. Though our absence had been but short, and our excursion not a perilous one, under the circumstances, our safe return was hailed with joy. Our adventures were listened to with eager interest and sympathy, especially the painful disappointment which Helfer and I had experienced at Baghdad, and all were glad that we were not too much disheartened by it to continue our journey.

Early next morning we reached Hillah, a flourishing mercantile town at the southern extremity of the district of Babylon. We cast anchor on the right shore, from which Birs Nimrod is seen towering up majestically in the distance. Unfortunately, I was unable to join the party who made an excursion to it, the exertions of the previous few days having enjoined rest. I could only form an idea of it from the reports of our party and the descriptions of former travellers.

The extensive mound of ruins, having a circumference of 762 yards, which forms a pedestal for the square pyramid of Belus, as it is called by Strabo, is three or four miles from Hillah. The eastern side of the mound rises in two platforms, 450 feet broad. Towards the west it rises, in the form of a dome, to a height of 200 feet; on the summit is a single pillar of excellent construction, still standing erect, but rent from top to bottom, the only remaining monument of ancient ornamental architecture in this region.

The tower of Belus of the Chaldeans is built with eight large platforms, reached by outside flights of steps, on which were resting places and seats. In the top was the throne, with the golden table and pedestals, long ago robbed of their statues. This was the great sanctuary of Bel, probably built before the time of Nebuchadnezzar, and at the same time the observatory of the astrologers of Chaldea.

This colossal structure has bidden defiance to time,

and although the upper half, with the statues of deities, was in ruins in the time of Cyrus and Xerxes, Alexander the Great, according to Arrian, was so struck with its imposing grandeur and the wisdom of the Chaldean astrologers, that, after his victorious return from India, he resolved to restore it in all its magnificence. But the 10,000 labourers employed could not, during two months. remove the rubbish accumulated by the destruction caused by Xerxes, nor bring the original foundations to light. Meanwhile the conqueror was smitten by death, and its restoration has never since been attempted.

At some distance from this edifice, there is a group of mounds of ruins, not so high as the pedestal of the tower, but much broader, being 414 feet in diameter. Here, according to Herodotus, stood the great altar of Belus, belonging to the tower, on which the animals were sacrificed, and on which, at great festivals, incense was burnt to the value of 1,000 talents.

As before stated, all these mounds are composed of ruins of masonry built of bricks, on which inscriptions are often found. On the top there are gigantic masses, which must have fallen from great heights, and have gradually crumbled away; some of them still exhibit bright dark-blue colours, or are veined with yellow, the colour having been preserved by their having been melted or glazed. Both ancient and modern explorers ascribe this to the destruction by fire from heaven, in accordance with the ancient legend.

There are various legends about this destruction, but all concur in considering it a divine punishment for man's audacity. Niebuhr's Arab guide told him, when he visited the ruins, that a king of the name of Nimrod built the palace; during a thunder storm, intending to wage war with God, he shot an arrow into the air, and, exhibiting a bloody arrow, boasted that he had wounded God. He was punished by being stung to death by insects, and his palace was destroyed by fire.

Our departure from Hillah, in spite of the friendly intercourse which we had had with the natives, was not to take place in peace. Without any reason that we knew of, the crowds on shore, many of whom had visited the steamer, suddenly assumed a threatening aspect; others pointed long guns at us from the roofs of the houses on both sides of the river. They refused to open the bridge, which they had before readily agreed to do, in order to prevent the steamer, of the power of which they had no idea, from going on, or in the intention of making a formal attack.

All attempts at an understanding were fruitless, as well as threats that we would force our passage through; shots, which fortunately did not hit anyone, were the only response. There was considerable delay, till the Colonel was convinced that words were useless, and that he must teach these ignorant people better by proceeding to deeds. He gave orders to go on with full steam on, and break the slender ropes by which the boats were fastened. Officers and crew had been impatiently waiting for this. With stentorian voice the Commander called out from the paddle wheel into the engine room: ' Go on with full speed ! ' and ' with full speed ' was echoed from below. In an instant the steamer passed through the bridge, scattering the light pontoons like spray, to the astonishment and terror of the gaping crowd, whose courage and threats it at once put an end to. To give them a still greater idea of the defensive powers of the steamer, as well as a proof of the magnanimity and friendly feeling of the English, a few thundering cannon shots were fired into the air. The inhabitants gazed long after us in amazement, perhaps puzzling their brains to discover how the beautiful boat could thus escape their hands.

On the same day, June 11, we glided down between date palms, without obstacle, to Dewanyeh, a town of a few thousand inhabitants, the limit of the pachalic of Baghdad.

The town is surrounded by a wall of earth surmounted by towers. There were numerous boats of various sizes on the river, by means of which an active trade is carried on, and many wares are conveyed to the bazaar.

The Pacha of Baghdad keeps a strong garrison here, partly to defend the town, partly to keep the refractory Arabs in order. Wellsted relates of these Agyl Arabs that they fought in the conquest of Spain, and have preserved traditions of that heroic period.

The existence of lions about here, which we had doubted, was confirmed, for we saw unmistakable imprints of their great paws on the shore. The crew saw many of their footprints while felling wood, but no lions. They rest by day in the thickets and go out by night to plunder or to drink. We heard them roaring at night, on board, which dispelled all doubts about their proximity.

It made me anxious about Helfer, who, never think-ing of anything but his researches, always landed directly we stopped. My exhortations to prudence were disre-garded; he only laughed, and said that in this respect he had become a true Turk. This only made me more anxious, and I resolved never to leave him, in order to compel him to caution by my presence.

I was full of these thoughts when, on June 13, we anchored at the town of New Lamlum. Up to this time the shores had been clothed with um-brageous date palms. Numerous settlements of agri-cultural Arabs are seen amongst the underwood, and give the idea of a considerable population.

The Euphrates here divides into several branches, and the low lying lands are under water during a great part of the year. This region reminded me of the Spreewald at home; numerous flocks, of which the wealth of the population consists, find pasture there as here, only here the dirty-grey buffalo lifts his ponderous limbs out of the bogs, while in the rich meadows of the Spree the sleek red cattle luxuriate.

This part of the Euphrates country is inhabited by the Khezail Arabs. Their huts of reeds and mud covered with mats stand on little hillocks in the marsh; they are liable to inundations, and are not seldom carried away, if the inhabitants are not sufficiently alert in getting the hut and its contents removed into safety on the backs of buffaloes or swimming oxen. If these are not at hand, the women fasten a bundle of reeds under their bodies, and swim across the water with an infant in their arms, while the elder children swim after them.

But as often as the floods wash away their huts, they always build again on the same spots. They are really amphibious, for they live as much on water as on land, and being so constantly in the water and marshes seems to have a decisive effect on their build, for their limbs are so long and thin that when you see them wading about you would think they were on stilts.

The main arm of the river is only 100 to 150 feet wide, and navigation was much impeded by a multitude of small boats, in which the inhabitants paddle about from house to house with great dexterity.

We had hardly landed when the people crowded round us, and a brisk trade began, which, welcome as it had been in other places, made us fear here that it would excite the natives' cupidity. Colonel Chesney knew them to be arrant thieves, from having been here in 1831, particularly the Shiahs, a Shiitic tribe of Persian origin, who have preserved many characteristics of their forefathers, and are said to be much given to plunder, although they are diligent agriculturists. During the night, therefore, there were guards appointed on board, as well as on shore, to keep off unbidden guests.

The stifling heat in the cabins made the nights a torment; sleep was out of the question. We had, therefore, for several nights slept on deck. With all our clothes on, and wrapped, heads and all, in linen sheets to protect ourselves from mosquitoes, and our eyes from the bright moonlight, we lay on the narrow cabin mattresses, and thus found the longed-for rest. That night my imagination had been excited by tracks of lions having been seen, and I dreamt about them. All at once it seemed to me that a lion was seizing me with his four paws and dragging me away. I could not disentangle myself from the folds of the sheet, and called out, ' a lion, a lion ! ' Helfer awoke, but swathed up in like manner he could not tell for a moment what was going on. He grasped my arm, still I was dragged farther towards the edge of the deck, not yet provided with any balustrade. Just then a shot was heard, then another, I heard a splash into the water, I was released. It was all the work of a few minutes, the whole crew were alarmed, and were by our sides. No one could account for the incident till Major Estcourt, who had spent the night on shore, came on board, and told us that a robber Schiah had tried to steal his clothes from under his head ; it had awoke him ; he had shot at him, and then fired at another thief whom he thought he saw on board. But there was no trace of a lion. My assurance that there had been one, and that he had begun to drag me off, was of course ascribed to a lively imagination, in spite of my assertion that he had sprung upon me, and that I still felt the clutch of his claws. Ashamed of having been caught in this weakness I held my peace, until daylight solved the mystery, and relieved me of my mortification.

It appeared that one of these amphibious Arabs had got on board, in spite of the watch, probably under water, and through one of the cabin windows. He had stolen a chronometer, pulled about everything of a glittering nature, and tried to get hold of it. Alarmed by the shot on shore, he must have rushed up the cabin stairs, and probably tried to jump into the water from just the spot where I was lying. In doing this, not being able to see me, he must have fallen upon me with hands and feet, got entangled in the sheet, and so pulled me along with him. But he even exercised his thieving propensities in this hasty flight, and stole Mr. Fitzjames's tarbush. So, though there had been no lion, there had been something which it was no wonder that at the moment I took for one, and my cries for help were justified.

After the chronometer had been restored, on our energetic remonstrances to the sheikh, and proper respect impressed on the robber crew, on June 16, we left this singular place with its queer inhabitants, who stood in crowds on the shore, and watched the movements of the steamer with astonishment and awe. Lower down we saw numerous huts, mostly under the shade of date palms, which grow in groups here. In the low lying lands there are rice fields yielding a hundredfold.

Unfortunately, among the many branches of the river, forming quite a network of channels, we took the wrong one, and after a voyage of some hours got aground. When we got off next morning we had to go back, in order to get into the right channel, near the village of Barblyah ; after this we went on without any hindrance.

In our rapid course we passed many ruins of fortified castles and large towns, of which we could learn nothing but the names. Among these, Irak-Jakal-el-Assayah, the Erech of the Bible, is said to be one of the most ancient.

Near El Khudhr, a large village of the Beni-Hakem, we came to a poplar wood, which promised to supply us with fuel as far as Basrah. The villagers were willing to fell it, and, incited by the promise of good pay, went to work at once. But the next day they showed unaccountable ill-humour, and could not be induced to work any more.

While Lieutenant Murphy had been taking observations in the castle of El Khudhr, and Mr. Ainsworth and Helfer were in the wood, we observed great excitement amongst the Arabs. They were evidently conspiring against us, sending messengers in various directions, probably to call upon their allies for help, and began a war dance, with wild cries, swinging their guns high into the air.

When asked through our interpreter, Seyd Ali, what was the reason of this conduct, they gave no satisfactory answer, but called the foreigners cowardly dogs, and threatened to butcher us all. They also threatened to capture those of our party who were on shore, but they were safely escorted on board by the Colonel and some of the crew.

The number and fury of the wild figures in the wood were continually increasing, we could hear their cries and insults on board. For our own safety, and to keep up our dignity, we had to avoid all signs of fear. For this reason, and in the hope of coming to an understanding, the Colonel had the steamer steered nearer to the wood. She was greeted with a shower of shot, which happily wounded no one, though the Colonel was in a very exposed place. Still he hesitated to return hostilities, though all longed to avenge the insult; but as the wild horde went on firing, a broadside of grape and canister was fired into the wood, and as this did not silence them, a second. The effect was fearful, as I could see from our cabin window. Mr. Fitzjames had taken me there by the Colonel's orders, when the fight began, while Helfer kept his place on deck. How many were killed and buried under the falling trees we could not discover; but we could see that only a minority of the war dancers saved themselves by flight. There had also been some firing from an old castle on the opposite shore, but a few rockets sufficed to drive away the foe.

This was the only time that actual hostilities occurred during the long voyage through a country inhabited by a wild quarrelsome race. We afterwards learnt that they were caused by our cutting down trees in what the Shiites considered a sacred grove.

Without any further disturbance, we passed through the main stream, which had become wide and deep by the influx of several canals, to the flourishing commercial city of Sheikh-el-Schuyukh. It is inhabited by the Montefek Arabs, a powerful tribe. We saw their well-built vigorous forms, not so dark as those we had seen before, moving about almost naked amongst rose bushes, fig and pomegranate trees.

Their chief occupation is breeding horses, in which they are so successful that they supply the English in India with the best race horses. They live chiefly on camel's flesh, and only cultivate rice and practise agriculture when compelled to it by the Pacha of

Baghdad. But they often shake off his yoke and domineer over the neighbouring tribes; they even sometimes venture as far as the gates of Baghdad. Their chief assumes the title of Sheikh-el-Muscheik, Sheikh of the Sheikhs.

In time of war the Sheikh's power is unlimited, but is not great in time of peace, when his chief duty is hospitality. When Captain Wellsted was the guest of Sheikh Agyl Ibu Mahomed, he kept open table daily for 300 to 400 guests. Thirty or forty slaves were constantly employed in grinding coffee. It is in hospitality like this that the Sheihk seeks renown, while he himself generally lives an extremely frugal life.

It is a difficult task for the Pacha of Baghdad to maintain his authority over those powerful vassals living in unapproachable marshes, and he tries to render it easier by exciting the tribes to mutual jealousies, that they may weaken each other by their feuds. Captain Wellsted found the same Sheikh Agyl, a few months later, in Baghdad, as guest of the Pacha. A handsomely furnished palace was assigned to him as his abode. He did not occupy the interior, but in true Arab fashion, pitched his tent on the flat roof. His followers, however, took possession of the purple velvet divans embroidered with pearls, cooked their food on the marble floors, and broke the costly mirrors, that each might take a piece away with him. They even allowed sheep and goats to run about in the splendid rooms. Agyl had with him a retinue of no less than 4,000 men. An equal number of the Jerboah tribe soon came to the city. They encountered each other in the cafés and bazaars, and quarrels ensued, which turned the streets into a battle field. This gave rise to a feud between the tribes, and they fought till their forces were exhausted. The Pacha could then bring his contumacious vassals into subjection again.

On our arrival at Sheikh-el-Schuyukh, a salute was fired in honour of the Sheikh, and friendly intercourse opened with him. He soon furnished us with the wood we required, so that we were able to go on early next morning.

The tide reaches to this point, and caused a strong counter current, which impeded progress; but we reached Kurnah successfully. At this important place the Tigris and Euphrates meet, and the two rivers take the name of Schat-el-Arab, till they flow into the sea below Basrah.

Kurnah is almost hidden among date palms, so that only the roofs of a few huts were to be seen. These trees begin to attain their highest perfection here, and form thick woods; their fruit is in great request as an article of trade, and is very profitable to the inhabitants. They are, however, not so much used here as food as in Arabia; it is said to be unwholesome to eat many of them.

I was delighted with these slender trees with their waving green cupolas, and could imagine nothing more beautiful. And yet they dwindle into insignificance compared with their tropical sisters, the cocoa-nut palms. It is only in the tropics that the palm is seen in all its glory.

A Turkish vessel was lying at anchor here, and we

gave her the usual salute ; but she was so ill equipped that she was unable to return it, a symptom of the fallen estate of the Turkish empire.

In default of sufficient fuel, though empty boxes and every bit of spare wood was burnt, we could only make the distance to Basrah, forty-five English miles, at half speed. But, slow as the manifold obstacles had rendered our course in the upper part of the river, the rapid current of the united streams now bore us swiftly on to our destination, too swiftly, indeed, to allow us more than a hasty glimpse of the scenery.

So we only saw from a distance the very ancient ruins which abound here ; among them, some which equal Birs Nimrod in vastness and antiquity. One of these is the tower of Magyar, rising to a height of 200 feet, out of an immense mound of ruins, on the former bed of the Pallacopas. The Pallacopas was one of those broad and deep canals, which intersected the country in all directions, turning rivers into new channels, feeding lakes, fertilising deserts, and floating fleets of ships. These magnificent canals still excite astonishment now that they are turned into swamps. They furnish still stronger evidence of the once numerous population of these lands, and the extent of their civilisation, than the vast ruins of colossal edifices.

Early in the morning of June 18, our steamer cast anchor in the roadstead of Basrah. The problem of the possibility of the navigation of the Euphrates by steam was solved, the end attained. We had at length, after a struggle of three months with obstacles and privations of every kind, happily completed a voyage of 1,500 miles on an untried river, whose shores were peopled with savage races of men. How could we but rejoice! We congratulated each other on having lived to see this day, and mournfully thought of the companions we had lost.

The day was celebrated by unfurling the royal standard, and the number of guns fired corresponded with the years of King William IV. of Great Britain.

The whole population of Basrah, merchants of all nations among them, flocked to the landing place, to assure themselves with their own eyes of the arrival of the steamer. Even the admiral of a Turkish man-of-war, lying at anchor, and M. Fontanier, the French consul, came to offer their congratulations, and openly confessed, that, for numerous reasons, they had considered the scheme absolutely impracticable.

Meanwhile, the joy at the success of the Expedition, to which all on board freely gave themselves up, was not unmixed with sorrow to Helfer and me. We had to part with friends, who had become endeared to us, whose guests we had been for nine months; they had honestly shared good and evil fortune with us; by the most delicate consideration they had lessened the discomforts of living in the confined space of shipboard for me, and, altogether, they had always maintained the fine tact of gentlemen, and had fully justified the confidence with which Helfer and I had joined their party by the truly brotherly kindness and attention with which they had treated us. I have pleasure in here offering to the survivors, after this long lapse of time, my sincere acknowledgments and heartfelt thanks.

In the roads, the brig *George Bentinck*, an English merchant vessel, bound for Calcutta, with a cargo of horses, was lying. She was just about to sail, and was to call at Bushire, in Persia, our next destination, to take in more horses. The kind offer of the Captain to take us as passengers was the more welcome, as it is but rarely that English vessels cross the Persian Gulf.

There was no time for sad thoughts and feelings. With a shake of the hand, and a laconic ' Good bye,' which, with the monosyllabic English, expresses all that other nations use many words for, we took leave of our comrades, and went on board the *George Bentinck*.

Wind and tide were in our favour, and land soon disappeared from view. The heat, however, rose to such a degree as I have never felt before nor since, not even beneath the rays of a tropical sun. This makes the climate of the Persian Gulf most dangerous to Europeans. At this season the sun's rays are reflected, with double force, from the abrupt and lofty walls of rock which surround it; they heat the water and turn its surface into steam, so that the atmosphere is like a vapour bath. You sigh in vain for a cooling douche. I sank into an almost unconscious state, and was only kept up by having sea water frequently thrown over me, and inhaling acids. I could not walk from the cabin to the deck, and had to be lifted through the skylight wrapped up in a sheet. Happily, the voyage only lasted forty-eight hours. He who gets through it without illness is congratulated, and is considered to be steeled against any other climate.

We ran into the harbour of Bushire, landed at once,

and went to the house of the English Resident. On the way, which led through a densely peopled part of the town, I had most unpleasant experience of the fanatical rigour with which the Shiites insist on the absolute seclusion of women. I was recognised as a woman by some of the passers by, and a crowd soon collected, who grossly insulted and even threatened to stone us. Fortunately, we were followed by the captain and some of the crew on foot, and under their protection we reached the consulate.

This was the first time on our journey, and after a year's residence in Mohammedan countries, that I had been insulted as a woman. Under the painful impression of it, the Persians, with their long, lean figures and stooping attitude, clad in caftans down to their ankles, and with tall pointed caps of black lambskin on their heads, appeared to me very ugly, though really they cannot be called so, for they have aquiline noses, and much brighter complexions than the Arabs.

Apprised of our coming and our intentions, the Resident, Captain Hennell, received us most kindly. In these remote stations, seldom visited by Europeans, travellers are very welcome to the Residents, cut off as they are from the civilised world. Although we were not English, he regarded us as being so, since we had made the arduous Euphrates Expedition in his countrymen's company, and we were hospitably entertained in his comfortable abode. The navigation of the Euphrates was of great importance to Captain Hennell, as, if regularly carried on, it promised to make Bushire a staple place of commerce Our communications on the subject therefore greatly interested him, and formed the chief topic of our conversation.

'In return for your information,' he said, one day, 'I can give you some that will interest you, and be a sort of satisfaction to you. Those Affghan princes, as they called themselves, who have so shamefully deceived you, have been at Bushire, but they did not show themselves to me; they went to Bombay and up the Indus on their way to their home on the Upper Ganges, of course without the least suspicion that warrants were issued to arrest them. Shortly after they reached Lucknow the warrant arrived. They had again played their part well as Asiatic princes, and succeeded in interesting our Resident there on their behalf, so that he executed the warrant with reluctance, and felt convinced that there was some mistake. This part of the story,' added Captain Hennell, ' will be most satisfactory to you, as it is calculated to lessen the mortification which few people can avoid feeling at having been taken in ; for if such a practised " Tiger " (a nickname for an Englishman who has grown old in India), as our Resident at Lucknow, was deceived by them, you need not blush to have been their victims.'

' But who then are these extraordinary people ? ' we eagerly asked, and received the following account of them.

They were the sons of a European indigo planter, and an Indian woman of one of the higher castes, in the district of the Upper Ganges ; they received a good education, but early showed a tendency to extravagance and roguery. At last they played a shameful trick on their father and one of his business friends. They had been entrusted by the former with a chest of gold coins for a banking house in Calcutta; they broke it open, took possession of the money, filled it with stones of equal weight, and sealed it with their father's seal, which they had surreptitiously got possession of. The banker suspected nothing, and gave them a receipt for the money. When he discovered the fraud, the thieves were on their way to Europe. For a long time, all trace of them was lost, as they assumed various names. But at last it was discovered that they were on their way back to Asia, and, having got through their money, were going home. Measures were taken for their arrest, and as soon as they were on the soil of India they were taken prisoners.

Thus vanished the last faint nimbus which had surrounded our hypocritical friends in our eyes; they were unmasked as vulgar impostors, and we were the richer by some dearly bought experience.

I have always been interested in observing the various methods by which people protect their dwellings from heat and cold in different climates. While in Baghdad they live half underground for the sake of coolness, I found that in Bushire, in order to catch the sea breezes, there are square towers, in the centre of the houses, from the basement to a good way above the flat roof, with small openings in each story, by which means a strong, cool current of air is maintained throughout the house. It produces a sensible coolness, and often obliges you to put on more clothing. Violent gales are not uncommon here. During the very first night, which here, as at Baghdad, we spent on the roof, such a storm arose that the light, wooden partitions were torn down, and coverlets and articles of clothing were whirled about, so that we were glad to beat a hasty retreat down the little staircase into the dressing rooms, where there were safer couches for those driven from the roof.

Our Captain, having more horses to ship, had to stay a week at Bushire. Helfer made entomological excursions. I wanted one day to beguile the time by drawing, and to take a sketch of the neighbourhood as a remembrance. In spite of warnings not to go out alone, finding that the gate, which was generally closed, had been accidentally left open, I ventured out and, choosing an elevated spot whence there was an extensive view, began my sketch. As it was close by the consulate I thought myself quite safe.

Engrossed in my work I did not observe that the space between the Residence and the beach was thronged with people, until wild yells reached my ears, and looking up I saw a crowd of men coming towards me, with angry and threatening looks. Terribly frightened, I rose up, and ran to the edge of the cliff. My situation was desperate; it appeared as if I must either jump into the sea, or be stoned by the enraged multitude. Just when the danger was at the worst, a number of the consular police came to my aid, and drove the ruffians away with loud cracks of their whips. I was saved, but all my pulses throbbed, and my heart beat audibly for a long time.

When the incident was discussed at dinner time,

Captain Hennell said to me : ' You have had a specimen to-day of the dangers to which a European lady is exposed in this country.' And, turning to Helfer, he continued : ' I have refrained before from giving you my opinion about your idea of making some stay in Persia, but I take this opportunity of strongly advising you against it.' He then drew such a repulsive picture of the hatred of foreigners by the populace, and of the perfidious, and quarrelsome character of the higher classes, that it dispelled all my illusions, and even Shiraz with its fragrant rose gardens lost its attractions.

Helfer also was convinced that under these circumstances his plan of settling as a physician in a Persian town was impracticable. It was definitively given up. Whither then should we turn our steps ? We considered every alternative without coming to any decision.

In the meantime, Captain Eales, of the *George Bentinck*, came in, and, hearing of our dilemma, proposed to us to go on with him, and make Calcutta our next station.

Calcutta, the star of the East, the city which the concurrence of European and Asiatic luxury has made the dearest in the world, had never, in view of our limited resources, entered into Helfer's calculations. How could he reckon upon lucrative practice among the English, who have no confidence in any doctors but their own ? And what prospect did it afford him for the prosecution of his special objects in travelling ? These were important considerations, and weighed heavily in the scale. On the other hand, we recurred to the pleasant time we had spent in the society of the

English officers, and to the confidence with which their conduct had inspired us, so that the idea of again passing some time with their countrymen, and under their protection, became more and more attractive, and finally gained the day. Trusting to the good genius which had hitherto guided and watched over us, we agreed to Captain Eales's proposal.

The day before sailing we had the joyful surprise of seeing the *Euphrates* run into the harbour of Bushire. Colonel Chesney, not finding the means of refitting the steamer at Basrah, had risked the sea voyage in her, though she was constructed only for river navigation, and it was said by seafaring men to be madness. But it succeeded, as many things do succeed with the courageous which are never achieved by the faint-hearted. Great was the pleasure of this unexpected meeting. We told our friends of our intentions, which met their cordial approval.

The next morning the last farewells were spoken, and we embarked, on board the *George Bentinck,* for Calcutta.

END OF THE FIRST VOLUME.

LONDON : PRINTED BY
SPOTTISWOODE AND CO., NEW-STREET SQUARE
AND PARLIAMENT STREET